THE SEARCH

THE SEARCH

Christopher Nicole

This first world edition published in Great Britain 2001 by
SEVERN HOUSE PUBLISHERS LTD of
9–15 High Street, Sutton, Surrey SM1 1DF.
This first world edition published in the USA 2001 by
SEVERN HOUSE PUBLISHERS INC of
595 Madison Avenue, New York, N.Y. 10022.

British Library Cataloguing in Publication Data

Nicole, Christopher, 1930–
    The search
    1. Terrorists
    2. Women detectives
    3. Suspense fiction
    I. Title
    823.9'14 [F]

ISBN 0-7278-5742-8

Except where actual historical events and characters are being
described for the storyline of this novel, all situations in this
publication are fictitious and any resemblance to living persons
is purely coincidental.

Typeset by Palimpsest Book Product'
Polmont, Stirlingshire, Scotland.
Printed and bound in Great Britain b
MPG Books Ltd., Bodmin, Cornwal

Be vigilant; because your adversary the devil, as a roaring lion, walketh about, seeking whom he may devour.

The First Epistle General of Peter

The Bomb

The sand was cool and firm along the waterline, the sea untroubled. The still dawn had ironed smooth the unimportant ruffles of the previous night, as each almost imperceptible wavelet erased the footprints of the few early risers, leaving Jessica to make her own fresh impressions on the new day. She dragged a toe, making a shallow rut, and wondered if her presence here in Spain would leave any further lasting impression. Probably not. No more than her absence might have on Tom . . . or was that being unfair? She wasn't sure.

As the sun swung above the horizon, beaming a blinding path of pure gold across the Mediterranean, Alicante glowed. It was known historically as the White City, and if that no longer had any meaning in the context of a mass of high-rises and hotels fronting the sea, the title was still evocative.

Jessica Jones was walking barefoot along the beach, carrying her shoes in her hand. The night shift had ended at six, but there was little point in going to bed while the adrenalin was still pumping. It seemed to make more sense to walk the beach, breathe the salt air. Relax. It was more peaceful now than it would be for the rest of the day, occupied only by distant tractors moving slowly to and fro along the shore, levelling the half-collapsed sandcastles and filling the laboriously dug moats as it scooped up debris abandoned by yesterday's tourist

1

invasion. Men were emptying litter bins, and one portly gentleman was risking arrest by walking his dog on the precious brown sand.

Jessica bent over and with one hand splashed water on to her face and hairline, then lifted her eyes to the eastern sky. Already the sun was warm enough to dry the soft droplets. In another hour or so the crowds would arrive, brawny young men and bare-breasted young women, anxious to see and be seen. Parents would trail the bucket and spade brigade across the road, tinies wearing sun cream and over-large sunglasses. They would all go into the sea with giant plastic sharks, bright red dinghies and multicoloured beach balls, splashing, shrieking, laughing, burning. Crying and fighting.

It was not Jessica's scene. For one thing her figure, if neat, was not of the *Baywatch* variety, and for another, being required to spend so much of her working life in the midst of large numbers of people, watching and waiting for possible catastrophes, she hated crowds. By the time the sun-worshippers appeared she would be sleeping in preparation for her next shift.

But it gave her private amusement to imagine how any of those beach people might react if they knew that, in the bag swinging so nonchalantly from her shoulder, there was a Skorpion 7.65 M-61 machine pistol. The dainty-looking shoulder strap was reinforced with a steel strip, not only to prevent it being cut by any opportunist thief but also because the tiny blowback weighed roughly three kilos fully loaded with twenty cartridges, which it could deliver at a rate of seven hundred rounds per minute over seventy effective yards. It was her personal choice, since it had been established that most man-stopping weapons, such as Magnums, were considered too heavy for female operatives.

Jessica knew there were few more unlikely people in the professional protection business than herself. At thirty-five, her smooth-skinned delicate features and air of fragile innocence was enhanced by long, very pale blonde hair. Small and slim, she was the type that men automatically wanted to take under their wing. Actually, beneath the cotton shirt and trousers she had well-developed muscles, kept trim by regular workouts in a gymnasium when at home. These, together with equally regular training in unarmed combat and the frequent practice sessions on the firing range, had made her one of the most skilled operatives of either sex in the division.

That skill had all but got her killed, two years ago. It was not an occasion she would ever forget. But she had protected her principal, and been commended for it. Which made assignments like this, rated a low risk factor – according to Control – the more welcome.

Yawning, she looked at her watch: seven thirty. She was at last beginning to feel sleepy. Walking up to the back of the beach she used one of the convenience showers to wash the sand from her feet, and slipped into her canvas shoes.

Not for the first time, as she sauntered along the pavement below the overpass leading north towards the harbour and the hotels, she wondered what she was doing with her life. Being in Intelligence had been fun at first, but not compatible with a normal existence. It had led to the breakdown of her marriage, and, on the downside of that, to the end of her immediate career.

Tom had rescued her. He was in Protection for the Special Branch. Big stuff – presidents and foreign potentates. She had not attained such dizzy heights, yet. In any event, her brief necessarily had to be women. Not that Protection allowed her any more of a personal life. Tom's erratic schedule was likely to take him on a weekend in the Outer Hebrides at a moment's notice, a decision he was not allowed to relay home. So one sat and waited for an eventual phone call which might be entirely reassuring or be a catastrophic end to a relationship.

Now that she was a proven survivor, Jessica felt she was more able to cope with the possibilities that had not yet happened. And she had been fortunate in her recent assignments, as she had graduated from general duties to specific individuals. Margaret Lewton was Britain's first female Foreign Secretary, a very sensible woman, happily married and with a large family, who would no more consider a sudden weekend in the Outer Hebrides than an unscheduled visit to Karakorum. That she was chairing this European conference on Methods of Combating International Terrorism at a hotel in Alicante on the Costa Brava in June was, certainly in Jessica's eyes, a testimony to her good sense.

Mrs Lewton was protected by four operatives, two men and two women.

Presumably the other delegates were also well protected, mostly by men; the various divisions were not encouraged to get too close to each other – one was only aware of being surrounded by groups of steely-eyed men with their jackets flapping open. Possibly the men were equally aware of the two steely-eyed women, however small and blonde one might be, with their swinging shoulder bags.

But today was the last of the conference; this afternoon she would be on a plane home to her Docklands flat overlooking the river, and hopefully Tom . . . unless he was in the Outer Hebrides.

Megan Lynch peeped out over the coarse sheet, eyeballs rolling from one side of the room to the other, trying to remember where she was. Then she grinned and hugged herself as an exciting awareness swamped her mind. Spain! With Daddy and Mummy! An unfamiliar snort from the next bed gave an additional reminder. And Nan!

4

Spain! The birthday surprise they had only told her about yesterday morning. Hot Spain! She pushed back the sheet and thin coverlet revealing the head of Winnie-the-Pooh on the front of her T-shirt nightie, and let all the events of yesterday roll through her mind.

It had been almost unbelievable. Daddy and Mummy seldom took more than a couple of days off work, when it was essential to cram as much activity into their 'quality time' as possible. Those occasions were usually quite fun – unless her parents were into fighting mode and spent all day either arguing or not speaking to each other – but there never seemed to be time just to be together . . . talking. Unless they said, Let's talk! And she couldn't think of anything to say, couldn't remember any of the questions stored up in her mind. Of course Mummy and Daddy talked a lot, though seldom to her. So she had wondered, often, if they really rated her as a person, or was she just an appendage, a frequently irritating interruption to their busy lives. Like each of her parents at various times, Nan had tried to explain the situation. But perhaps now, in Spain, there would be time to be together when they weren't Doing Something, like going to a cinema or Legoland.

Megan suddenly remembered the sea, just out there across the road. They could go on the beach and wade out into the water together. Sliding her feet out on to the bedside mat she tiptoed across the cool, tiled floor to the window, and tried to peer out through the roller shutter; better not to wind it up till Nan was awake. The room was a long, narrow box, identical to all the other rooms she had seen through open doorways on the long trek from her parents' room last night, with the bathroom and wardrobes right at the inner end next to the corridor. Responding to a sudden need she disappeared into the bathroom and closed the door.

*   *   *

Two floors down, Margaret Lewton was sitting up in bed gazing into the space above her laptop, thinking. This morning's closing speech had been written last night; only the summing-up needed completing . . . with a few resounding punches aimed at the doubters and ditherers.

There was a knock on the door and Coralie carried in a tray of early morning tea. They greeted each other, commenting on the heat and the unrelenting sunshine, while the Special Branch woman rolled up the blinds to admit a pink glow from across the sea. Nearly six feet tall, Coralie was the complete antithesis of Jessica, with wide shoulders and thighs like tree trunks; her fashionably cropped black hair did little to soften the heavy line of her jaw and piercing dark eyes.

'Would you see if they can send up my breakfast within fifteen minutes, dear?' Margaret asked.

Coralie nodded. 'Shouldn't be any problem. Want me to turn on your bath?' She had been assigned to the Foreign Secretary several times and become used to her habits. 'Did you sleep well?'

'Yes, once the drunken Brits down on the front finally packed it in. Why do they always behave so appallingly abroad?'

'Because of our drinks culture, imposed I suppose by the licensing laws, which dictate that once given the opportunity, one should drink as much as possible as quickly as possible. I would estimate that your average Spaniard drinks far more than your average Brit, but he does it slowly. And throughout the day and into the night. He's relaxed about it.' She stepped on to the narrow balcony, frowning, then turned to her principal. 'Ma'am, I think there may be a problem . . .'

Margaret threw back the covers and dropped her feet to the floor. 'What's the matter?'

Suddenly the alarm of Coralie's mobile was shrieking.

The Search

* * *

They were a team of four officers, six hours on and eighteen off and, when the Minister was out in public, they were backed up by two extra male colleagues.

Today, in a break from normal routine, Jessica was due to relieve Coralie at two, allowing her only eight hours off, but as far as she knew Mrs Lewton was not leaving the hotel until she was ready to go to the airport. By the time she reached the hotel, she reckoned the Foreign Secretary would just be getting out of bed, to dress and prepare for her closing speech to the conference. Death and damnation to all terrorists. Everyone said this over and over again, but very little progress was being made in stamping out this unending guerrilla war between normal world citizens and the crazed aggression of murderous fanatics.

She strolled along the pavement past the customs area, the huge mound of Santa Barbara Castle behind her now, and on to the Ramblas. This was one of the most attractive aspects of the city. Huge palm trees swayed above the wide promenade of terracotta and white paving, laid to give the impression of uneven waves, waiting for the gypsy stallholders and the artists to set up their wares for the day. To her left the harbour opened up – ocean-going ships alongside the distant docks, and closer at hand the Royal Alicante Yacht Club with its rows of pontoons where several million pounds' worth of sea-going dreams nodded lazily at their warps.

On her right, the various seafront bars and restaurants were just coming to life, the waiters unfurling canopies and putting out chairs, and doing a brisk trade with those who believed in beginning the day with a cup of coffee and a Poncho. Delivery vans hurried to unload panniers of bread and trays of fresh-plucked chickens; Coca-Cola bottles rattled as their red and white truck was backed into

7

a parking slot. Pigeons strutted ahead of her, hoping the sweepers had missed a few crumbs.

Now the hotel was in sight, a vast and not very attractive structure, rising like a whale amongst the minnows to either side, painted a hideous yellow. All the front rooms had their mini-balconies looking out over the sea, and were doubtless priced accordingly.

About to cross the road, Jessica paused to let a car go by, somewhat slowly, followed immediately by another. She waited, patiently, watched the first car turn into the entrance to the hotel car park, which was reached by an arched tunnel through the very centre of the building.

As it swung into the archway, it stopped, and three men got out.

Instantly Jessica's instincts were roused; she was trained to be suspicious of anything unusual. The second car had also stopped, on the road, not fifty feet from where she stood, and the three men hurried towards it.

As did Jessica. Immediately her hand reached into her bag. 'Wait there!' she shouted, and realised she was speaking English, not Spanish. The men checked, and looked at her. The one nearest was fair-haired and fresh-complexioned – not a Spaniard she reckoned, and she had no recollection of ever having seen him before . . . but there could be no doubt that he recognised *her*!

'Fucking bitch!' he shouted.

Memories tumbled through her mind.

The man was reaching for his inside pocket, but before he could draw a weapon one of his companions had seized his arm and was bundling him into the waiting car, shouting something in Spanish. Jessica only caught the word *segundos*.

Then the car was swinging up the street.

Seconds! Robert Korman! That was impossible! But . . . Jessica stared at the parked car, which was now being investigated by the hotel doorman as it was blocking the entrance.

Seconds! Hand on her pistol, Jessica glanced at the receding car, but Protection was not basically a business of drawing guns and blazing away with a risk to the lives of innocent bystanders. Weapons were only to be used for the direct protection of one's principal – and then only if the would-be assailant was known to be armed.

Her principal! Not to mention Coralie. And everyone else in the hotel. Jessica turned back, finger pressed on the alarm button on the mobile in her bag, realising there was nothing she could do except possibly save one or two lives on the street . . . and her own.

'Leave it!' she shouted at the doorman. 'Run!' she screamed at the people nearby. 'Take cover!'

With that, she threw herself across the Ramblas and into the ditch on the far side, arms round her head.

The car had swung round the corner in the few seconds before the explosion. Even so, it was rocked by the blast. So was everyone around them. Other cars swerved to and fro, some even collided. People fell off their bicycles. Several pedestrians were knocked over. Glass shattered from windows high above them and the shards showered the street.

For just a moment following the explosion there was an eerie silence save for the rumbling aftershock, then the morning exploded into a paean of sound: people shouting and screaming, dogs barking, sirens wailing.

'Drive, drive, drive!' Claus said. He was seated in front next to Hamid. Up till then, no one had spoken. With the exception of the Chief, they were new to the business, as shocked as anyone by what they had done.

'Not too fast,' Albert said from the back seat. 'We don't want to attract attention.'

They were, in fact, the only car travelling away from the waterfront; all the others going in that direction had stopped.

'They will remember us,' Hamid said. 'Someone will remember us.'

'Someone will remember the car,' Claus said. 'And that is not important.'

'Do you think Nicole got out?' Claus asked.

'Of course she got out,' Albert said. 'She knew the timing.'

'If they pick her up . . .'

'They will not pick her up.'

'It is that other woman,' Hamid said. 'She knew what we were doing.'

Albert looked at the Chief, sitting beside him. Like his companions, he both worshipped and feared the Chief. The man was not only a legend, he was also a cold-blooded killer. And his temper was the most frightening thing about him. But Albert could not help being curious. 'What happened back there, Chief?'

The Chief had been locked in a brown study, eyes half-shut. Now he seemed to be awake. 'I would have killed her. Why did you stop me killing her?'

'I knew we had to get away. Every second counted. Why did you wish to kill her?'

'The bitch recognised me.'

Albert frowned. 'That is not possible.'

'I tell you, it is possible, and it happened.'

'Had you ever seen her before?'

'She is a British policewoman. Special Branch Protection Section. Yes, I have seen her before. At the Slavonian Embassy siege. She shot at me, from a range of a few feet.' His smile was cold, in keeping with his face; it was a curiously non-committal face – nose, chin, lips moulded into an unidentifiable pattern. 'A flesh wound.'

'But . . .' Albert was puzzled. 'The Slavonian Embassy siege was before Buenos Aires. Before . . .'

'My face surgery?' the Chief asked. 'Yet somehow she identified me.'

'Well . . .' Albert shrugged. 'Perhaps she got blown up by the bomb.'

'She *must* have been blown up by the bomb,' Claus said. 'She was too close to escape.'

'We must find out,' the Chief said.

'It will be too dangerous to go back,' Claus protested.

'We still must find out. Do you not understand? Our entire strategy is built upon the fact that no one in British Intelligence or the Metropolitan Police or any other police or intelligence service in the world knows who I am or what I look like. But now this woman . . .'

'One split-second glance . . .'

'She will be trained to remember what she sees even in split-second glances.'

Albert looked at Claus, who had turned round. Despite their respect for the Chief, knowing he was the best in the world, they both also knew he was paranoid. 'All right,' Albert said. 'The first thing we have to do is make the rendezvous and get out of the country. Then we can set about finding out if the woman survived. If she survived, there will be much publicity. Her name will certainly be revealed. If she is English, we can trace her to her home, and eliminate her.'

'You are talking of at least a week,' Hamid commented, twisting the wheel to and fro as he drove as fast as he dared; but they were now well away from the waterfront and nearly out of the city. 'Think how many descriptions and identikit pictures she will have given by then.'

'No one was ever caught by an identikit picture who wasn't already a part of the community,' Albert said. 'We will get to her in time.'

11

'I do not want her killed,' the Chief said. 'I want her alive.'

Once again Albert and Claus exchanged glances.

'I need to know how she recognised me,' the Chief said. 'There were other policemen present at the Slavonian Embassy. If something was overlooked in my surgery they too will be able to identify me. I have to know how she knew it was me. I want her brought to me. It is the Will of God!'

The Victims

The man had a kind face, although he was frowning. Jessica did not suppose he was even as old as herself, but he was doing his best to add years by wearing a walrus moustache to go with his white coat. 'Can you hear me?' he asked.

Jessica realised that she could, although his voice seemed to be coming from a great distance, and through the strains of what might have been a brass band.

'Where am I?' she asked, not sure she could actually hear herself over the banging in her brain.

'You are in hospital. You are lucky to be alive.'

Disjointed memories trickled back, and Jessica believed him. She looked past him at an anxious nurse, realised there were many more people in the background. She looked down at herself, and the green hospital robe, and suddenly became aware of pain. 'How bad?' she asked.

'For you, nothing more serious than the cuts, at the moment. We'll know more when we have the results of your scan,' the doctor said.

'Cuts!' Suddenly she was aware of a thousand little pinpricks all over her body. Instinctively she put up her hand to her face.

'Your face is all right,' the doctor said. 'You were lying on it.'

But the arms she had held over it, revealed as the sleeves of the gown slipped back, were a mass of tiny red marks.

'It is your back that suffered most,' the doctor said. 'But the cuts are all superficial. I do not think there will even be any scarring. You are very fortunate.'

'So you said. And were others fortunate?'

He shook his head. 'It is bad. Very bad. There are some people who wish to speak with you.'

There are so many people I have to speak with, Jessica thought, looking past the doctor and the nurse at the waiting men. But not these. These had policemen written all over them. One even wore Guardia uniform. The man who came closer at a nod from the doctor wore a suit and was disturbingly young. That was the trouble with reaching half the allotted span: everyone was so young.

He drew up a chair, sat beside the bed. 'Miss Jones?' He spoke excellent English.

Jessica nodded, and winced; something was wrong with her neck.

'You are lucky to be alive.'

'Yes,' Jessica said. Presumably she was going to hear this from everyone for the foreseeable future.

'Or perhaps you knew what was going to happen,' the inspector suggested.

'I realised what was going to happen,' Jessica agreed.

'You knew these people, these terrorists, eh? Perhaps you were one of them, eh?'

'Oh, don't be absurd,' Jessica snapped. 'Tell me what happened.'

'You do not know what happened, Miss Jones?'

'I remember throwing myself into a ditch. Then . . . waking up here.'

'You do not know that the Ocean View Hotel has been destroyed?'

'The . . . the whole hotel?'

'The entire front collapsed after the bomb went off in the archway, and the rest followed. We estimate there must

14

have been something like a thousand pounds of explosive in that car. Do you understand that because of that ditch, you are one of the few survivors within several hundred metres of the explosion? And it appears you have only a few cuts.' He seemed to find this deeply offensive.

But the hotel! Mrs Lewton! Coralie! And all the others. 'Are there many casualties?'

'A great number. Almost everyone in the front of the hotel. The list may run into hundreds. Many are still missing under the rubble.'

Robert Korman!

'You were staying in the hotel,' the inspector said. 'We found your bag, and in it the key to your room. But fortunately for you, you were not in the room, eh? You were outside, sheltering in a ditch. That was very fortunate for you, eh? Unless you knew it was going to happen.'

'I realised what was going to happen, seconds before it did. Listen—'

'We think you knew. As I told you, we recovered your bag. So tell me about this heavy calibre automatic weapon you were carrying. Our female tourists do not usually take early morning walks armed with such things. I would like you to tell me where you got the gun, and for what purpose you were carrying it.'

'It's licensed.'

'I do not think it is licensed in Spain.'

Jessica knew she would have to break cover, or they would probably lock her up.

'All right. If you recovered my shoulder bag, and will now look in it again, you will find a small disc that has a number on it. If you will then call the British Consulate and give them that number, the whole thing can be sorted out very quickly.'

He peered at her. 'You are saying that you are connected with the British Consulate?'

'I am asking you to telephone them and give them that number. Then you will be given your answers.'

'I will do that. But you will have to remain under guard, meanwhile.'

'Well,' she closed her eyes, 'I don't suppose I'm going anywhere in a hurry.'

But lying in bed was growing more uncomfortable by the moment, even if she spent most of her time on her stomach. The nurse arranged two mirrors so that she could look at her back; she had been covered in antiseptic cream but it was still horrendous.

'What else is the matter with me?' she asked.

'I don't think there is anything serious, but we are still waiting for the result of your scans. You could have internal injuries. And in any event, all of those cuts . . . Your ditch was full of broken glass, they say, with you underneath it. You are lucky to be—'

'Don't tell me . . . *alive*.'

'I was going to say, to be free of cuts to your face.'

'Thank you. When can I get out of bed?'

'Well . . . you can move about if you wish. But though you may feel reasonably well, you are undoubtedly suffering from shock and could quite possibly black out at any time over the next forty-eight hours. Don't try to walk far alone. And of course, you understand you cannot leave the hospital.'

'Because I am technically under arrest.'

'Because you have no clothes, Miss Jones. Yours were torn to pieces by the glass.'

'Shoot! And none left in the hotel, either. Tell me, are you English?'

The young woman grinned. 'My parents retired out here. I finished my schooling here and then studied nursing.'

Jessica nodded, and winced. The pain in her neck

was worse. 'Are there any other victims in here with me?'

'More than we know how to cope with, scattered through various wards, and even in the corridors.'

'Any English?'

The nurse leaned over and whispered. 'The little girl in the next ward, and her grandmother. The parents were both killed, and the grandmother may have to have her legs amputated.'

'Heck,' Jessica muttered. 'The girl . . .'

'She has some cuts, like you, but also some severe bruising. And three stitches in her scalp. They say the room she was sharing with her grandmother was right away at the far end of the hotel. The child was found in the midst of a heap of marble in the remains of what would have been the bathroom.'

'May I visit her?'

The nurse looked uncertain. 'I'm not sure that would be a good idea, until things are sorted out.'

'You mean, until I can prove I wasn't one of the bombers,' Jessica said.

The nurse's face twisted. 'I'm just obeying orders.'

Jessica supposed she was right. In a place like Spain she could well be lynched if people got the idea she might be guilty of so horrendous a crime. It kept banging through her mind. Mrs Lewton. Coralie. All the acquaintances she had made during her week here.

And Robert Korman!

'My name is Harrison,' said the man behind the horn-rimmed spectacles. 'Would you mind telling me just what the hell is going on?'

'Are you from the Consulate?' Jessica asked.

She was, as had become a habit, lying in bed on her stomach, which seemed to disturb him.

'I am from the Embassy, in Madrid. Drove down here this morning.' That seemed to have upset him even more.

'I need to contact Control,' Jessica said. 'And these people won't let me use a phone, or anything.'

'They think you're guilty of planting that bomb,' Harrison said.

'And you know I'm not, Mr Harrison.'

'Convince me.'

'I am . . . was . . . a part of Mrs Lewton's protection squad. Didn't my number prove that?'

'Unless you got it off someone.'

'Oh, for God's sake,' Jessica exploded. The pain in her neck made her wish she hadn't.

'Simmer down. You look like the right person. How come you weren't in the hotel?'

'I came off duty at six, when I was replaced by Coralie Wilkinson. I went for a walk before going to bed. I always do this. I like to walk on the beach. I was on my way back when I saw the cars. There wasn't time to send more than an alarm on my mobile, then duck.'

'But you knew they were terrorists.'

'I recognised one of them: Robert Korman.'

Harrison stared at her for several seconds, then he took off his glasses and polished them. 'The doctor says that you weren't badly hurt, but that you might have concussion.'

'I do not have concussion,' Jessica snapped. 'And what has that got to do with it, anyway?'

'My dear Miss Jones, Robert Korman was killed, over a year ago.'

'His body was never identified.'

'No, it wasn't. When people are blown up by their own bombs, there is seldom a lot left.'

'It obviously wasn't him who got blown up. He is alive, and he planted that bomb yesterday morning.'

18

'You mean the day before yesterday morning. You really aren't thinking very clearly.'

'Two days ago? Shoot! Then he's probably out of the country by now.'

'You still think it could have been Korman?'

'It *was* Korman,' she shouted.

Harrison considered. 'You recognised him? You mean you've seen him before?'

'Yes. We got far too close for comfort at that embassy siege two years ago.'

'And you recognised him at the time of the explosion.'

'No, not exactly.' Jessica frowned. 'That's the odd thing. I didn't recognise him. His face was quite different, as if maybe he'd had a plastic job.'

Harrison threw up his arms in despair.

'But I recognised his voice,' Jessica said.

'I see. You had a conversation, while he was planting the bomb.'

'No, Mr Harrison,' Jessica said wearily. 'But he shouted at me. He shouted "fucking bitch". Those were the exact words he used at the embassy siege when I shot at him.'

'Two years ago,' Harrison remarked, his tone suggesting that he was surprised she hadn't been called that more often. 'The man is dead, Miss Jones. You are suffering from shock. I'm not blaming you. You've had one hell of an experience. You're lucky—'

'Don't say it. All right, Mr Harrison. You tell me this. Since that embassy siege I have lived a relatively quiet life. I have not had to take any risks at all, my principals having been women of good sense and regular habits. To the best of my knowledge, I have not laid eyes on a terrorist in those two years. But that man yesterday morning . . . er, the day before yesterday . . . recognised me. Tell me how he did that?'

Harrison stroked his chin. 'I think we had better get you out of here,' he said.

Harrison had one of the women from the Consulate come in to take Jessica's sizes and buy her a new outfit. By the following morning, when the clothes were delivered, the sense of shock was wearing off, but her various cuts still stung and the pain in her neck was still excruciating; the doctor insisted that she continue to wear a neck brace as a precaution.

She found it difficult to believe that it had really happened. But the evidence was all around her. Harrison had contrived to get the policeman withdrawn, and while waiting for her new clothes Jessica was able to go into the next ward and sit with Megan Lynch, the little girl whose parents had been killed in the blast.

The child lay against the pillows, white as a sheet, her huge violet eyes sunk into the dark circles under her puzzled frown. Jessica put her least bandaged hand over the small one lying on the coverlet.

'Hello, Megan.'

The small, cropped head didn't move. Only the eyeballs swivelled towards the visitor. 'Are you Miss Jones?'

'Yes, Jessica Jones. But you can call me JJ. Everyone else does. Are you beginning to feel a bit better?'

The violet eyes stared. 'Why did they do it, JJ?' Megan asked. 'Why did they do it?'

Jessica sighed. 'They were just very bad men, Megan.'

Megan's frown deepened and she turned away. 'That's baby talk. I'm seven, you know. Why haven't Mummy and Daddy come to see me?'

Oh, God! She didn't know they were dead! Jessica's mind raced. But not fast enough. 'Were they hurt?' continued Megan.

'Yes, I'm afraid so.'

20

'Nan, my grandmother, is hurt too. Her legs are very, very bad.' She moved her head slightly to stare back at Jessica. 'Are my parents very, very badly hurt?'

'Yes.' Then she quickly asked, 'Have you anyone who can come out here to Spain to see you?'

'No.' The child's voice was hardly a whisper.

'What about an uncle or aunt?'

'I haven't any.'

'Older brothers or sisters?'

'No. There's only Nan.' Pause. 'And my parents. And you.'

God! What was going to happen to the kid? Did Harrison know about her?

'Have you seen your Nan yet?'

'No. She is in another section of the ward. The nurse I asked could only speak Spanish. I think I have heard one nurse speak English but she hasn't been in here to me today.'

Shoot! What the hell was she to do? She couldn't leave the poor kid here all alone amongst foreigners. 'I'll go and see what I can sort out.'

The strange thing was, the child hadn't asked to be taken to see her parents. Did she sense the full extent of what had happened?

Staggering down the ward past the flowered cubicle curtains to the nurses' station, Jessica ached in every muscle, every bone. Her head throbbed and her mouth was parched. '*Enfermera inglesa*?' she asked hopefully.

'*Si, si, señorita. Momento.*' The Spanish nurse hurried away and a few minutes later the English girl appeared.

Jessica explained, and the nurse looked shocked. 'Oh! How ghastly! I'll see if we can get her into a wheel-chair and take her to her grandmother. Leave it with me.'

Later, the English girl said her mother would visit the

child. 'She quite often comes in to see English patients who haven't any visitors.'

Next morning Harrison returned to check her out of hospital. She knew he was coming and was up and dressed in her new clothes, uncomfortable in her collar. 'You're on this afternoon's flight,' he said.

Jessica nodded. 'I'd like to see the hotel. It could be important. Jog my memory, you know.'

It was something she had to do, however unpleasant. The area was cordoned off, but Harrison had his pass and they were allowed through.

Jessica gazed at the fallen palm trees, broken chairs and tables tangled in their fronds; glass crunched beneath her feet, and to either side of the hotel the restaurant frontages were fragmented. The centre of the hotel itself was simply a vast crater.

'There's not much chance of finding any more survivors,' Harrison muttered, watching sniffer dogs at work.

Or even bits of survivors, Jessica thought. If she hadn't gone for that walk on the beach, she'd be in little bits, too. She shuddered.

'You'd better come and have a drink before lunch,' Harrison suggested. 'You don't look too good.'

As the car wound its way up the narrow streets to the Consulate, Jessica told him about Megan Lynch. 'I can't bear to think what is going to happen to the child. She is only seven and apart from a legless grandmother, she has no one in the world to care for her. What will the authorities do? Fly her back to England and put her in an orphanage?'

'Surely there must be someone who can look after her. Maybe when the grandmother is fit enough to fly back she will take her into her own home.'

'I only hope so.'

*   *   *

They ate an early lunch together, then it was time to go.

Harrison had deputed one of the secretaries from the Consulate to accompany her; Jessica wasn't sure if it was for her protection or to make sure she didn't do, or say, anything stupid.

The woman's name was Karen, and she was highly nervous, especially when they were taken into a special room before boarding so that Jessica's gun could be given to the pilot – who looked equally nervous.

Their flight to Gatwick took a couple of hours. They didn't speak much; Jessica replied to Karen's conversational attempts in monosyllables, not because she felt antisocial but simply that she wanted time to think.

She was still uncertain of what had happened. Uncertain of herself. Her brain remained unable to assimilate the fact that all of those people were dead, or the fact that young Megan was suddenly an orphan. That the child's grandmother was now legless. The poor woman had survived the horrific operation, but like nearly everyone involved, she would never be the same again.

So where did she go from here? Months of tests and rehabilitation programmes; the department was meticulous. This was not merely because it cared for its operatives; it cared more for the people the operatives were supposed to protect. All operatives had to be one hundred per cent fit in both mind and body.

One thought dominated her emotions: Robert Korman. Even if they had only seen each other twice, she was beginning to regard him as her evil genius. She wondered if she actively hated him, decided that she probably did. She had never actually hated anyone before. But was it possible not to hate Korman, now that she had seen the Lynch family destroyed? Special Branch operatives were not meant to get emotionally involved, of course. But looking at Mrs

Lynch senior – a lively, active woman in her mid-fifties – how could one help feeling fury and hatred? And as for the trauma which would distort the rest of young Megan's life . . .

Jessica's eyes were moist, her fists tightly balled, the nails digging into her palms.

'We're landing,' Karen said.

Jessica fastened her seat belt. 'Thanks for looking after me.'

'Are you all right?'

'I have no idea,' Jessica confessed.

'There'll be somebody to meet you.'

'I'm glad of that.' Even if it would mean a debriefing, and God alone knew what else, when all she wanted was to get home to her flat and go to bed for a month.

Hopefully with Tom. She had no idea if he would be there, or even if he knew of the bomb attack yet. She longed to lie wrapped in his arms and forget the world.

'Miss Jones?' The hostess bent over her as the plane taxied gently to a halt. 'Would you leave the aircraft first, please?'

Jessica nodded, and looked at Karen, who grinned. 'I'm just an ordinary passenger.'

'Would everyone please remain seated,' the hostess announced over her phone.

There was some discontented muttering as Jessica promptly got up and hefted her new overnight bag. 'I'll see you,' she told Karen, and hurried for the door.

The head stewardess was waiting for her. 'I think this is yours,' she said, as nervous as the rest of the crew.

Jessica took the bag containing the gun. 'Thanks for looking after it.'

'Do you really use it?'

'When I have to.'

There were two men at the foot of the steps, obviously – to her trained eye – fellow operatives, although she didn't recognise either of them. A car was parked only a few feet away.

'I feel like royalty,' Jessica confessed.

'The Commander is waiting for you,' one of the men said. He did not seem to appreciate her quip.

They sat on either side of her for the drive into town. Now she almost felt as if she were under arrest. My God, she thought. Perhaps I am.

'Must've been nasty,' remarked the man on her right.

'Very nasty,' suggested his companion.

'Yes,' Jessica agreed.

'Survival, that's the secret,' the first man opined.

'It's an art,' his companion pointed out.

'Listen,' Jessica said. 'I didn't set out to survive. It just happened.'

'Lucky to be alive,' the first man said.

Jessica ground her teeth.

At last they were at New Scotland Yard. The Commander, Cyril Adams, was there together with an Assistant Commissioner and two other men. But not Judith. That was disconcerting.

'JJ,' Adams said, shaking her hand, smiling. 'Do sit down.'

Jessica obeyed. It was a straight chair before their desks and made her feel that she was being interviewed for a job.

'Assistant Commissioner Proud can't be here right now,' the Commander explained. 'But I know she'll be in touch. Are you all right?'

'I think so, sir.'

'Well, you have an appointment with a doctor when you leave here. Can't be too careful, eh? Always the possibility of internal injuries.'

'I have no pain or discomfort, sir, save for some cuts and bruises and a stiff neck.' She touched the pink neck-brace.

'Can't be too careful,' he repeated. 'And then, I think a good dose of R and R, eh?'

'Yes, sir,' she agreed.

'So, apart from making as full and detailed a report as possible to Arthur, tomorrow, as of now you are relieved of duty until further notice. I'm afraid you will probably have to return to Spain to give evidence at the inquiry into the explosion, but that won't be for some weeks. Probably months, eh?'

'Yes, sir. About Korman . . . I mentioned it to Mr Harrison.'

'We'll talk about Korman in due course, JJ. We all understand that you have had a terrifying, traumatic experience.'

My God, she thought. He doesn't believe me. None of them believe me.

But did she believe herself, any more? Yes, she told herself fiercely. It *had* been Robert Korman. The most feared terrorist in the world, when he was alive. But he *was* still alive. And only she knew that. Or at least, was prepared to believe it.

'There'll be a commendation,' the Commander said winningly.

For what? she wondered. For not being there when I was needed? But that meant not being blown up when I should have been.

'Thank you, sir.' She stood up.

'And I think, as you are going off duty, that it might be a good idea for you to turn in your weapon,' he suggested.

'Yes, sir,' Jessica said. She wondered if she was actually in the process of being fired.

Dr Arnold was as kind and thoughtful as ever. He didn't

26

even say she was lucky to be alive, contenting himself with, 'Quite an experience. But you came out of it very well. Pretty sore, eh?'

He had been peering at the cuts on her back and bottom.

'Oh, they're bearable,' Jessica said. 'It's this bloody brace.'

'Hm.' He removed it, peered at her neck, and moved her head to and fro.

'Ow!'

'Severe?'

'No. Just irritating. Do I have to wear it?'

'Might be an idea, whenever you're about to do anything vigorous. I think the tendons are just strained. There's no structural damage.' He sat behind his desk while Jessica dressed herself. 'You will have to see Mrs Wright.'

'Oh, sh— . . . shoot,' Jessica commented. 'I don't think she likes me.'

'I don't think she regards it as her business to like anybody. But until and unless she gives you a clean mental bill of health you are not employable. I'll be in touch with her, and she'll be in touch with you in a day or so.'

Jessica put on her shoes. 'Do you think I'm mentally affected by what happened?'

'Of course you are. Everyone would be. As I think you are a sensible woman, I also think you will recover from it. It's Mrs Wright's business to tell us when you have.'

An official car was waiting to take her home. She smiled to herself. This was possibly the last time she'd get VIP treatment. The driver carried her bag into the lobby and left her waiting at the lift doors.

Jessica's home in East London could not have offered a more striking contrast to the home of her childhood. She had been born in the heart of Herefordshire, where she had been surrounded by oak beams, dilapidated antique furniture covered in chintz, two golden retrievers and three cats of indeterminate origins, and where every window had opened on to aspects of lush greenery.

Here, a south-facing plate-glass wall revealed only a few sparse sycamores amidst concrete and bricks across the river. It was not a panoramic view, as they were only on the third floor, but ever changing and interesting. A white four-seater settee was placed at the window end of the oblong room with two black swivel armchairs and a plate glass and graphite occasional table. At the rear of the room, next to the open-plan kitchen, was the dining area, the furniture a continuation of the glass and graphite theme, all much as it had looked when she and Tom had bought it fully furnished . . . and she still wasn't sure she really liked it. It was akin to being in a stunningly different holiday apartment done over by an expensive interior designer, but one didn't necessarily want to live with it.

Tom, bless his heart, wasn't really bothered how it looked, just so long as they could be there together – from time to time. 'Change anything you like, sweetheart,' he had told her.

She went along the corridor to the bedroom, hoping against hope he just might have returned unexpectedly. All she saw was her own weary image across the white duvet, reflected in the mirrored built-in wardrobe on the far side of the room. It was all exactly as she had left it five days ago. Cautiously she removed the neck-brace while kicking off her shoes; she felt more comfortable without either.

Back in the living room the black-faced clock indicated a quarter past eight; she adjusted her watch to English time, registering that it was really too late to start drinking tea . . . but nevertheless that was what she wanted. A lovely big mug of properly made English tea. Of course it wouldn't taste so good with long-life milk but – she filled the kettle – better than the insipid stuff she'd had in Alicante. She carried the travel bag provided by the Consulate into the bedroom, left it on a chair, and returned to the kitchenette.

She had picked up a copy of *The Daily Telegraph* from the car seat, discarded by one of the men on the trip from Gatwick, and was interested to see if they were still covering the bombing in Spain. They were, extensively, putting the whole episode into new but not very informative perspective. The tea had a remarkable reviving effect, so much so that the thought of food became bearable. She selected a microwave meal from the freezer and sat at the dining table, using the newspaper instead of a mat to avoid the irritating clatter of cutlery on glass. As she finished the meal she remembered she hadn't checked the computer for messages and e-mail. Only one message came up on her screen: *Love and kisses from Tom to JJ.* She grinned, cleared away her plate, and decided to run a bath; the idea of a long hot soak in her own bath gel was irresistible.

She lay back, pondering the strange relationship with Tom and their mutual, possibly off-key use of the word *love*. Were their feelings for each other really love? Or was theirs merely a convenient arrangement to satisfy their respective mental, financial and sexual needs? She sighed, sat up, and began shaving her legs. Tom didn't really approve of nightclothes; this was an ideal opportunity to indulge in the sensuous luxury of the coffee-coloured silk and lace confection she had bought in Bond Street more than a year ago, in a fit of madness. The long fair hair took ages to dry – so much longer than in the warm morning sun on her hotel balcony just four days ago in Alicante.

While running the fingers of one hand through the strands to maximise the benefit of the hot air from the dryer, she dared let her mind wander back again over the intervening days, the sad waste of life. The tragic death of Margaret Lewton, such a great political figure, an adored wife and mother. And the death of Coralie and so many others; many of them, especially her fellow operatives, had known they were in the line of fire, but not the Lynches! The image of little Megan's traumatised face as she leaned back against her pillows, waiting to be told her parents were both dead, made Jessica quiver with rage again. Bloody Robert Korman!

She flung the hair dryer on to the bed, picked up the nightdress and slipped it over her head before wandering into the kitchen for a cup of coffee and a cookery book to take to bed with her. Though not a culinary enthusiast herself, she found cookbooks very soothing and soporific. Switching out the lights behind her, she carried the mug and the book to the bedside table, turned on the weird, bent metal bedside light, and then hunching down under the duvet she sipped, read, and at last turned off the light, inviting sleep.

There were distant sounds: a boat siren, cars. And then a much closer sound. A neighbour, maybe? No, nearer than that.

Jessica listened, heart pounding. There was someone in the flat with her.

The Raid

J essica sat up, heart pounding. The sound had not been repeated. But it had been a door closing.

'Tom?' she called.

There was no reply.

Panic was neither in her nature nor her training, but she was still feeling the effects of the Spanish trauma, and her heart was pounding quite painfully. Slowly she eased her feet out from beneath the duvet, stood up. She resisted the temptation to switch the light on again, because she knew the room, and the whole flat, better than any burglar possibly could. And this had to be a burglar, surely.

And she had no weapon. She was well trained in unarmed combat, but apart from still feeling thoroughly battered, she knew that only in movies did the little heroine get the better of a large man – certainly if the man happened to be armed.

There was another sound, in the corridor outside the bedroom door. She needed to make a decision. To retreat into the bathroom would be to trap herself, with limited space to manoeuvre. To climb out of the window on to the balcony and thence the fire escape was to surrender – and it was a chilly night. She had to risk the phone. But first, the door. She tiptoed across the room to turn the key . . . but it burst open with such force that she was sent flying. She landed sitting on the floor, momentarily breathless.

There was more than one person in the room with her.

31

Desperately Jessica rolled away from the door, rose to her knees.

Someone spoke sharply, but not in English. Hands lunged for her, but she reached her feet and leapt further into the room.

Another decision, but there was nothing for it, now.

Jessica ran for the window and threw it open as the light came on. She could not resist the temptation to look back, and saw to her consternation that there were actually four people in the room: three men and presumably a woman, judging by her hair, which was long and black. They all wore black tracksuits and balaclavas. Oddly, although they were all armed, for the moment the pistols and knives remained in their belts.

But now a gun was drawn, and levelled. 'Come back inside, Miss Jones,' one of the men said, his voice only slightly accented.

The pistol had a silencer. To attempt to continue her escape would be to die.

Perhaps she was going to die, anyway. But she was trained to look for survival, and chances of counter-attack.

Against four people?

Slowly she withdrew her leg and re-entered the room, carefully straightening her nightgown.

'Close the window,' the man said.

Jessica obeyed, brain churning. They knew her name, so she could forget any idea that this was an ordinary burglary.

'What do you want?' she asked.

The man smiled. 'We want you, Miss Jones.'

Jessica licked her lips. 'Whatever for? Who are you?'

'We are the Will of God,' the man said. 'Gabrielle.'

The woman was carrying a small bag. Opening it on the floor, she took out a hypodermic. At the same time, the other two men moved forward. Jessica knew immediately that she was going to be sedated . . . and kidnapped. She had to react, and quickly.

She hurled herself forward as the two men converged on her. One of them caught her nightdress and she felt it rip. But she was past them and at the woman, who had just snapped the glass tube over the needle and was only now getting up. Jessica struck her with pumping arms and knees and knocked her over again; she landed on her back with a shrieked curse.

The door was still open and Jessica ran for it. The man with the gun swung it at her, but she ducked and was through into the darkened corridor, only twenty feet from the front door of the flat but hampered by the nightdress gathering round her knees and fluttering from her right shoulder where it had been torn. She reached the door, scrabbled for the latch, and heard their breathing as hands grasped her shoulders. Again she was flung to the floor with a force that drove all the breath from her body.

One of the men kicked her in the ribs, and she gasped with pain. He drew back his foot to kick her again, but was checked by a sharp command from the leader.

Instead he and his companion seized her wrists and dragged her back into the bedroom. This was hardly less painful, as her ribs still ached and she was bumped along the floor.

In the bedroom she was released. She collapsed in a heap, aware that her nightdress was in rags, and that they were all staring at her.

'That was stupid of you,' the leader said. 'I am allowed to shoot you, Miss Jones, if necessary. But it is the Will of God that you should be taken alive, if possible. So now, please, do not resist us further.'

Jessica panted, as she watched the woman Gabrielle carefully squeeze clear liquid up through the needle of the hypodermic . . . and again heard the sound of the front door lock being turned.

Gabrielle hesitated, looking at the leader, who made a quick gesture with his right hand. Gabrielle came forward, while the leader moved to the door, and one of his men reached to turn out the light. But that meant he had to release Jessica, and the fact that they were not expecting anyone else left her certain that it could only be one person at the door.

'Tom!' she screamed, at the same moment pulling her other arm free and again swinging at the woman.

Gabrielle gave another shriek and dropped the hypodermic. Jessica swung her free arm and struck the remaining man across the side of the head. He grunted and relaxed his grip.

The leader now finally lost patience and fired, but the room had been plunged into darkness as the light was switched off, and Jessica had no idea where the shot went. She was hurling herself forward, rolling across the carpet to come to rest against the wall, trying to hold her breath, wanting to shout again to warn Tom but knowing that to do so would be to die.

The flat was almost quiet, except for gasping breaths seeping through the darkness. But slowly Jessica's eyes became accustomed to the gloom. It was impossible to identify individuals, but she could see one figure moving towards the door, while another crouched in front of it. A third had backed against the wall. The fourth she couldn't see.

For the moment they were ignoring her, until they had disposed of this fresh threat.

She saw an arm raised; the watcher had identified a movement in the corridor. Now his hands came together, clearly holding a levelled gun. Jessica swept her hand left and right over the floor and found one of the shoes she had discarded earlier. She picked it up, drew a deep breath, and hurled it, in the same movement rising to her knees and again throwing herself across the room, seeking shelter behind the bed and shouting, 'Tom! Four of them! Shoot! Shoot to kill!'

If it was Tom, at this hour he would surely have come straight from the airport, and therefore would not have checked in his weapon. She hoped and prayed.

The night exploded into sound. The first terrorist's weapon, silenced, made only a thud. Ton's reply was a huge bang, followed by a shout from the man he had hit, who now fell to the floor with a crash that seemed to shake the entire building.

The woman Gabrielle shouted something, and then ran round the bed, seeking Jessica. The leader also fired, but was forced against the wall as Tom's Magnum exploded again.

Gabrielle was standing above Jessica, holding a gun in her right hand. Jessica kicked with both legs, and Gabrielle shrieked another curse as she lost her balance and fell across the bed. Jessica was up in an instant, grappling with her, seizing her right wrist to bend it to and fro. Gabrielle grunted and fought back, scratching at Jessica's face with the nails of her free hand, but Jessica had buried her face in the woman's shoulder while continuing to exert all her strength on the wrist. The gun went off, even as she felt the nails biting into her back. But then the fingers relaxed and the gun fell to the floor.

Instantly Jessica was rolling on to her back, reaching for the gun with one hand, kicking with both feet. The woman snarled at her, but received Jessica's heel in her chest and stumbled backwards.

It was time to worry about Tom. Jessica was aware that he had fired again.

Now she rolled across the carpet, Gabrielle's pistol in

her hand, anxious to see but afraid to switch on the light in case she dazzled Tom. All around her was movement, noise, both inside and outside the flat, people shouting, sirens wailing. The telephone by the bed buzzing. Then there were screams and shouts closer at hand, and another shot from Tom's Magnum, sounding like a cannon at such close range.

'Tom!' Jessica shouted.

The light came on from the switch by the door, and he was standing there, the heavy, menacing revolver in his hand, normally friendly features distorted with angry concentration, lank black hair drooping left and right. Around him was a scene of carnage. One man lay at his feet, absolutely still, surrounded by a pool of blood; Jessica didn't need a second glance to know he was dead. Another man, lying on his face halfway down the corridor, also appeared dead. Of the leader and the woman Gabrielle there was no sign.

But the front door was open, and beyond it the heads of other residents of the apartment block had emerged from their front doors, gathering on the landing, gaping at the dead man and, Jessica realised with consternation, along the corridor at her virtually naked body. Then a woman screamed, and they all started shouting at once.

Jessica dashed to the bedroom door to fetch her dressing gown from its hook, and was enveloped in Tom's arms.

'Are you all right?'

'Yes,' she said. 'I think so. Tom . . .'

Cautiously at first, people were venturing into the flat, and one of the women saw the second dead body. 'Aaagh!'

'Call the police!' someone shouted.

'He has a gun!' shouted someone else.

Tom laid down his Magnum, released Jessica, and went into the corridor. 'The police will be here,' he said. 'Now, please . . .'

The police had already arrived. A large uniformed constable was pushing through the throng. 'What's going on?' he demanded, and then himself saw the first corpse. 'Holy Jesus Christ! That man's dead!'

'I'm afraid he is,' Tom agreed. 'There's another in here.'

'But how . . .'

'I shot them,' Tom explained.

The policeman stared at him, gulped, and unhooked his mobile.

'Look out for his gun,' one of the women shouted.

'Would you mind asking those people to leave?' Tom asked. 'Then we can discuss this in a civilised manner.'

'*Do* you have a gun?' the policeman asked.

Tom picked it up and held it out, butt first.

'Just put it down again, will you?' the policeman requested, and began speaking into his phone. 'Yes,' he said. 'A serious incident. Two people dead. I need support and Forensics. Yes, I have made an arrest.' He grimaced at Tom. 'I am about to.'

'I have a gun too,' Jessica said, emerging from the bedroom and laying Gabrielle's pistol on the table beside Tom's.

The policeman goggled at her.

'I think you should put on something more substantial,' Tom suggested. 'We are about to be arrested.' It was part of their training never to admit, in public, who they were.

The policeman advanced down the corridor and peered at the second dead body.

'These people are wearing masks,' he remarked. 'Burglars, were they?'

'In a fashion,' Tom agreed, and reached for the first balaclava.

'Just don't touch anything,' the policeman said.

'What about the other two?' asked one of the onlookers still bunched by the door.

'What other two?' the policeman asked.

'There were two others,' a man said. 'Running down the stairs like mad people.'

'One was a woman,' someone else remarked.

The policeman removed his cap to scratch his head.

'Listen,' Tom said, 'if you will allow Miss Jones to get dressed you can take us down to the station.'

The policeman replaced his cap, suspiciously. He had never encountered two people who were actually asking to be arrested. 'You go ahead, miss.' He regarded the body lying half in and half out of the bedroom doorway. 'I'm afraid we can't touch anything until Forensics have had a go.'

His back-up had already arrived. Sirens were wailing and there was a great deal of noise on the street. Jessica retired to the bedroom, gathered up some casual clothes, pants and a jumper, and went into the bathroom to dress. Her brain was spinning, teeming with apparently unrelated thoughts and images. There was so much that needed thinking about, so much that needed doing, so much that needed explaining.

But miraculously, her neck had stopped aching. Whatever had been put out by the explosion must have been put back in by her more recent manhandling.

The apartment was now full of people. The onlookers had been ushered out, and the hall door closed, but they had been replaced by policemen, ambulance men, detectives, a police surgeon, and various senior officers, all muttering at each other.

Fully dressed now, Jessica sat on the bed. She was not upset by the presence of the dead man – she had seen sufficient dead men before – save for the nagging fear that when the balaclava was pulled off she would find herself looking at Robert Korman. Or should that be a hope?

Tom sat beside her, put his arm round her shoulders. 'You okay?' he asked again.

'A bit shook up. Tom . . .'

'I know,' he said. 'But keep it.'

An inspector was standing in front of them, looking at a notebook. 'Mr Bainbridge?'

Tom nodded.

'You the owner of this flat?'

'We own it jointly.'

'But it's actually in my name,' Jessica said.

The inspector looked at her and then at his notes. 'Miss Jones, is it?' His tone indicated that he did not consider her the least bit important in the context of what had happened.

'Yes,' Jessica said.

'Right. Now you are . . .' Another glance at his notes. 'A police sergeant, Mr Bainbridge?' His eyebrows shot up but he didn't comment. 'And you returned here tonight . . .' he paused.

'About half an hour ago,' Tom said.

'And entered the flat, and found these two men assaulting your, ah, partner. Is that right?'

Tom squeezed Jessica's hand to make her keep silent. 'That's right.'

'So you promptly shot them dead. Do you normally carry a point four five Magnum revolver in your pocket?' He sounded genuinely interested.

'I have a shoulder holster, as a matter of fact,' Tom said, and opened his jacket.

The inspector was not amused. 'I assume you have a licence for it?'

'I do,' Tom said.

'But not a licence to kill, eh?' Now he was pleased with his little joke.

'As a matter of fact, I do,' Tom grinned back. 'When it's a matter of life and death.'

'I'm glad you find this funny,' the inspector sneered. 'Because I am going to have to arrest you on a possible murder charge. And you, young lady, with being an accessory. That gun . . .'

'I took it off one of them,' Jessica explained.

Photographs, measurements, and a pathologist's preliminary inspection completed, a police sergeant joined them.

'We'll be taking the bodies out now, Chief.'

The inspector nodded.

'Wait a moment,' Jessica said. 'I want to look at their faces.'

The inspector raised his eyebrows. 'You're not serious?'

'I am very serious,' Jessica said.

The inspector looked at the sergeant and shrugged. The other policemen stood around looking embarrassed at such ghoulishness. Carefully Jessica raised each balaclava in turn. One of the faces was vaguely familiar, but she couldn't be certain. The other she had never seen before.

Neither was Robert Korman.

'Thank you,' she said.

The bodies were removed, followed by the policemen. Several of them remained in the hall, but for the moment Tom and Jessica were alone with the inspector.

'Friends of yours, were they?' the inspector asked.

'I think it would be a good idea to shut the door,' Tom suggested.

'My dear Sergeant Bainbridge . . .'

Tom felt in his breast pocket and took out his badge.

The inspector peered at it. 'Special . . .'

'The door, Inspector,' Tom said.

The inspector closed the door. Jessica produced her badge from her desk drawer.

'Good God!' the inspector said. 'Well . . . are you claiming this shooting was in the line of duty?'

'We haven't found that out, yet,' Tom said. 'But it is something we need to do, very fast.'

'I should think you do,' the inspector said. 'But I am still going to have to arrest you in connection with two unlawful killings, until you can prove otherwise. I don't suppose you have any idea of the reason behind this attack, if it wasn't a burglary?'

'We need to work on that, Inspector,' Tom said. 'Do we have to come down to the station?'

'I'm afraid you will have to. I'll try to make it as quick as possible. Is there someone you should telephone?'

Tom looked at his watch: it was nearly midnight. 'I think it had better wait until tomorrow. You weren't thinking of keeping us locked up overnight, were you?'

'I should,' the inspector said. 'This is a serious incident. But I'll let you come home as soon as we've completed the formalities. If you undertake to remain here.'

It was three in the morning before they got home. It had been a very long three hours, coming on top of an even longer evening. They had been stared at by the other residents of the building as they left, some of whom Jessica knew quite well, but all of whom had suddenly seemed anxious not to know her at all.

'Drugs,' she heard one woman whisper. 'That's what it was. Drug related.'

Then they had been surrounded by a crowd on the street, muttering and rumbling. By the time they reached the station the media had arrived, asking questions and trying to get photographs and video coverage. Jessica had followed Tom's example and covered her face with the blanket thoughtfully suggested by the inspector before they left the flat.

'What are you going to give them?' Tom asked, listening to the paparazzi's clamour.

'Simply that there has been a shooting and that two people are helping us with our inquiries.' He glanced at Jessica. 'Don't worry, your names will not be released. But I imagine they'll obtain those easily enough from your neighbours.'

'Yes,' Tom said. 'It may be time to move on.'

'You're going nowhere without my say-so,' the inspector said.

At the station they were photographed and fingerprinted. It was all such a farce, as both their photographs and their fingerprints together with DNA samples were already on file, a very special file, and these would have to be destroyed as soon as they were correlated.

'Routine,' the inspector explained. 'Now, as I said, I will let you return home, but there will have to be a policeman on duty outside your flat for the time being.' He gave one of his disarming grins. 'Who knows, it might be for your own protection.'

'A reassuring thought,' Tom said, closing the door behind them, having said a cheery goodnight to the constable. The latch had been damaged by the intruders so the front door could not be locked. At least the various onlookers had gone back to bed.

'Whew!' Jessica kicked off her shoes. 'One of those nights that never seems to end.' She looked at the various bloodstains, the chalk marks on the floor. 'I feel like a stiff drink. There's some Hine Antique in the sideboard.'

'At three o'clock in the morning? Don't you think this might be setting a sinister trend?'

'Only if you expect to find dead men lying about the place whenever next you come home. Do you reckon I'm

42

allowed to clean this place up, or do we have to sleep in a morgue?'

'As they've left, I reckon we can tidy up a bit. But no cleaning. The forensic boys will be back tomorrow, no doubt, trying to lift any more fingerprints they can find.'

He half-filled two balloon glasses, gave her one, and stood a fallen chair back on its feet.

Jessica gazed at the bullet-ravaged bedroom walls. 'We need a major repair job.'

'First things first.' He took a deep swig of brandy. 'I don't suppose you'd care to tell me just what and why?'

Jessica sighed, and sat on the bed, suddenly aware of how exhausted she was.

'Have we the rest of the night? Where did you blow in from, anyway?'

'Singapore. So where have you spent the last few days?'

'How did you know I was away?'

'Darling . . .' He sat beside her. 'Before I got involved in Protection, I was a detective. I still am, officially, Detective-Sergeant Bainbridge. And detectives are supposed to notice things. Like that half-unpacked overnight bag lying in the corner, which, incidentally, is not yours.'

'I was given it by the Consul in Alicante. To replace my things which I lost.'

'Shit! You were in Alicante? With the Lewton woman?'

'I didn't do a very good job, I'm afraid.'

'You're alive. Thank God for that.' He hugged her and kissed her as she rested her head on his shoulder. But his detective's brain was still working. 'You think this was connected to that?'

'I'm afraid so.'

'But no one has claimed responsibility. I mean, for Alicante.'

'Not yet.'

'But you think these were the same people, tonight?'

'From the same people. One of them might have been there; his face was vaguely familiar.'

Tom finished his brandy and got into bed. 'But why? Why come after a humble Protection officer?'

'Because I have information about them which no one else does. That bomb in Alicante was planted by Robert Korman.'

Tom sat up. 'But—'

'Don't say it,' Jessica begged. 'Robert Korman is dead. But I saw him, Tom. And what's more, he recognised me.'

'So . . . you recognised each other. Must have happened pretty quickly.'

'It did. And he recognised me. I recognised his voice.'

'But not his face?'

She shook her head. 'He must have had plastic surgery since last I saw him. Do you believe me?'

'Of course I do.'

'No one else does.'

'Well, we're going to have to make them. Okay, so Robert Korman is alive, and well, and living in' – he waggled his eyebrows – 'Spain?'

'I haven't the faintest idea, although I should think it's unlikely. The important thing is that he doesn't want anyone to know he's alive.'

'So he sent four goons after you, because he knows you recognised something about him. His voice. But they didn't just kill you.'

'I think they meant to kidnap me.'

'For what reason?'

'That's something I really do not wish to think about at this time in the morning. Let's get some sleep.'

'Will you be able to?'

'And how.'

'And here I was, panting back from Singapore looking for a large piece of nooky.'

'Tonight? You'd be better off with a rubber dolly. Slightly more animated.'

'I can wait.' He kissed the back of her neck and switched off the light.

But even with the effects of the brandy and the comforting knowledge that Tom was only inches away, sleep was a long time coming. Incredible to believe that this time yesterday she had still been in the hospital bed in Alicante feeling quite weak. Not that she was feeling very strong right now; waves of panic swept over her every few minutes, making her pulse race, heart thump. She couldn't stop listening for threatening sounds. Then miscellaneous, unrelated thoughts would invade her mind; she remembered the postcard she had written on the plane to little Megan Lynch. Another line of unwelcome thought. So much had happened in the past twenty-four hours. So many people had looked at her as though she had gone potty whenever she mentioned Korman. But she knew she had seen him, and what was more, Robert Korman knew he had been recognised, and clearly felt she was too dangerous to live. But he had not ordered her assassination, which could have been so easily accomplished. He had wanted *her*. That in itself could give anyone terrifying nightmares if one dared fall asleep. And so far, no one believed her; she even had her doubts about Tom, although he had so gallantly claimed he did.

Robert Korman! She remembered the siege of the Slavonian Embassy as if it had been yesterday. Practically her first assignment. She remembered being told on the radio that the building was surrounded by terrorists, determined to wreck the peace talks being held there. She remembered the initial feeling of panic, and the reassurance from Eileen, a moment before her partner,

Ted, had been shot dead. She remembered looking up at that handsome, smiling, cruel face, and realising that she was next in line. She remembered thinking that she was about to die, drawing her own weapon with the speed that had made her an outstanding pupil at training college. The picture remained vivid in her memory, of firing, and hearing the man shout, 'Fucking bitch!'

She didn't know whether she had actually hit him or not. He had been dragged away by his companions as the morning had filled with police sirens and personnel. But she had never forgotten those two words shouted at her as she had levelled her gun. And now, after two years, they had come back to haunt her.

But Korman had been killed a year later, when a bomb he and his people had been about to plant had prematurely exploded. At least, that was what everyone had supposed; no trace of his body had ever been found but pieces of his clothing were subsequently identified. And he had not been seen or heard of since. So had it been his ghost, in Alicante?

She must have fallen asleep eventually, only to be awoken with a start by noise; someone was ringing the bell and knocking at the same time.

'Shit!' Tom commented, sitting up. 'Don't tell me the media are here.' He rolled out of bed, dragged on his boxer shorts, and padded down the corridor. 'It's not actually locked,' he said as he opened the door. 'Oh, my God! I beg your pardon, ma'am.'

Jessica sat up and clutched the duvet to her throat as she watched the woman come down the corridor to stand in the bedroom doorway and look at her.

'I gather you had a busy night, JJ,' the woman remarked. Assistant Commissioner Judith Proud did not only hold a unique position for a woman; she also held a unique stature as a disciplinarian. She hardly looked the part, as she was tall and slender, had soft, attractive features and a wealth of curly dark hair, but there was not a man or a woman in the department who was not terrified of her, and that included the Commander. As was her custom, she wore a smart suit rather than uniform, and carried a briefcase.

'Yes, ma'am,' Jessica agreed.

Behind the AC, Tom was fluttering like a startled bee. 'Coffee?' he suggested. 'Would you like a cup of coffee, ma'am? I was about to make some.'

'Please,' Judith said. 'Join me.'

She went into the lounge and sat down. Jessica put on a dressing gown and hurried behind her. 'I'm sorry we're not dressed, but . . .'

'You've had a very long night. You understand that there is going to be hell to pay? I have a meeting with the DPP later on this morning, but I'm sure you realise there is deep public anxiety about policemen shooting people unless there is a very good reason.'

'There was a very good reason,' Jessica assured her.

'First things first,' Judith said. 'I take it the two men who were shot were armed?'

'The police have their guns, and the one I took off the woman. They also had knives.'

'That's something, I suppose. And were you able to identify them?'

'One face was familiar. He might have been one of the bombers in Alicante. But I couldn't swear to it.'

'But you have an idea as to their organisation.'

'Well . . .' Jessica looked up as Tom came in with a tray and three steaming cups.

'I have read the report on Alicante,' Judith said. 'And Harrison's. I was going to call you in today, anyway, to talk about it. But under the circumstances, I thought I'd come down here instead. You realise you're going to have to move out. Who and what you are is blown. There is no possibility of keeping that a secret, even if I manage to talk the DPP into dropping charges. Anyway, you'd have to go simply because those goons might come back. How did they know where to find you, anyway?'

'The flat is in my name,' Jessica explained. 'And I was recognised in Alicante.'

'By the man you claim was Robert Korman.'

'With respect, ma'am, it *was* Robert Korman.'

'Who then sent his people . . . to kidnap you? Why?'

'That I don't know. But I would hazard a guess that he wants to know if and how many people I might have informed of his reappearance.'

Judith drank some coffee. 'If Korman is alive,' she said, 'that is about the most serious news we have had in a very long time.'

Tom sat beside her on the settee. 'Just how much do we know about this character, ma'am? And why is he so dangerous?'

Judith opened her laptop and punched a few keys. 'Robert Korman,' she said. 'Born 1 December 1950, Istanbul, of Hungarian parents. One of twins. This is important. Involved with sister Arsinoe in anti-government activities as a student, in 1968. Shot and killed a policeman and forced to flee the country. Uncertain whether Korman or sister actually fired the fatal shot. Jointly involved in German terrorist activities in the early seventies, linked to Baader-Meinhof gang and may have been involved in the Munich Olympic massacre. Fled Germany on break-up of the Baader-Meinhof gang, either offered their services or were recruited by the IRA in late seventies. Became their master bombers on the continent, carrying out several attacks on British Army personnel and property. It was in one of these that Arsinoe was shot and killed by a British soldier. This led Korman to declare undying hatred of

Britain and all things British. Although several of his close associates were in time taken, he always avoided capture. In fact he has been so skilful at evading arrest that there are no fingerprint records on him at all, and the few photographs in which he appears are so blurred as to be virtually unrecognisable. Broke with the IRA at the time of the first ceasefire in 1994, disappeared. Surfaced again in connection with the siege of the Slavonian Embassy in 1997. No group ever claimed responsibility for that attack, but Korman was captured on a security video. As usual, it wasn't a very good image, but it could be related to earlier shots.' She looked up. 'That was the time you and he had a close encounter, JJ.'

'Yes, ma'am. I shot at him, and appear to have missed any vital organ.'

'Pity. However, he does not appear to have taken that personally, or considered it important, at the time. He didn't come after you. As I said, we had, and have, no idea who he was working for, and we found it very disturbing. None of the Slavonian dissident groups claimed responsibility; in fact, they all dissociated themselves from the terrorists. And of course we now definitely wanted him for murder, as he was seen to shoot and kill Detective-Sergeant Ted Parsons. But then he disappeared again, only to surface for the blowing up of the conference centre in Buenos Aires last year. He was supposed to have gone up with his own bomb. In fact, the Argentinian police were told he had by one of his accomplices, who survived, briefly: both his legs were blown off.' She gave a quick smile. 'The fellow died well, apparently. When asked about Korman, he said, "It is the Will of God."'

Jessica frowned.

'So, with Korman officially dead, it seemed we could all relax. Until Alicante. Now, according to Harrison, JJ, although you said you were positive it was him, you also said that you didn't recognise the man, although you were quite close to him, and had been very close to him outside the Slavonian Embassy two years ago.'

'I think he must have had facial surgery,' Jessica said, only half-concentrating.

'Which would make sense if he had been blown up in Argentina and survived,' Tom suggested. 'He must have been pretty badly injured.'

'Possibly,' Judith remarked. 'But you think you recognised his voice. You must admit that is a pretty long shot, JJ.'

'He used exactly the same words and the same tone as the first time,' Jessica insisted.

'You'll agree you were pretty stressed out.'

'No, I wasn't,' Jessica said. 'Not then. The bomb hadn't gone off yet. And there's something else, something you said.'

Judith raised her eyebrows.

'You said that after Korman had been officially blown up,' Jessica said, 'and one of his people was found dying, the man said it was the will of God.'

Judith nodded. 'He seems to have had a macabre sense of humour.'

'No, ma'am. He was making a confession.'

Judith frowned. 'In what way?'

'I don't know. But when I asked the kidnappers what they were doing, why they were kidnapping me, their leader said, "It is the Will of God." In fact, they used the phrase twice.'

Judith regarded her for several seconds. Then she said, 'You were fairly stressed then, too.'

'He said it,' Jessica insisted. 'Like the Argentinian police, I just thought it was a remark, at the time. But . . . the same phrase? Twice? Related to Robert Korman?'

'Theory?'

'That that is the name of their organisation.'

'The Will of God? We have never heard of it.'

'Because they haven't made any claims.'

'The Will of God,' Tom said. 'You know, with international terrorism, one automatically thinks of Muslims. But surely they would say the Will of Allah.'

Judith regarded them both for several seconds more. Then she shut down her laptop and closed it. 'Pack up,' she said. 'I will have a car here for you as soon as possible. It will take you to a safe house, where you will remain until further notice. And until further notice, you will remain completely out of sight. Understood?'

'Does this mean you believe me?' Jessica asked.

'This means I am trying to keep you alive while I do some investigating.'

'I'm supposed to have a session with Mrs Wright today,' Jessica said.

'Do you feel in need of psychiatric evaluation?'

'Not right now.'

Judith nodded. 'I'll arrange something.'

'I'm also supposed to make a detailed report to Arthur.'

'Leave that with me. But first things first. The vanishing act. That includes you, Tom Bainbridge.'

'Yes, ma'am,' Tom said. 'Do we get our weapons back?'

'No. You are both officially under suspension. Just remember that you need to disappear, utterly. Your food and other requirements will be brought to you.'

'That may be a problem,' Tom said.

'The driver who picks you up will take a list of anything special you may need for the next few days.'

'You sure about this, ma'am? We have expensive tastes.'

Judith ignored the quip. 'You will remain in this bucolic idyll until someone comes for you. I expect this order to be obeyed. Honeymoon.' She allowed a slight twitch of her lips, not quite a smile.

51

'Whew!' Tom said when he closed the door behind her. 'She's only supposed to visit people at home when they're getting the push.'

'There's no guarantee we aren't. We'd better get a move on.'

Jessica went into the shower. Tom followed her into the bathroom to shave. 'I'd say she believes you.'

'Then she's unique.'

'I believe you,' he said in an injured tone.

'You're also unique.' She stepped out, towelled, blew him a kiss. 'Let's hope she can persuade Adams et al.' She put on her undies and began packing. 'I had grown quite fond of this place.'

'Bullet holes and all?' Tom called from the shower.

'Adds character. What about all our pictures, the cutlery and the glasses? Are we supposed just to abandon them?'

'We'll have them stored until we get settled again.'

'Brrr.' Jessica pulled a T-shirt over her head and got out a pair of denims. What she most wanted to do was sleep for a week, in her own bed.

'Look at it this way,' Tom said, putting his arms round her waist from behind and nuzzling the soft hair on the nape of her neck. 'We have each other.'

'Are you organised to do something about our gear?' Tom asked the police driver.

The driver surveyed the four suitcases. 'You mean there's more?'

'That's our home,' Jessica pointed out. 'All our personal belongings.'

'My business is to deliver you. The rest you'll have to take up with your boss. You did lock it up?'

'I'm not sure how much good that's going to be,' Tom said. 'The lock's broken.'

The driver made a face. 'I'll report to division and they'll have a new one fitted.'

'Then there's the matter of the champagne,' Tom said.

'What champagne?'

'We were told to equip ourselves with whatever we needed to disappear for a week. A case of champagne is a must. There's an off-licence just over there. Don't worry, I have my cards.'

'You must be stark raving mad,' the driver said. 'You start using cards and they'll trace you in a tick. I'll check out the situation and see if I can get you some bubbly.'

'Bollinger.' Tom winked at Jessica. 'We only drink Bollinger.'

Two hours later, after endless narrow country roads, the car turned on to a track through fields, winding down through a valley and up the far side to a farmhouse. The track was rough and stony, and they could feel the car exhaust dragging through the ridge of grass between the ruts. They came to a sudden halt beside a small barn full of rusting machinery.

'Looks sort of isolated,' Tom commented.

'And very muddy,' Jessica remarked, seeking dry footing as she stepped down.

'It'll dry when the weather improves.'

'You're saying we're going to be here a long time,' Tom suggested.

'Haven't a clue, mate.'

Jessica was surveying the fields behind the house. It was all rather beautiful. But . . . She blinked at the cows in the distant pasture. 'We don't have to milk those things, I hope?'

'No problem. Those fields are rented out. All you have to do is be a young couple taking a rest from the rat race. Nervous breakdowns, eh?'

'Never was a truer word spoken in jest,' Tom said. 'You were going to give us some cash.'

'Nearly forgot.' He felt in his breast pocket and took out a roll of notes. 'You have to sign for it.'

Tom did so.

'Five hundred pounds,' Jessica said. 'That sounds as if we *are* going to be here for more than a week. And if we can't go into the village, what are we to spend it on?'

'Play gin rummy,' the driver laughed, dumping their bags near the farmhouse door.

'Don't forget the champagne,' Tom called as the policeman backed his car round the side of the barn and bounced off down the track.

'Now what?' Jessica tried the unresponsive door handle. 'Can't get in.'

'Let's try round the other side.' Tom led off along a slippery brick path with Jessica close behind. The whole place was rather overgrown with neglected creepers smothering sheds, hedges and bushes. It had rained recently and everywhere was dripping. Then the scene changed as they turned on to a paved patio facing south with an open view across a valley to the downs beyond. A sliver of sea glinted in the far distance.

'Not too bad from this angle, is it?'

Startled, the pair swung round, alert, looking for the origin of the voice. A bucolic-looking character edged through a wooden gate. 'Better in fine weather, o' course. Then you can see ships in the English Channel. Nice at night, too, with the coast all lit up.'

Tom smiled politely, noting the soiled dungarees and mud-caked boots, the floppy hat. 'I'm sure. So tell me, do you live near here?'

'Aarh!'

That he took for an affirmative. 'My wife and I will

be staying a few days. Name's John West.' He held out his hand.

'You bloody liar!' The rustic straightened his back and took off his hat to run his hand through his tangled hair. Then he laughed. 'You're Tom Bainbridge and Jessica Jones. Harry Philpotts, C Section. Glad to see I had you fooled, there.'

'Shoot! You did, too. What are you doing here? Sent to see we behave ourselves?' Tom shook his hand.

'Sort of. It's my spell on watch. Seeing you're comfortable, like.'

Jessica laughed. 'That shouldn't be too difficult. All I want to do is get into a bath and then sleep for the foreseeable future. By the way, how do we get in?'

'Here.' Harry led them through a French window into a snug sitting room.

Jessica looked around appreciatively. It was all very simple: white-washed walls and rough, dark-stained wood; cretonne curtains and matching chair covers; hair-cord carpet and scatter rugs and pictures of hunting scenes. A comfortable, liveable look. The kitchen was old-fashioned with flagstones and a patterned oilcloth on the table, but the stove and fridge were gleaming white, obviously new. Upstairs, inner walls of lath and plaster divided the floor space into three bedrooms and a large, airy bathroom. 'Which is your room?' she called down to Harry.

'I don't have one,' he replied. 'I'm not here to sleep. My replacement arrives at eight. He won't be sleeping, either.'

'What about food?' Tom asked.

'There's stuff in the fridge and freezer. And if you give me a list of anything else you want and some money before I go, I'll see you get it tomorrow. I gather Control don't want you waltzing around the neighbourhood inviting visitors.'

A honeymoon for three! Jessica grinned to herself.

She lay in the bath with a mug of tea made with real milk, and as the water was still hot Tom stepped in as she stepped out. By the time he came downstairs she had revved up a couple of frozen pizzas, made a salad, and even found a bottle of Australian wine in the cupboard. Harry was replaced by Brian Tupper – who shared the feast at the kitchen table – and then the three of them carried mugs of Nescafé into the sitting room to watch the news.

Jessica had begun to relax, but the continued media coverage of the Alicante bombing made her tense, angry and desperately sad for the relatives paraded on screen for viewers to wallow in their grief . . . and especially for Megan Lynch, who fortunately was not screened.

The next week there was to be a memorial service for Mrs Lewton. Jessica wondered if she'd be allowed to go.

'See you in the morning,' Brian said.

'I'd feel happier if you'd leave me some hardware,' Tom said. He had spotted the Magnum in the shoulder holster under the jerkin.

'Sorry, chum. Orders. But here . . .' He gave Tom a mobile. 'If I can't handle it, press that alarm and you'll have half the Sussex force here in ten minutes. Not that anyone except us knows you're here.'

'Presumably we're still under suspension,' Tom grumbled as they went to bed.

Sleep eluded Jessica for hours; it was impossible to get Megan's desperate plight out of her mind. Her body pounded with anger.

The sun awoke them, late. Brian had already been replaced by Harry and they shared fried bacon and tomatoes, then lay out on sunbeds while he pretended to garden, maintaining the rustic caretaker image.

Tom wanted to hear Jessica's story in detail.

'Not that I can tell you much,' she pointed out. 'I've learned more about it from the TV than I gleaned out there. The one thing quite positive in my mind is that Robert Korman is alive and was responsible for the bombing. His face was quite different, but there was absolutely no doubt about his voice. And anyway, if it wasn't him, why would those Will of God fanatics want to kidnap me?'

'There can only be one reason, my love. He wants to know if you recognised him, and if he's had a facelift or whatever, how. Equally, he wants to know who you've told and described his new face to.'

'No one, yet. No one has wanted to know. No one believes me.'

'Well, I do. So tell me about him.'

Jessica sat up, smiling. 'Well, thanks for that. You've never seen him, have you? You won't remember his bony, Roman nose and heavy brows that virtually met in the middle, and his fleshy lips. Those have all gone. Of course I didn't have time to examine him closely . . . it was all over in a matter of seconds. But his nose is definitely smaller, and so is his mouth, and his chin was less pronounced. The whole impression was one of blandness; there were no distinguishing marks.'

'They'd all have been taken out by the surgeons. It's difficult to accept you're so sure it was him, from just a couple of words.'

'Like listening to a voice on the radio, I suppose. The first time I heard that voice I was utterly traumatised. He was pointing his gun at me and I thought I was going to die. Then Ted Parsons caught his attention and he shot Ted instead. But I'll never forget that voice. And to hear it again in virtually identical circumstances.' She shuddered. 'It brought me up in goose pimples. But the really important thing is that he recognised me. That's the clincher.'

'What colour was his hair?'

'I can't say for sure but I have an impression of pale brown. And curly. It used to be almost straight black. But any competent hairdresser could have done that.'

'Height?'

'That hasn't changed. About five foot ten, I'd say.' She was silent for a moment, then stretched her arms. 'I need some exercise. As we're not suppose to go walking I think I'll find some music on the radio and do some aerobics. Want to join me?'

'Absolutely not. Not my scene.'

They were watching television after dinner on the second night when they heard a car bumping down the track to the farmhouse.

'Tom!' Jessica said. 'Visitors!'

He got up and went to the window, peering round the curtain. 'Can't see them yet. And not a weapon between us.'

'Oh yes, there is,' she said. 'There's a bloody big carving knife in the kitchen – though a fat lot of good that would be against a Kalashnikov. Where's Brian?' She fetched the knife.

'Patrolling outside, I think. How do we know if these people are sent down from Control or if they're here by the Will of God?'

'No idea. There's an axe, too, in the scullery.'

He brought it in, grinning at her. 'Prehistoric. Wouldn't even be much good against a penknife.'

'We have to make them come in.' Jessica switched off the lights, plunging the entire house into darkness. As she did so she heard a car door slam. 'They're not being very subtle.'

'You take the back door and I'll take the front.'

They listened to footsteps on the back path, and a moment later there was a knock on the back door.

'You can open up,' Judith called. 'We know you're in. We saw the lights.'

Jessica switched the lights on again while Tom came through to unlock the door. Judith gazed at the axe and the carving knife. 'Ready for everything, I see. Have you been enjoying the bucolic life?'

'Ma'am, you just scared the shit out of us,' Tom said.

'I've brought you back your gun, Tom, and yours, JJ. May we come in?'

Tom stepped back, and Judith came into the house, looking as always incredibly chic in a black shirt and chinos with a gold-buckled leather belt. Behind her were Brian and three men, one of whom Jessica had met before; he was a high-ranking chief superintendent. The other two were considerably younger; one wore a pale moustache and looked somewhat effete, the other was beetle-browed and heavy. This last carefully closed the door behind them.

'All well?' Judith asked. 'No alarms?' She wandered about the kitchen and went into the lounge, almost as if expecting to find the odd dead body lying about.

'Up to this minute, none, ma'am,' Jessica said.

'Good. Sit down.' She did so herself, and the men with her found seats for themselves. Jessica and Tom sat together on the settee.

'Have you ever seen this before?' Judith asked, and placed on the coffee table what looked like a very small cross. 'You may pick it up.'

Very cautiously Tom took the tiny piece of metal; it was about as long as the last joint of his index finger. It had also been at some time recently exposed to severe heat, judging by its blackened and generally tarnished appearance. 'Never saw it before in my life.' He glanced at Jessica.

'Me neither.'

'Tell me about it,' Judith commanded.

'Well . . .' Tom considered. 'It's a cross.'

'Go on.'

'I'm not all that big on crosses, ma'am.'

'It's an inverted cross,' Jessica said. 'I think.'

'Absolutely correct. It's an upside-down cross, you might say. Have you any idea where it came from?'

Jessica had an inspiration. 'The wreckage of the hotel in Alicante.'

'Spot on. It has an inscription on its back.'

Jessica picked up the little cross and stared at the back. The letters were so small as to be indistinguishable.

'You'd need a magnifying glass,' Judith said. 'The inscription is in Turkish. It says, The Will of God.'

Jessica looked at Tom.

'Here's its mate.' Judith placed another little cross on the table. 'One of its mates, I suspect.'

The second cross was identical to the first, save that it was undamaged; there was an inscription on the back of this as well.

'Same thing?' Tom asked.

Judith nodded. 'Now where do you suppose we found that one?'

Another inspiration. 'On the body of one of my would-be kidnappers,' Jessica said.

'That's right. Here's *its* mate.' She placed the third cross beside the other two. 'Presumably the two who got away were also wearing these.'

'Where?' Tom asked.

'On a chain round their ankles. So it would appear that your suspicions have been confirmed, JJ. The attack on your flat was linked to the attack in Alicante.'

'Hold on,' Jessica said. 'The men I saw in Alicante all got away. None was blown up.'

'Quite. This was taken from the body of a young woman – or what was left of her after the explosion and the fire.

60

She has not been identified, although it is presumed from the scraps of clothing remaining that she was a member of the staff. Several members of the staff are known to have died, but identifying them has proved difficult. In any event, finding this indicates that the bombers had one of their people inside the building. I don't suppose we'll ever know whether she committed suicide, was supposed to get out in time and didn't, or was simply regarded as expendable by her employers. However, the point is that these crosses – one in the hotel and two in your flat – give credence to your belief that the man you saw, and who shouted at you, outside the hotel in Alicante, was Robert Korman. There can be no other possible reason for him to send a kidnap squad after you. Would you recognise his new face again?'

'Oh, yes,' Jessica said.

'He is obviously aware of that. So it's a case of get Jones. We'd like an identikit right away.'

Jessica nodded, absently. 'Does this mean I have to go into hiding for the rest of my life, or until you catch up with him?'

'Which you never did in the past,' Tom put in, 'even when half the Division had some idea what he looked like.'

'Well, now we have someone who *knows* what he looks like. We are going after Mr Korman in a big way. Not necessarily for your sake, JJ. The point is, if he's alive, as we now believe he is, and is working with this group which calls itself the Will of God, he is once again perhaps the most dangerous man on earth. We know he has recently been targeting only British institutions and British people, but there is no pattern to it. They are almost like wildcat, mood-of-the-moment strikes, and yet planning explosions like those in Buenos Aires or Alicante takes some time. They also cost a great deal of money to set up. We know

61

nothing of his funding. And the fact that no one, not even this Will of God, has ever claimed responsibility for any of his actions, is the most sinister thing of all. We know nothing whatsoever about what is going on, save that, thanks to you, we can be pretty sure that Korman is involved. So, JJ, this is your pigeon. I am seconding you to Captain Merryman's outfit.' She indicated the fair-moustached young man. 'SAS Special Unit. Your business is to find and destroy Robert Korman. And the Will of God.'

'A woman! An ordinary policewoman. And a pint-sized one at that.' Robert Korman stared at the two people standing in front of him, and they trembled; they knew what his rages were like. 'Now two of my men are dead. Albert! What is she – Supergirl?'

'She didn't kill them, Chief,' Albert said. 'She had a back-up.'

'She's shacked up with another cop,' Gabrielle explained. 'Unfortunately, he just turned up, armed with a Magnum.'

'You were four to two,' Korman said. 'Four to two! I trained you to kill, not be killed. You are shits! All of you. Useless lumps of shit! Well, you will have to go back again.'

'Ah . . .' Albert glanced at Gabrielle.

'She has gone,' Gabrielle said. 'They have gone.'

'Gone?' Korman inquired. 'Gone where?'

'We don't know. After the shoot-out, there was a great deal of police activity. There was no time for anything but to get out. When we tried to check the next day, they had gone, and the apartment was under police guard.'

'Did you not find out where they had gone?'

'They went off in a car. We reckoned it was a police vehicle, judging by the description one of the neighbours gave. Anyway, they have vanished.'

Albert and Gabrielle gazed at their master, and insensibly moved closer together as they watched Korman's expression. His entire face seemed to change, his mouth widening and his nostrils flaring. Neither had seen him before the plastic surgery, but they knew they were looking at a monster.

'Two men dead.' Korman's voice was like dripping vitriol. 'And the target disappeared. What do you call yourselves? Fools? Pigs? Idiots? Shitbags! You . . .' He flung out an arm, pointing a finger at Albert. 'Return to England. Find that woman.'

Albert licked his lips. 'I don't know where to start. She could be anywhere.'

'She must surface somewhere. She must have relatives. She must have friends . . . Listen, she was in hospital in Alicante for a few days. Check that out. The English are great for making friends. Find out who she met in hospital, people she will have kept in touch with, will wish to contact again.'

'I will require assistance.'

'Then get assistance. Go to Mehmed. Tell him what you need. Take what you need. But I will change your instructions. Do not bother to kidnap her. That has already proved too costly, and whatever she has been able to tell the British police will already have been done. Just kill her. That is all you have to do, Albert. Just get her in your sights and blow her away. Avenge your comrades.'

'I will take Gabrielle again.'

'You will not. Gabrielle stays here. You . . .' This time the pointing finger was directed at the woman. 'Get in there.'

Gabrielle looked at the doorway indicated. She knew that it led to Korman's private apartment. She knew what he intended.

'You said there would be none of that.' Her voice was a low whine.

'I have changed my mind. Get in there!'

Gabrielle looked at Albert for aid. But he was already backing across the room.

'You have no right to do this,' she said.

'I am Robert Korman,' he sneered. 'I can do whatever I wish. It is the Will of God!'

The Plan

Jessica looked at Merryman. She didn't much care for him, and nothing about him suggested he might live up to his name.

Tom obviously felt the same way. 'Am I to be seconded too, ma'am?' he asked, hopefully.

'No. You will be returned to ordinary duties, Tom. We have no reason to suppose that Korman has you specially targeted, or that he even knows who you are, beyond the fact that you are JJ's partner. Obviously he'll know she has described him to you, but from what she has said, he no longer has a very describable face, so I doubt that will worry him too much. Right. I think we need to be on our way. Your transport will be here in a couple of hours, Merryman. As usual, I am not going to ask you how you propose to handle this; your only priority is haste. Good luck, JJ.'

Jessica swallowed. 'When do I surface?'

'When Korman is caught. Or dead. And this time I mean, guaranteed dead.'

'But . . . that could take years.'

'It had better not.' Judith went to the door. 'Fetch your things, Bainbridge. You're coming with us.'

Tom obeyed, came down the stairs a few minutes later with his hastily packed carry-all. 'I feel as if I'm abandoning you to the wolves.'

'Never was a truer word spoken in jest,' Merryman agreed.

Tom kissed Jessica. 'Are we allowed a get-together?' he asked Judith, who was waiting, somewhat impatiently, by the door with the superintendent.

'It may be possible to arrange a brief break,' Judith said. 'But not for a week or two.'

'There's to be a memorial service for Mrs Lewton,' Jessica said. 'Am I allowed to attend?'

'Certainly not.'

'I feel I should send Mr Lewton a card or something.'

'You can do that when this is over. Come along now.'

Brian went with them, closing the door, and Jessica was alone with the two SAS men. 'What happens now?' she asked, indeed feeling that she was surrounded by wolves.

Merryman looked at his watch. 'As the lady said, our transport will be here in a couple of hours. But as we don't have a moment to waste, we may as well start now. This is Sergeant McAdoo, by the way. My second-in-command and your immediate superior.'

The beetle-browed sergeant nodded.

'Pleased to meet you,' Jessica said. 'Would anyone like a cup of coffee? Tea?'

'Forget it,' Merryman said.

'Oh.' He seemed determined to be hostile. 'Well, then . . .' She sat down.

'I did not give you permission to sit, Jones.'

Jessica stood up again, and to attention, while he slowly walked round her.

'My first task,' he said, 'is to evaluate you.'

Jessica waited, but she was taken by surprise when he suddenly hit her, just above the right buttock, an agonising blow which drove all the breath from her body as she collapsed to her knees.

'Maybe we will have that cup of coffee after all, Sergeant,' Merryman said. 'You make it.'

Jessica was still kneeling as the pain slowly receded. But a red mist floated in front of her eyes – mainly outrage.

'I am sure you can get up now,' Merryman said.

Jessica pushed herself up, standing straight with difficulty.

Merryman sat down and crossed his knees. 'There are some things you should know,' he said. 'And for God's sake stop shaking. First, my outfit is outside the norm. Even of the SAS. Our business is to seek and destroy, quickly and efficiently, and without identification. That is why we do not wear uniform, and if any of us falls into the wrong hands, alive, we never divulge who we are, even under severe interrogation. Not even the Big Four: number, rank, date of birth, name. Understood?'

'Yes, sir,' Jessica said, having difficulty getting the words out between her gritted teeth.

'You do not refer to me as sir. I am boss. Understood?'

'Yes . . . boss.'

'Two,' Merryman said. 'As we exist in conditions of extreme severity, it is necessary, and I demand, that we are one hundred per cent fit at all times. We call it the Beast. Understood?'

'Yes, boss.'

'We'll check you out on that, later. Three. You need to know that I do not like employing women, and I never have before. Now I am stuck with two, at least in the short term.'

Jessica could not stop her head from turning. 'Two, boss?'

'It seems that the great lady feels you should have a chaperone,' he said distastefully. 'However, it is very necessary for you to understand why I have been forced to employ you. It is simply because you appear to be the only person able to identify Robert Korman. Now I don't know if it is ever going to be practical to have you meet up so that you can pick him out. As far as I am concerned, you are just bait. Judging by that attempt to kidnap you, he believes you could be dangerous to him. Therefore, if we go after him, with you stuck out in front of us, the odds are that he is going to flush cover and come after you again. That's when we will get him. You with me?'

'Yes, boss.'

'That idea scare you?'

'Yes, boss.'

'But you'll go through with it?'

'Yes, boss. Am I allowed to ask a question?'

'Shoot.'

'Why did you hit me?'

'That was part of the evaluation process, Jones.'

'And what did you learn?'

'A whole hell of a lot. You did not dissolve into moans and tears. You did not even properly fall down. And you did not turn round and attack me back. So now I know that you're a whole lot tougher than you look, and that you have yourself under good self-control. Ah, coffee. You may sit, Jones.'

Jessica sat, took the cup of coffee from the Sergeant. Self-control, she thought; she felt like throwing the boiling liquid in the bastard's face.

'Of course,' Merryman said, 'one brief test is far from sufficient. They tell me you're thirty-five.'

'Yes, boss.'

'That's one hell of an age to be going into the field, even if you don't look it.'

'Thank you, boss.'

'You are really going to have to prove your fitness.'

'I will do so, boss.' But she could not resist a smile.

'What's so funny?'

'Simply that, as I understand it, you're stuck with me whether I'm fit enough for you or not.'

He scowled at her. 'Quite a smarty-pants, aren't you?
Right. I am informed that you are a first-class shot.'

'Yes, boss.'

'Something else we can test tomorrow. And also that
you have a top ranking in CQB.'

'Yes, boss.'

'Right. Have a go at the Sergeant.'

Jessica looked McAdoo up and down. He was a big man.
'I don't think I could defeat the Sergeant, boss.'

'Why not?'

'He is about twice my size, and I have to assume he is
also trained in Close Quarter Battle.'

'So what would you do if he confronted you?'

'If I made the assumption that he was going to kill me,
I would shoot him, boss.'

'But you don't have a gun, Jones.'

'Then I would run like hell.'

He regarded her for several seconds, then suddenly
grinned. 'At least you're a realist.'

'There's a car,' McAdoo said.

'I assume it's Wilcoxon. But just check it out. Okay,
Jones, get your gear.'

Jessica went upstairs, packed her bag, and looked at the bed
where she and Tom had spent the better part of two very
pleasant days. She wondered when they would have the
opportunity to do that again, for all Judith's promise. And
before then . . . quite apart from the danger of the operation
to which she had been seconded, she was going to have to
put up with the ultimate male chauvinist pig, who was also
a bully and a thoroughly unpleasant character. If she forgot
that for a moment, her aching back would remind her.

She grinned. Maybe, when it was all over, she'd be
able to get him on a harassment charge. She carried the
bag downstairs, where she was greeted by a large young

woman with curly black hair. 'Jessica Jones? I'm Monica Wilcoxon.'

Jessica was immediately reassured. Monica Wilcoxon looked a very sensible and no-nonsense person. She shook hands.

'I'm to look after you,' Monica said. 'He been giving you a hard time?'

'He said it was necessary.'

'He always does.' As with her companions, Monica was in plain clothes – in her case a dress. Thus it was impossible to determine her rank. But she certainly seemed on very easy terms with the Captain. 'I'm told this is a rush job.'

'She has to be ready by tomorrow night,' Merryman said.

'That is probably an impossibility,' Monica said. 'But we'll see what we can do.'

The car was a Land Rover. There was a driver, who was not introduced. McAdoo sat in front beside him. Jessica found herself in the middle of the back seat, wedged between Merryman and Monica.

'I'm told you have a pretty impressive CV,' Monica remarked.

'Thirty-five,' Merryman remarked, disparagingly. 'I wouldn't even have a man on my team who was thirty-five.'

'He likes them young,' Monica explained mischievously. 'That should mean he'll keep his hands off you.'

'But not his fists,' Jessica said.

Monica looked past her at Merryman. 'You didn't.'

'Just testing.'

'Well, maybe, when she's ready, we'll let her test you back.'

She was growing on Jessica with every moment.

They drove for perhaps an hour, then pulled into what

70

might have been a deserted airfield from the Second World War. All that remained were a couple of grass-infiltrated runways and several Nissen huts. One was clearly a mess centre; it glowed with light and issued some noise.

'We have one to ourselves,' Monica said, and led Jessica into the first of the huts.

The interior was hardly less primitive than the outside, but there was a free-standing heater, its flue disappearing through the wall, and a small camping gas stove, together with two cots as well as an open hanging cupboard and a few shelves.

'Home,' Monica said, putting some coal into the smouldering fire. 'This place is *damp*. You wouldn't believe it was flaming June.'

Her gear was scattered about the place.

'How long have you been here?' Jessica asked.

'Moved in this morning. I only received my orders at breakfast. That's the way they do things.'

'Are you part of the team?'

Monica shook her head. 'I'm here to make sure you're ready and able. And please, don't start telling me what you're about. I'm not supposed to know, and I don't want to know. Nightcap?'

'What are you offering?'

Monica grinned. 'Don't sound so hopeful. I'm talking about Horlick's, not alcohol. Alcohol is out while you're with me.'

'Then I'll settle for Horlick's.'

Monica put the kettle on. 'Now strip off and let me look at you.'

Jessica obeyed.

Monica walked round her, slowly. 'Apart from miscellaneous scabs and scars from the cuts you had, you look in pretty good shape. Let's see . . .' She bent over Jessica's bruised back. 'It's coming out.' She pressed the area. 'Does it hurt?'

'Yes.'

'He really is a bastard. But I'm afraid that's the way the cookie crumbles. This is a man's show. Once you volunteer to join it, you have to play by their rules. That bother you?'

'No. Save that I didn't volunteer. I was seconded.'

'Then there's clearly more to you than meets the eye. Uh-uh . . .' She held up a finger. 'No confidences.'

'Has he ever hit you?' Jessica asked.

'No fear. I'd have him on a charge.'

'Eh?'

Monica winked. 'I'm his superior officer. We both hold captain's rank, but I have seniority . . . I'll put something on that.' She sprayed an aerosol on to the black and blue flesh.

'Tell me something,' Jessica said. 'Is he likely to hit me again?'

'I should hope not.'

'Because if he does, the next time I'm going to hit him back.'

Monica grinned. 'I don't think that would be a good idea. At least, not until you hold a captain's rank as well. I'll have a word with him.'

'If you're a captain,' Jessica said, 'I should be calling you ma'am.'

'Forget it. I only use my rank when I have to.' She washed her hands, and then brewed up the Horlick's. 'Drink that, and then let's get some sleep. We have an early start tomorrow. Like I said, this body of yours looks in pretty good shape, but we still have to see how it works.'

Monica meant what she said; she had Jessica out of bed just before dawn and doing fifty press-ups. Then they went on a fifteen-mile run. There was no sign of Merryman or McAdoo. Probably they were still in bed, Jessica thought bitterly.

When they got home, they breakfasted, after which a jeep arrived with a doctor and nurse, who subjected Jessica to a thorough physical examination. She expected them to comment on the bruise, as well as the myriad small cuts resulting from the explosion in Alicante, but they did not, preferring to concentrate on her blood pressure and reflexes and general health, which seemed to please them.

Then it was a session of Close Quarter Battle, in which Jessica discovered she had a lot to learn – Monica was an expert even above the top ordinary level. Next they went to an open range and engaged in target practice, Jessica being required to use a small calibre pistol and draw from a belt holster and fire at a succession of moving cardboard targets set up by an attentive corporal.

'That is really very good,' Monica said, and presented the evidence to the male members of the group, who had now appeared, looking fresh and spruce.

Merryman inspected the various large sheets of cardboard, each bearing the outline of a man. 'Hm. Not bad. That fellow would have been able to shoot back, though. And that one.'

'I think,' Jessica ventured, 'that if we are to be part of a team, whose lives may depend on the ability of our comrades, we should all have a go. Just to assess,' she added vindictively.

'Jones has a point,' Monica said. 'One needs to have complete confidence in one's comrades.'

Merryman raised his eyebrows, but armed himself, fitting on the earpieces, while McAdoo signalled the distant corporal. The targets began passing again, and Merryman started shooting. Faster than herself, Jessica realised . . . and more accurately as well.

'I really hate to admit it,' she said as she and Monica lunched. 'But you were right. The bastard is good.'

Monica grinned. 'He may even grow on you.'

'Somehow I doubt that,' Jessica said.

That afternoon she was visited by the identikit expert, who had her go through all his drawings, slowly recreating the face she remembered from Alicante – trying various shapes of jaw, various hair styles – to arrive at a picture that satisfied her.

'Good-looking guy,' Monica remarked. 'If a trifle wild-eyed.'

'I suspect I was pretty wild-eyed myself at the time,' Jessica admitted.

That evening she was summoned to Merryman's hut. Monica went with her, which gave her a little more confidence, especially as Merryman was alone.

'Well?' he asked.

'I would say she is both fit, and good at her job,' Monica said.

'At thirty-five.'

'You wouldn't really know it. She won't let you down.'

'I'll have to take your word for it. Okay, Monica, thanks a million.'

Monica got up, and Jessica rose also.

'You stay,' Merryman said.

Jessica looked at Monica in alarm.

'I'm afraid that's it, as far as I'm concerned,' Monica said. 'You're on your own, now.'

Jessica gulped.

'She is not on her own,' Merryman pointed out. 'She is now part of my team.'

'Well . . . the best of British.' Much to Jessica's embarrassment, Monica gave her a hug and kissed her on both cheeks. 'Maybe we'll meet up again, some time.'

*   *   *

The door closed behind her. Seldom had Jessica felt so alone.

'Sit down,' Merryman invited.

Jessica sat down.

'I need to assume we're ready to go,' Merryman said. 'Robert Korman.' He spread the identikit portrait in front of him. 'So this is our man. Not the sort of face you'd remark on in a crowd.'

'It's as good a likeness as these things ever are,' Jessica claimed.

Merryman laid a photograph beside it. Obviously the print had been taken from a larger photograph, and was in any event indistinct. With a ballpoint pen he outlined the features and the shape of the head, behind a shock of dark hair.

'Less hair, that's reasonable. He must have lost quite a lot in that blast, quite apart from surgery afterwards. Different colour, obviously. Different bridge to the nose. Again it was probably broken. Different mouth. Hm.' He traced the line of the chin, then peered at the identikit portrait, using a magnifying glass. 'Similar. Hard to change the shape of a man's chin. Anything about him you'd recognise?'

'The eyes. I remember the eyes.'

'You didn't mention that before.'

'It didn't register at the time. Things were happening too fast. But when I thought about it . . .'

Merryman shook his head. 'No good. That's at least half imagination, and half memory of the previous time you saw him, before he had the face change. But you say you'd recognise his voice.'

'Definitely.'

'We must get him to shout at you.'

Was this really the thug who had nearly ruptured her kidney?

'Now,' he said. 'You've seen his CV?'

'AC Proud outlined it to me.'

'Here's a copy.' He laid it on the table. 'With one or two additions. There's no use attempting to dig back further than the Slavonian Embassy. That was the first time he surfaced after breaking with the IRA; before then his activities are fairly well documented, as was his motivation. With the Slavonian Embassy siege he moved into a new area, one about which we still know too little. Although we knew he was there, because he was identified by three other officers as well as yourself, he got away and no group ever claimed responsibility. Nor was there any obvious motive for the attack – in the past Korman had never had any links or contact with any Slavonian group. While that situation was still being studied, along came Buenos Aires, and with him reported as officially dead by the Argentine police, his file was closed with great sighs of relief all round. Now it has been re-opened. I may say that I was not involved in any of the previous investigations. I only received the file yesterday. And I think I have immediately turned up something of the utmost significance.'

He took a sheet of paper from his briefcase and placed it on the table and tapped it. 'I have here a list of the guests at that dinner party at the Slavonian Embassy two years ago. As I have said, at the time we supposed the attempted coup was directed against the Slavonian Government, who had been having troubles at home, and two of whose members were in England on a mission, and attending that dinner. It seemed obvious that a dissident Slavonian group had recruited Korman, then at a loose end since splitting from the IRA. That such a group was not actually known to exist, and that no group ever claimed responsibility for the attack, was accepted as being because the attack had been a failure. But such a group as might have carried out such an attack has *never* been identified. The lack of a claim was also mystifying, as there are generally only two objectives in terrorist activity. One is publicity. That requires a claim. The other is an attempt to force the government you are attacking to change direction. But in the absence of any group making a claim or a demand, there was no direction towards which the Slavonian Government was going to turn, even supposing they ever would. So I came to the conclusion that the Slavonian Government was *not* the target of that attack.' He pushed the paper across the table. 'Read it.'

Jessica picked it up, scanned the list 'Quite a diplomatic Who's Who. Any of these characters might have been worth killing by a dissident national.'

'An entire hit squad hardly works for an itinerant dissident national. And Korman's attempt to get in and kill somebody, or perhaps the lot, foundered on the alertness of our security guards and protection squad, which included you, Jones.'

'Thank you for those few kind words.'

'You did a great job. However, it remained a total mystery as to what they were at and who was directing them. So to Buenos Aires. Another failure from Korman's point of view: the charge exploded prematurely. From our point of view, apparently the best possible result. However, again, what was the motivation and who was behind it? On the surface there was no possible connection between the Slavonian Embassy in London and the International Culture Centre in Buenos Aires.' He pushed another sheet of paper across the table. 'Here is the guest list for the reception to be held in the Culture Centre on the night of the explosion. Compare the two.'

Jessica did so. 'I'm afraid I don't understand. I assume you're looking for the same name on both lists, which might suggest Korman's target. But there's no one on both lists.'

'So forget names. Try titles and jobs.'

'Again,' Jessica said. 'There's no one . . . we had a minister at each.'

'Did any other country?'

'No,' she said thoughtfully. 'But ours weren't the same minister. The Minister for Trade and Industry was at the Slavonian dinner party; the Minister without Portfolio was at the Argentinian reception.'

'What do they have in common?'

'Not a lot. As I remember, they dislike each other.'

'But they do have one thing in common, Jones. Tell me what it is.'

'Ah . . . they're both members of the Cabinet, I suppose.'

Merryman pointed. 'You have it.'

'You think Korman is out to eliminate various members of the Cabinet?'

'Why not all?'

'Come again?'

'Can there be a more effective way of attacking a country, short of war, than to eliminate, one by one, its entire Cabinet? At the very least, if he's successful enough, he'll have people looking over their shoulders and hesitating before accepting one of the jobs.'

'He hasn't been too successful thus far.'

'One could say he's had some bad luck. Running into you at the Slavonian Embassy . . .'

He was growing on her, moment by moment.

'And then being blown up by his own bomb in Buenos Aires. But he was certainly successful in Alicante. And if you look at the list of those attending that conference, and compare it with the other two, again you will find that the only thing they have in common is the presence of a British Cabinet Minister.'

'But . . . why? Who is he working for?'

'That is one of the things we need to find out. But I have a notion that he's working for himself. That is why there has been no claimed responsibility. Korman blames the British Government for the death of his twin sister. Those responsible for British Government policy are the members of the Cabinet. No responsibility has ever been claimed for any of these attacks because this is not a group seeking either publicity or making a political statement. It is simply out for revenge.'

'And you think it is his group, recruited by him.'

'Yes, I do. All right, so he had to give it a name or a symbol. That's necessary morale for people engaged in a highly dangerous operation. But it's his group all right. And we know absolutely nothing about its composition, about its financing – and somebody has to be putting up the money – about where it gets its weaponry, and most important of all, about where it has its headquarters. Until this last week. Thanks to the discovery of those little crosses, we have a pretty good idea that the group is located in Turkey, or has Turkish connections. And thanks to you, we know it is headed by Korman. But nothing else. Neither of the two dead terrorists is on any file that we have been able to trace, photo, fingerprint or DNA. That's what's driving the powers-that-be out of their minds.'

'But . . . if you're so sure about what Korman is after, surely all we have to do is put all our Cabinet Ministers under round-the-clock protection.'

'Wouldn't you have said Mrs Lewton was under round-the-clock protection in Alicante?'

Jessica gulped.

'We're doing the best we can in that direction,' Merryman said. 'We can seal up their homes and the Palace of Westminster, but there is no way we can prevent senior members of the Government from appearing in public, or from travelling abroad as and when required. We simply have to get Korman before he gets anyone else.'

'Are the members of the Cabinet aware of the collective threat?'

'Only the Prime Minister, the Deputy Prime Minister, and the Home Secretary have been informed of my theory, and it was their decision not to tell their colleagues. I mean, as I just said, while every prominent politician must know that he or she is a possible target for an assassin's bullet, it would be most inhibiting for them to know a man like Korman is after them. It is the Prime Minister's personal directive that this matter must be cleaned up just as rapidly, and decisively, as possible. So, let's see just what we have. These for starters.' He spread out the little crosses. 'The Will of God. What do they tell you?'

'As you said, the inscription is in Turkish, so there's a Turkish connection.'

'Trouble is,' Merryman said, 'Turkey is not only a very big country, it is riddled with dissident groups and incipient revolutionaries, and houses quite a few terrorists. But it's something. Go on.'

'Well . . .' Jessica considered. 'That the organisation is linked to religion, probably Christian or Jewish rather than Muslim.'

'I wouldn't be too sure about the religious angle. Our friend Korman does not appear to have had any religious affiliations in the past. But he may be using it as a recruiting factor. However, we have a possible Turkish base and a possible religious involvement. Next?'

'Well . . . Alicante. Spain in general.'

'Bit of a dead end. The getaway car was found by the Spanish police, but unfortunately everyone was so confused and panic-stricken by the explosion that it wasn't until several hours later. They had plenty of time to change to another car and reach the French border. Even more unfortunately, as you know, there are no longer passport checks at the borders between France and Spain, under normal conditions. By the time the Spanish police got around to closing the border, they were long gone. And I may say that the car yielded nothing. Not a print, not even a thread of fabric. We need always to remember that Korman is the ultimate professional.'

'But . . . Turkey is not a member of the Common Market,' Jessica said. 'So if they were travelling on Turkish passports, they would have been held up somewhere.'

'We don't know what passports they were using, but I'd bet they weren't Turkish, if that's where they were heading. I'm afraid under modern conditions it is really very simple for terrorists to move from one country to another.'

'You say there were no fingerprints on the getaway car. But it had to come from somewhere. And have national plates.'

'It had Spanish plates. The police traced it easily enough. It was hired in Valencia the day before the explosion. The man who hired it had an international driving licence in the name of Georges Dubois, which, as I'm sure you know, is not the most uncommon name in France. He paid cash.'

'Description?'

Merryman shrugged. 'Medium height, medium build, no distinguishing marks.'

'Could it have been Korman himself?'

'I think not. Monsieur Dubois had dark hair.'

'Okay, what about the second getaway vehicle.'

'Not a clue. I would say it was driven over the border from France, with French plates, and merely returned there.'

'Well,' Jessica said. 'It doesn't look as if we have much to go on.'

'We have two things, Jones. We have the Turkish

connection. And we have you. Someone Korman wants to get hold of, very badly.'

'So you are sending me to Turkey? Wouldn't it be simpler to stay here, and expose me? Suitably covered, of course. If Korman really means to get at me, he'll come again, and this time we'll be prepared.'

'That approach is too passive. I told you, we want him, now, before he blows up anyone else. We may be certain that he wants to eliminate you, but if we don't force his hand, he draws up the agenda. We could be sitting on our asses for a month or more, while he makes plans, and maybe has a go at his next target. There's another point: he didn't come himself to your flat. He sent his people. So there is no reason to suppose that if, for instance, you returned there, he would come after you himself. He is the man we want, JJ. Not his goons.'

'So, Turkey. I hope we're going to travel in strength.'

'We are. You'll have to be on your own, of course, officially. But my team will be right behind you, and around you, at all times.'

'I hope so. Do I get to meet these guys? My life insurance?'

'Not a good idea. Otherwise you might just be tempted to recognise one of them and give the game away. Just be sure they'll be there.'

'I suppose I'll have to . . . be sure, I mean. What am I supposed to be doing?'

'Just being there will be sufficient, I hope. However, we want you to be as obvious about it as possible, and as threatening. You have taken leave from the police after what happened in Alicante, but instead of putting your feet up on some beach, you have taken it into your head to do some investigating. This is because while you are sure it was Korman you saw in Spain, no one here believes you.'

'Near enough,' Jessica commented.

'So, your various investigations have led you to Istanbul, for a start. How you managed to trace Korman to Turkey is your business, but now you are probing. You are particularly interested in the financial angle. Korman has recruited a team. We don't know how many, but even one man, or one woman, costs money. We know he employs at least four, and that is assuming the four people who attacked you were the same as those in Alicante.'

'There was no woman in the car in Alicante.'

'Exactly. So, more than four. Plus the one blown up in the hotel. Then there is the matter of his base, and how and where he obtains his explosives. He and his people also travel extensively. It all comes down to money. Now, we have a team working on this, making up lists of known wealthy subversives who may possibly be financing him. We hope to have that list available to you before you depart. Once you have it, you will pursue whatever name takes your fancy openly.'

'In Istanbul, with you or someone standing constantly at my shoulder.'

'You don't like the idea.'

'Just checking. I've never been quite so exposed before.'

'Of course you have, JJ. Every time you went about your duty as a protection officer. You know the rules, get yourself killed rather than your principal. Now the role will be reversed and you're going to be getting the protection yourself, even if not quite so obviously.'

Jessica hoped he was right.

The helicopter dropped out of a cloudless blue sky, stirring the dust of the semi-desert as it settled. For as far as the eye could see there was nothing but arid hillsides and sudden valleys sheltering beneath overhanging peaks. Situated some forty miles north of the city of Konya – known to history as Iconium, famous for its whirling dervishes – this was one of the most desolate parts of an always desolate country.

Yet there was life here, if one knew where to look.

Once Turkey had been a green and pleasant land. That had been a thousand years ago, before the coming of the Seljuks. The Seljuks had been nomad warriors from the steppes of Asia. Their only creed had been destruction, and after they had shattered the Byzantine army of the emperor Romanus Diogenes at Manzikert in 1071, they had swept across the peninsula, killing every living creature, pulling down every house or church or wall, uprooting every crop, every tree, every bush. The Seljuks had destroyed Turkey, and after a thousand years it was still recovering.

But people always survive, in however limited numbers. The Byzantine farmers and their wives and children subjected to the storm had had nowhere to flee; they could only hide themselves as best they were able. They went down, dug into the soil, and created amazingly large and elaborate villages and even towns under the earth's surface, where they lurked and waited for the wild horsemen to go away. The remains of several of these troglodyte societies have become tourist attractions. But not all have been found, or are open to the public.

As he stepped down from the helicopter, ducking away from the turning blades, Rashid ben Khalim supposed, not for the first time, that such an underworld was an entirely suitable home for a man like Robert Korman. Every time he came here he felt he was descending into the pit of hell, to dine with the devil.

But it was his devil, he thought with some pride.

Rashid ben Khalim was a tall, slender, good-looking and clean-shaven man in his early thirties. Even when walking across the desert he was impeccably dressed in a three-piece suit, with gleaming shoes, close-knotted tie and white soft hat. His two servants hurried behind him with the suitcases; even if he did not intend to spend more than a few hours here, he would wish to change before starting the journey home.

In front of him there seemed to be nothing but desert, but now two men appeared from amidst the rubbled stones and boulders at the foot of the hill. 'Ben Khalim.' They saluted.

Rashid nodded to them and waited while a stone was rolled aside, to reveal steps leading down. Below him was light and cool; he could hear the hum of the generator and the air-conditioning plant, their exits as cunningly concealed as the entrance itself.

'What is the news from London?' Rashid asked as he reached the first level. He was now in an antechamber, from which corridors led away in several directions.

'It is not good,' one of the attendants said. 'Two of our people have been killed.'

Rashid snorted, and went down the corridor that led to Korman's apartment. He opened the door without knocking. A guard sat in the inner lobby, and started up, pistol in hand, then stood to attention as he recognised the intruder. Rashid opened the inner door, entered a well-furnished lounge. He crossed this, opened the bedroom door beyond and gazed at the bed; Korman was just getting up and putting on a dressing gown. The woman lying beside him was naked, her body a mass of red and white blotches, her black hair tangled. As there were no covers on the bed, she rolled on her side, away from the two men.

Rashid jerked his head, and returned to the lounge. Korman followed, banging the bedroom door behind him.

'I understand things have not gone well in London,' Rashid remarked.

'We were unlucky.'

'I still think that woman is irrelevant.'

'To you.' Korman went to the sideboard, opened the fridge, poured two glasses of white wine. 'Not to me. I have sent my people back. They will get her.' He grinned. 'They will kill her.'

'She is also a distraction. Have you forgotten Kuala Lumpur?'

Korman drank. 'Who is it?'

'The Minister for Trade and Industry. And it is only a week away. You leave tomorrow.'

'I am ready.'

'With two of your people dead, and some more still in England, have you sufficient? You had better call the people in England back. They can meet you in Malaysia.'

'I have sufficient. I have Gabrielle, and Hamid, and two more. That is sufficient.'

Rashid frowned at him. 'Gabrielle. Is that her in the bedroom?'

'Yes.'

'She did not look very happy. I thought you never had sex with any of your people? I thought you *could* not have sex, with anyone, after Buenos Aires.'

'I cannot,' Korman said. 'In the sense you mean. But I can still enjoy women.'

The Child

'Just to let you know there will be a delay in start-ing the operation,' Merryman said across the desk. 'Damned annoying. Anything from twenty-four to forty-eight hours.'

'Any particular reason?' Jessica asked.

'Nothing for you to worry your head about. But we must have all our people ready and in place. Meanwhile you can keep yourself busy with a bit of extra time in the gym.'

He was back to being a patronising bastard, when only last night she had come close to admiring him. 'Yes, boss.'

He looked up after a moment, obviously wondering why she hadn't accepted his silent dismissal. 'Something on your mind?'

'Yes, boss. That delivery of back post I received this morning contained a letter from one of the nurses in Alicante. She tells me that the child, Megan Lynch, who lost both her parents in the blast, has been sent back to her grandmother's house in England. I would like to contact her, and if we are going to be delayed, visit her.'

'Whatever for?'

'Because she has no adult friends or relatives here.'

'She has her grandmother.'

'Who had both legs amputated in Spain and is still in hospital there. The child is with a housekeeper.'

'So what? You don't want to get involved.'

'I already am involved. We were in adjacent wards and talked together. She was quite traumatised and had no one else English to speak to.'

Merryman hissed. 'Do you know where this grandmother's house is?'

'No. But I can find out.'

'How?'

'Through the British Consulate in Alicante.'

'That would leave a direct trail for Korman to follow.'

'He won't find a connection to me if it's done through a third party on a clean line. A well-wisher interested in the child's welfare.'

He hissed again. 'Very well.' He flicked the phone switch. 'Corporal, send Patrick to me.'

'He won't be back from Southampton for nearly an hour, sir,' a voice replied through the box.

'Well, send him in when he comes.' Merryman switched off. 'Well, you can run along for now.'

Why do some men need to talk to women as though they were children? Jessica wondered. Silly bastard!

She was working up a good sweat on the walking machine when Patrick joined her. 'Miss Jones?' The tall, thin young man with close-cut hair and a scar on his chin introduced himself.

'Hi, Patrick.' She held out her hand. 'Please call me JJ. Everyone does.'

His fingers were like steel clamps. 'Okay, JJ, and I answer only to Pat.'

'Has Merryman told you what I want you for?'

'In a manner of speaking.'

She could imagine just what that 'manner' was. 'Let's go across to the mess and I'll fill you in on the way.' As they walked down the hot tarmac she told him about Megan's plight.

'Shit! I beg your pardon, but God that is awful.' Really

88

shocked, he went on to explain how he felt as a father. 'I have twins of eight, a boy and a girl. I can't imagine what would happen to them in similar circumstances.'

Jessica couldn't believe he was old enough to have fathered eight-year-olds. 'At least they would have each other,' she commented, pleased he was sympathetic.

They entered the mess hut through the kitchen and dining area, continuing to the group of club chairs arranged round a coffee table at the far end.

'I'm feeling dehydrated after that workout.' Jessica threw her towel on to a chair. 'I'm going to have a large orange juice. Want one?'

'Yeah, thanks. Now, you will have to take me through this, step by step,' he said.

There was a row of low cupboards ranged along one wall and sitting on top of them were two phones, one red and the other green. As she instructed, he picked up the red phone. 'Bob? Can you get me a Mr Bartlett at the British Consulate in Alicante?' Pause. 'I don't know. You'll have to ask directory inquiries through the switchboard at Headquarters. This has got to be a clean line.' Pause. 'I'm with you. Okay, I'll hang up and wait for you to call back.'

'It'll take some time,' Jessica warned. 'Spanish Telefónica have to be experienced to be believed.'

They were on their second glasses of orange juice when the red phone buzzed. 'Mr Bartlett?' Patrick asked. 'I'm calling on behalf of the Ministry. We're trying to trace the whereabouts of a minor who was injured in the bombing down there. Name of Megan Lynch. We're told she left the hospital, and that you might have her current address here in England.'

Jessica smiled at him, nodded and raised an approving thumb. She sat close by with a notepad on her knee, ballpoint poised.

They waited while a clerk found the appropriate file, and then as Pat repeated the agent's dictation, she wrote down the address.

'Yes, thank you, sir. That will be a great help. And we will get back to you if we require any further info pertaining to the child or the grandmother. Ah . . .' He listened, frowning. 'Is that so? Yes, it's nice to know there is some additional interest. Goodbye.'

'What was that?' Jessica asked.

'I was the second person in the last couple of days to inquire after Megan Lynch's health, and where she is now. You reckon that's important?'

'I hope not. Did they give the address?'

'I'm afraid so. Well, they gave it to us.'

'Hm. Southley, Somerset,' Jessica mused. 'How far is that from here?'

'I think there's a road atlas in here somewhere.' Pat opened and shut two of the cupboards before locating it. 'Here we are. Hm. No direct major road so I guess it would take about an hour and a half to two hours, cross-country. Want to go there? This afternoon?'

'If Merryman will wear it.'

'You can only try him. You going to tell him about the other inquiry?'

Jessica considered. It couldn't possibly have been Korman's people. Surely. Just some genuine well-wisher who had read about the little girl's plight in the newspapers. And even if it *was* Korman . . . She took a deep breath. She would have to face him some time: why not now, to save herself the trouble of going to Turkey? She would be well-guarded enough and, she thought stoutly, it was worth the risk if her visit might mean something to Megan. But in any case, Merryman was probably better not told. 'No. I don't want to excite him.'

They drained their glasses and left them on the bar

counter before stepping out into the sunshine again. 'And the best of luck,' Pat said as she headed back to the admin hut.

Merryman was preoccupied with other matters. 'As long as you keep your eyes skinned I suppose you can go.' He waved a hand vaguely at her. 'Don't give the kid or anyone else any information about yourself and get back here by this evening.' With one hand he shooed her away, while the other switched on the phone and he began barking orders to the unfortunate corporal in the outer office.

Bathed and changed, Jessica joined Pat and a group of personnel she hadn't met for lunch in the mess. 'Whew! Weather's hotting up,' she commented. She had scooped her pale blonde hair into a ponytail to keep it off the back of her neck; together with her diminutive figure, it made her look like a stunning teenager. Her all-male companions were obviously impressed.

She sat in the back of the muddy, green Range Rover with Pat, the windows opened wide to invite in whatever slipstream they could achieve on the narrow, winding roads, just sufficient to ruffle the map pages. Their driver, a thick-set man with heavy brows and a Burt Reynolds moustache who had lunched with them, kept an eye on his rear-view mirror but was sure they were not being followed. But all were armed, just in case.

After Pat's inquiries at a Southley village shop they located the house without difficulty. A warm, greystone building, it was surrounded by trees and a greystone wall and privet hedges which separated it from similar neighbours on either side.

'I'll be back in an hour,' the driver said, and drove back into the village.

From the gravelled car park in front of the garage, Jessica and Pat walked across the front garden to the door.

'Isn't it pretty?' she remarked, admiring the festoon of yellow roses over the trellis round the entrance. She thumped the brass lion-head knocker.

There was a long pause before they heard footsteps approaching and the door opened. A tall, thin, beak-faced woman said, 'Yes?' rather bleakly.

Not a good start. Jessica smiled sweetly. 'Good afternoon. We have called hoping to see Megan Lynch. Is she here?'

'Who are you? What do you want with her? Are you from some newspaper?'

'No, no! My name is Jessica Jones. Megan and I were in hospital together in Alicante.'

'JJ!' a small voice called from the corridor beyond, and the child wriggled out round Beaky's attempted blockade.

'Hi, Megan. How are you?' Jessica held her hand.

'I've had the stitches out of my head. It didn't hurt, you know.' She was suddenly aware of Beaky still standing there, blocking the doorway. 'JJ is my friend, Miss Lovelace. Please can they come in?'

'May they,' the woman corrected. She eyed the pair of visitors so casually dressed in jeans and shirts hanging out, loose. 'I suppose so,' she said reluctantly, little realising what Pat's shirt or Jessica's shoulder bag concealed. She stepped aside, closed the door behind them, and followed as Megan led the way through the house, through a sunny conservatory, and out into the back garden, where weathered teak furniture was arranged in the shade of an ancient oak. There were books on the table and cushions on two of the chairs. 'You'd better bring out more cushions, hadn't you?' Miss Lovelace told her charge.

'Have all your bruises gone?' Jessica asked once they were all seated.

'Just about,' Megan told her, pulling up the leg of her

flowered shorts to display a yellowish patch on her thigh. 'What about yours?'

'Mine were all cuts, remember? They're just about healed up now, but I will have a few nasty scars for a while.'

An awkward silence followed, and while she was trying to think what to say next, Jessica covertly assessed the child's face. The violet eyes set deep in new dark hollows, and the big white teeth, seemed too large for the little face that had visibly shrunk.

'Did you know my parents were killed by that bomb?' The child's voice was barely audible.

'Yes, Megan, I did.'

'Did you know when you spoke to me in hospital?'

'Yes.' Jessica took hold of the child's hand, stroked it, and drew her close.

The big violet eyes were wet. 'I think I sort of knew, too.'

Jessica felt her eyes stinging. Her arm slid round Megan's waist. 'Yes, I thought you did, in a way.'

'I didn't want to believe it,' she gasped, and turned her face away.

Instinctively, Jessica pulled her against her side and hugged her. 'Look at me. There is no need to be ashamed of tears. Crying is good for you. Let it all spill out.'

Miss Lovelace clicked her tongue and stood up. 'I imagine you would like some tea. I'll go and put the kettle on.'

Jessica continued to hold the thin little body, which shook with great sobs.

'I haven't got a hankie,' Megan sniffed.

Silent witness to the tragic scene, Pat handed over a large, folded handkerchief, grateful for something to do to relieve his helplessness.

Megan blew. 'Miss Lovelace doesn't like me to cry. She keeps saying I have to be brave.'

Jessica stopped trying to conceal her irritation with the woman. 'Well, maybe Miss Lovelace has never had to be brave. Perhaps she's never lost someone she loves – or perhaps nobody ever loved her.'

'What, not even her mother?'

Could even a blind mother have ever loved her? 'Well, maybe, a long, long time ago. And ever since then she's had no one to hug.'

'I never thought of that. You mean she's been loveless for years and years.' The child's voice dropped to a whisper. 'That should be her name, shouldn't it? Loveless?'

Jessica grinned and nodded. 'I guess so, but we won't tell her, will we,' she whispered back.

'No. And I'll try to like her a bit more.' A little sigh. 'I do wish Nan would come home soon. You see, no matter how late Mummy got home from work at night, she would still come into my bedroom and give me a hug. Now I have no one, except you.'

'And Miss Loveless,' Jessica added as the woman appeared in the doorway of the conservatory behind them.

'You joke,' the child hissed in a very grown-up voice.

Patrick jumped to his feet, smothering a laugh, and carried the tray out for Miss Lovelace. He admired the way Jessica had coped with the child, but was left wondering what her next move might be.

When the cups and biscuits had been handed round, Megan dashed off inside saying she wanted to find a photo of Nan to show to JJ, who had never seen the lady without bandages over her face.

When she was out of earshot, the unloved spinster suddenly said, 'Would you have any idea, Miss Jones, how long it might be before Mrs Lynch is able to come home? I've tried telephoning the hospital in Alicante, but I haven't got very far. I don't speak Spanish, you see.'

'I'll see if I can find out, although I shouldn't think it'll be for some time yet. And when she does she will be a nursing case, I imagine.'

'Oh, dear. I don't know if I could cope with that side of things, all by myself. It might be better if she stayed in hospital until she can walk.' She flushed. 'I mean . . . well . . . get about on her own.'

'I'm sure you wouldn't have to cope alone. Nurses would be made available. Even with artificial limbs it will be months before Mrs Lynch could attempt to walk on her own, and in the meantime, Megan needs her, desperately. The child wants someone to hug her and comfort her as the waves of misery flood in. She needs a shoulder to cry on, Miss Lovelace. Have you ever lost someone very dear and precious to you?'

'Look, JJ, this was taken last year at Weston-Super-Mare.' Before the astonished woman could reply, Megan ran across the lawn proudly waving a small framed snapshot of herself with a quite glamorous woman in a colourful bathing suit that showed off an excellent figure. 'It was on Nan's bedside table.'

'My, doesn't she look young.'

'Everyone says that. She's fifty-four. Will she be able to walk when she comes home? She told me they were going to give her tin legs.'

Jessica decided honesty was the best policy. 'No, not for a while. The stumps will have to be completely healed before the prostheses can be fitted. That's the tin legs. They are really very clever, you know, with proper joints in them like real legs.'

'That's right,' Pat added. 'A friend of mine trod on a landmine and had his leg blown off.' Miss Lovelace grimaced, but he ignored her. 'He plays golf and dances, swims . . .'

'Swims?!' Megan exclaimed. 'Doesn't it matter if it gets wet?'

95

'Oh, he doesn't wear it in the water. Just sits on the edge of the pool, unstraps it, and leaves it on the side while he goes in. He's quite good at water polo, too.'

Jessica finished her tea and stood up. 'I think we ought to be going, Pat. Our car will be back in a few minutes.'

'Oh, no! Must you?'

'Yes, Megan. But I promise I'll keep in touch. I have to go away on business, shortly. But when we get back I'll come and see you again. Thanks for the tea, Miss Lovelace.'

Megan came with them through the house, and at the door Jessica gave her a hug and a kiss. There were tears in Megan's eyes as she closed the door.

There was no sign of their driver.

'Poor kid,' Pat remarked. 'When you—' He stared at the strange car suddenly blocking the small drive. 'Take cover!' he shouted.

Pat accompanied his shout with a push that sent Jessica stumbling into the flowerbed beside the door. He went the other way.

There were three men in the car, and two of these now got out, carrying large machine pistols, with which they opened fire. Bullets scattered across the drive and slammed into the front of the house. Even as she opened her shoulder bag and drew her own weapon, Jessica heard screams from inside the house, and saw the front door begin to open.

'Shut it!' she yelled. 'Get down.'

The door stayed half-open as bullets shattered the glass panels. Oh, my God, Jessica thought. That poor little girl . . .

Pat had also drawn and was returning fire, with deadly accuracy. He carried a nine-millimetre Browning, and one of his bullets slammed into the nearer of the two men. He threw up his arms and fell backwards. The other swung his gun and fired into the bushes, and Pat gave an exclamation of pain.

The driver of the car was shouting in a foreign language, obviously reminding the gunman who his target was, because now he swung back to where Jessica crouched, changing magazines on his pistol as he did so. Jessica drew a very deep breath. She had only ever once in her life aimed to hit another human being. That had been outside the Slavonian Embassy and her target had been Robert Korman. She had missed, because for all her training, she had not really wanted the responsibility of taking a life. But now her own life was on the line, and besides, these thugs might just have killed Megan.

She levelled her Skorpion and beat the terrorist to the shot, a burst of four bullets slamming into his chest and sending him tumbling back beside his companion.

Jessica turned her gun on the car, but the driver was already backing down the drive, and the sound of the shots was bringing people out of their houses. She lowered the pistol, panting, sweating, and very slowly stood up. She had to keep watching the two men, but they were both undoubtedly dead.

Her knees felt weak, but there was so much to be done. There was always so much to be done. She ran to the bushes on the other side of the door. Pat was slumped against the wall, blood marking his shirt.

'Is it bad?' She knelt beside him.

He forced a grin. 'I'll live. It's somewhere in the rib area.'

'I'll get help.' She ran to the door, pausing to glance at the steadily growing crowd by the gate, staring first at the dead bodies, then at her. She felt she should tell them something, but for the life of her she couldn't think what.

Besides, she was more interested, and afraid, of what might be lying inside the door.

*   *   *

She pushed it in, blinked in the sudden gloom of the hallway, looked down it, and saw the body at the inner end. Breaking out in a fresh rash of sweat, she stumbled forward and dropped to her knees. It was Miss Lovelace. There was no sign of any blood, and she was breathing, if stertorously. She had fainted.

But the child . . .

'JJ.' It was hardly more than a whisper.

Jessica swung round and saw the little girl, who had rolled into the open lounge doorway. She scrambled up, ran to her. 'Are you all right?'

'Oh, yes,' Megan said. 'But Miss Lovelace . . .'

'She'll be all right. Listen, just stay tight.'

She took her mobile from her bag. 'Where the hell are you? I need a doctor, and I need you.'

'Five minutes,' the driver said. She suspected he might be in the pub.

'I don't think that's going to be a lot of help,' Jessica said, and replaced the phone. 'Do you have a first-aid box?'

Megan nodded. 'In the kitchen.'

'Don't move,' Jessica reminded her. She went to the kitchen and fetched the box, then went outside to where Patrick lay.

The crowd at the gate had grown, and one or two had actually stepped past the dead bodies to enter the garden.

'You shot him,' a man said. 'I saw you shoot him.'

'Well,' Jessica said, 'if I hadn't, he'd have shot me.' She knelt beside Patrick. 'I don't know if there's anything in there,' she said. 'I'm just going to bind you up to stop the bleeding until the doctor gets here.'

He nodded, his face tight with pain as the shock wore off. 'Everything under control?'

Jessica listened to the wail of a siren. 'Nothing is under control,' she said.

'Of all the stupid, fucking, foul-ups I have ever heard of,' Merryman said, 'this takes the cake.'

'Would you mind watching your language,' Jessica said.

Merryman glared at the little girl standing beside her. 'Who the fu— . . . effing God Almighty is that?'

'I don't think she goes much for blasphemy either,' Jessica pointed out. 'This is Miss Megan Lynch.'

'The kid from Alicante? Oh, holy sh— . . . sugar. What's she doing here? This is a top-secret establishment.'

'I saw a man shot dead,' Megan confided. 'Two men. JJ did it.'

'Only one,' Jessica countered.

She hadn't started to shake yet, but she knew it was going to happen. She had shot a man, dead.

'Is that why you brought her along?' Merryman asked, his voice sinking to a deceptively low tone. 'You want her locked up or something. Is that it?'

'I do not want her locked up,' Jessica said. 'I want her put somewhere safe. Listen, boss, her parents were murdered in Alicante. Her grandmother is still in hospital there. Now the lady who was looking after her is in hospital in a state of catatonic shock. She has no one, and nowhere to go. I regard her as our responsibility.'

'What do you think I am running? An effing kindergarten?' He pointed. 'She is your responsibility, Jones. And we leave tomorrow. That's before the police can nail you down. So you had better get rid of her, pronto.'

'Is he a bad man, too?' Megan asked.

'Oh, very,' Jessica said, smiling sweetly at her superior. 'I think I need to make another phone call.'

*   *   *

'Let me get this absolutely straight,' Judith Proud said, looking around Jessica's Nissen hut with some distaste.

But at least she was here, Jessica reflected. She hadn't brushed her off over the phone.

'You have managed to get yourself engaged in another shoot-out, which has all Somerset buzzing and is giving the media another field day, not to mention the Opposition . . . I believe a question is going to be asked in the House. God knows what the Government is going to say, as they're committed to keeping this whole business under wraps, at least until Korman is eliminated. And this happened because you went to see' – her gaze softened slightly as she looked at Megan – 'this young lady. Another Alicante survivor.'

'Are you a bad woman too?' Megan asked.

Judith looked at Jessica, eyebrows arched.

'It's a long story,' Jessica explained. 'What I don't understand is how those thugs got Megan's address.'

'Oh, come now, JJ. How did you get it?'

'Patrick telephoned the Consulate in Alicante . . . How is Patrick, by the way?'

'They got the bullet out and he'll be all right. He won't be on duty again for a few months, though . . . You were saying?'

'Patrick telephoned and pretended to be from some ministry arranging for her care . . . and they gave it to him.'

'Small world, isn't it. You do realise that was a serious breach of security.'

'Captain Merryman authorised it.'

'I must have a word with him. Well, again, one has to say you're lucky to be alive.' She frowned. 'Now that's odd.'

'That I'm alive?'

'In a manner of speaking, yes. The last time Korman's

people came after you, they wanted to kidnap you. Now they've abandoned that idea. They just want you dead. Well, I must say, the scoring is pretty good so far: four of his dead to one of ours wounded. He'll be tearing his hair. But you do realise that if you're just a target now, the odds on survival are getting longer.'

'I'm told I shall be wearing all manner of protective clothing, ma'am.'

'In the Turkish heat. And the best of luck. You leave tomorrow, I understand.'

'Yes, ma'am. Now about Megan . . .'

'Can't I come with you on your business trip, JJ?' Megan asked.

'Ah, no. I don't think that would be practical. We need to find you some place to stay until I get back.' She looked at Judith.

'It'll have to be some place very secure,' Judith said. 'And where what she has to tell the people around her won't matter.'

'You mean about how I saw JJ shoot that man? I won't tell anyone,' Megan protested.

'I know you won't, my dear,' Judith said. 'Not intentionally. But it might slip out.' She brooded for a few moments, while Jessica all but held her breath. 'I think you had better come and live with me for a few days.'

'Oh!' Megan looked at Jessica.

Who was utterly surprised. She knew Judith, like herself, had been divorced several years earlier. Again like her, there had been no children of the marriage. But there the similarity ended. Very unlike her, Judith was a high-flying career woman. That she had not become a mother had been a deliberate choice. It was an aspect of her personality that was reflected not only in her senior position but also in her dress and perhaps most of all in her flat. Jessica had only been there once, but had been overwhelmed by the neatness and pristine cleanliness of the place, the ornaments and bric-a-brac that littered every incidental table, the carefully leather-bound books in the cases, and beyond, a bedroom in which the bed might never have been slept in, and a bathroom which had clearly never been contaminated by human contact.

'Are you sure?' she asked.

'Of course I'm sure. You'd like to spend a few days with me, wouldn't you, Megan?'

Megan looked at Jessica. 'If JJ thinks it's all right.'

'That was awfully kind of you, ma'am,' Jessica said when they were alone for a moment, Megan having gone to the bathroom before she and Judith departed.

'Not at all. I'm looking forward to it. She seems a bright, intelligent girl.'

'She is. She's also, well, pretty lively.'

'I don't consider that a problem.'

'What she really needs more than anything else is bags and bags of TLC. Hugs and kisses and that sort of thing.'

'I'll bear that in mind,' Judith said. 'Have you had a chance to look at those names?'

'Just a glance. I'll study them on the plane. This fellow Salahin Izmir seems a good bet. Known terrorist connections, pretty wealthy . . .'

'Forget him,' Judith said. 'His terrorist connections are all with the Kurds. He's a Kurd himself. I think the man you want to keep in mind is Rashid ben Khalim. He's a millionaire, and he certainly has terrorist connections. Or he had. What makes him interesting is that he dropped out of sight, as far as terrorism is concerned, just over two years ago, and has remained out of sight, apparently concentrating on his legitimate business interests. Just over two years ago would take us back to just before the raid on the Slavonian Embassy.'

102

'Bit of a long shot, isn't it? Could be an entire coincidence.'

'It could. But we are dealing in long shots. And perhaps it's just too *much* of a coincidence that Korman started working anonymously as regards claiming responsibility and Rashid dropped out of the business at virtually the same time. Anyway, it's my suggestion, for what it's worth.'

'I shall certainly follow it up, ma'am.'

Judith nodded. 'And JJ, do come back to us in one piece, and *not* in a wooden box.'

She actually sounds as if she's fond of me, Jessica thought.

The helicopter dropped from the sky, scattering dust and dirt. Korman and Rashid were waiting some distance away, with Gabrielle. Only one man got out.

'Dino?' Korman frowned. 'Where is Albert?'

'Dead,' Dino said.

'And Fritz?' Rashid asked.

'Dead.'

Korman stared at him incredulously.

'How did this happen?' Rashid asked. 'You were not even supposed to get close to the woman. Just to kill her.'

Dino swallowed. 'She was armed, and she had a back-up. As before.'

'Four of my people, dead,' Korman said. 'And you said I was taking her too seriously.'

'She certainly seems an unusual young woman,' Rashid agreed. 'Do you have a photograph of her?'

'No,' Korman said.

'But she does not appear to be difficult to find. I think, Robert, your problem is that you have not recruited very well.'

'Albert was one of my best men.'

103

'Exactly. And he has blundered twice and cost you four lives, including his own. I think you should leave the young lady to me.'

'You?' Korman snorted. 'Have you any experience of this sort of thing?'

'Me personally, no. But I know someone who does. He is a professional, and he will carry out his task with no fuss . . . and no failures, either.'

'I am inclined to go after her myself,' Korman said.

'And you too are a professional. But you are needed in Kuala Lumpur. This woman may be the most deadly of her sex, but she is still a sideshow. Leave it with me, Robert. By the time you return from the Far East, she will be history.'

Istanbul

'I don't want to be melodramatic about this, or give you the impression you're a female James Bond . . .' Merryman grinned. 'You haven't the build for it. But a few things are necessary if we are going to keep you alive. Right?'

Jessica considered his changes of mood were far more dramatic than anything James Bond might have done. The outburst of yesterday was entirely forgotten, apparently. Now he was all charm and consideration.

'Now,' he said. 'You will leave here with Sergeant McAdoo in half an hour. He will drop you, with your bag, in Guildford. It will be quite close to the station, but not in the station itself. You will walk to the station, and catch the bus to Heathrow. You have your tickets. You will check in, and fly to Istanbul. Now, one of my people will be on the bus, and one will be at Heathrow, and one will be on the plane. None of these three people will identify themselves to you, and you will make no attempt to identify yourself to them. They are purely a precautionary measure, as there is no reason for us to suppose that the Will of God have any conception that we will be carrying the fight to them, or would be so foolhardy as to send you to Turkey. Once you get to Istanbul, of course, and start making obvious inquiries, they will get the message soon enough.'

'But you will by then have me surrounded with protection,' Jessica said. She wanted to be quite sure about this.

'I have three people in Istanbul. They know the flight you are arriving on, and they know what you look like, and where you will be staying. I shall myself be following on a later flight. I assume it goes without saying that should you see me you will under no circumstances give any indication of knowing me.'

Jessica nodded.

'On arrival in Istanbul, you will go to your hotel – you have the necessary vouchers – settle in and behave in a perfectly normal manner, while beginning your inquiries. You will, as I have said, be monitored at all times. However . . . there is always the possibility that something may go wrong.'

'Cheer me up,' Jessica muttered.

'So I want you to take this.'

He indicated a small box on his desk.

Jessica opened it, peered at the capsule inside; it was about twice the size of an ordinary medical capsule, and was red and white. 'Cyanide? Something that big would kill a horse.'

'Hopefully, it will not even kill you, Jones. It is not a cyanide tablet. Look at it.'

Cautiously Jessica took out the pill, peered at it.

'You will note that on the underside there is a small black dot, about the size of a ballpoint tip. Once that dot is depressed, the battery inside will commence sending a signal, and will keep it up for forty-eight hours. Having activated the capsule, you will then swallow it. That way no one can possibly know you are carrying a homing device, but we shall be monitoring the signal, so that if we lose sight of you, we shall still know exactly where you are.'

'Ah . . . this is in case I am kidnapped, is that it?'

106

'That is one contingency, certainly.'

'Small point. On the evidence of what happened yesterday, Korman is no longer interested in kidnapping me, only in killing me.'

'All the more reason for knowing where you are, right?'

She didn't quite follow his logic, but something else was bothering her. 'You expect this business to be wrapped up in forty-eight hours?'

'That would be very acceptable. However, we are prepared to go on longer, until it *is* wrapped up.'

'You said the battery would only last forty-eight hours.'

He nodded. 'At the end of that time it will have to be replaced. However, if you look in the box you will see that there are three replacement batteries. All you do is unscrew the two halves of the capsule, remove the dead battery, and insert a fresh one. You will have to use plastic tweezers, but it is straightforward enough.'

'I'm sure it is. However, while I have four batteries, I only have one capsule.'

'Ah . . . yes. I'm afraid the existing capsule will have to be re-used.'

Jessica gazed at him, and he flushed.

'I'm sure you will manage, Jones.'

Jessica placed the box in her shoulder bag.

'Just remember,' Merryman said, 'not to activate until you are well *in situ*. And good luck. There'll be a commendation.'

What am I *doing*? Jessica asked herself as she sat in an uncomfortable economy-class seat – they were determined that she should be as inconspicuous as possible – and stared out of the window at the fleecy clouds building over the Alps. The plane had taken off at eight, but even so it would be noon before she reached Turkey, owing to the time difference.

107

Despite Merryman's warning, she couldn't help looking with interest at her fellow passengers, but none of them seemed the least interested in her. A good half were homeward-bound Turks, anyway. The rest were British holiday-makers – she gathered most of them were part of a single package tour.

She opened her cabin bag, took out the folder she had been given. It contained several names and resumés, but Judith had suggested she concentrate on this man Rashid ben Khalim, so she did. There was an apparently recent photograph. Rashid was a good-looking thirty-six-year-old, who had inherited a shipping firm from his father at the age of twenty-five, and in ten years had expanded it into a worldwide corporation, diversified not only into tankers and bulk carriers, but also the holiday industry. She smiled: he even had a controlling interest in the package firm her fellow passengers were using.

The links to terrorism were tenuous, but visible. He had been involved in internal Turkish politics, opposing the then regime, even before his inheritance. His involvement had not been of the active, stone-throwing variety, but he had been noted as a background figure by the Turkish police. He had even been gaoled, briefly, when his flat had been raided and subversive material discovered. His father had bought him out, and upon Khalim's death Rashid had immediately become a powerful figure in the financial world – too powerful, it seemed, ever again to be arrested. But the police had kept an eye on him, and he was known to have contacts with several international terrorist groups. These contacts had consisted mainly of subscriptions to their funds; there had never been any evidence, or even suggestion, that he took part in their activities, although he was suspected of smuggling arms and munitions by means of his ships, to wherever they were wanted. To the IRA, certainly, some ten years ago.

Jessica pinched her lip. Presumably that was when he had first come into contact with Robert Korman.

Then the Irish had opted for peace, and Korman had found himself unemployed.

Or had he? As Judith had said, all of Rashid's contacts with terrorism had ended at the same time; he had even stopped his various subscriptions. The Turkish police had, apparently, given a great sigh of relief, and closed his file. And since then, a matter of five years, he had simply been an impeccable, very rich, very successful businessman.

While all the time being more active than ever before, by means of Korman? Why? Korman had never had any ideals. He had never dreamed of a united Ireland, simply because he wasn't Irish. He had never opposed Communism, simply fled from it. When it had ended, he had never returned to Hungary. There was no trace of any parents or any family whatsoever. It seemed obvious that Korman had been a name assumed by himself and his twin sister from the moment they became active in terrorism. But the death of his sister was accepted as being the driving factor that had at last given him a reason for living – and killing. His personal war was with the British.

But how had he managed to enlist a man like Rashid to support him? Jessica turned the pages to reach Rashid's personal file. Father a Christian Arab. Educated at an English public school. Once again she pinched her lip. Bullying? Could be. Bullying in school was known to have driven many boys – and girls – to suicide. Could it have driven Rashid ben Khalim to a hatred sufficient to kill, a hatred that had found its outlet in the support he had given to any terrorist – and thus, by definition, anti-establishment – group that appealed to him? But which had slowly hardened, and tightened, into a determination to strike at the nation that had caused his humiliation? As a result of his meeting with Korman?

She turned another page and frowned. Rashid was married, and had two children. He had a large home just outside Istanbul. How did one have a wife and children while arranging for people to be blown up? Or was that just part of his façade? Did his wife know of his underground activities? Not necessarily.

But his home might be a good place to start.

The immigration officer thumbed Jessica's passport with interest. 'You are a British policeman?' he asked, in English. 'A British policewoman, eh?' He grinned, and allowed his gaze to drift up and down her diminutive jeans- and shirt-clad body.

'That is my job, yes,' Jessica said. 'But I am here on holiday.'

'Ah, holiday. Vacation, eh? You on tour?'

'I'm on my own. I just thought I'd browse around Istanbul for a day or two.'

'Oh, yes, very nice.' He stamped her passport.

She carried her bag through the throng, caught a taxi to the hotel; it was a fair drive from the airport. She had not been to Turkey before, and immediately found it fascinating, from the large numbers of troops to be seen around the airport – Yeşilköy was also a military establishment – to the walls built by the Greek defenders more than a thousand years ago to defend the city – but which had fallen to the Ottoman Turks in 1453 – to the mosques and old buildings inside the city itself. But the hotel looked modern enough, even if the street outside was perilously narrow for the constant two-way stream of traffic.

'Miss Jones,' said the reception clerk. 'We have a reservation. Are you with a tour party?'

'No.'

'Ah.' He seemed puzzled, and, like the immigration officer, allowed himself a slow inspection. Then he snapped his fingers and gave instructions, in Turkish, to a uniformed bellhop. 'You will find all relevant information on the inside of your door, Miss Jones.'

'Thank you.' Jessica followed the boy to the lift. He placed her suitcase on the floor and stared at her as they ascended. Jessica stared back. They stopped on the third floor and he led her along a corridor and showed her into number 307.

It was a somewhat small but well-furnished double, with twin beds; she wondered if Merryman was being generous or if the hotel simply did not have single rooms.

The boy placed the suitcase on the rack, and waited. Jessica had obtained some Turkish lire at Heathrow, and she held out a note.

He did not take it. 'You no have English money?'

'Ah, you speak English. Would you prefer to have English money?' She gave him a fifty-pence piece.

'Is better,' he explained. 'You no with tour party?'

'No, I am not with a tour party,' Jessica said, beginning to be slightly irritated.

The boy grinned. 'You wish man, to look after you?'

'In what way?'

He shrugged. 'I am man. I look after you very much.'

'Ah.' The penny dropped. 'No, I don't think that will be necessary.' She looked at her watch. 'What time is lunch?'

He gestured at the notices on the door. 'It is now, if you wish.'

'Right. I'll tell you what you can do for me. After lunch I wish a taxi, to take me to a place called Beken. Is it far?'

'Not far. To the north.'

Jessica nodded. 'Right. I would like you to arrange it for me. I do not speak Turkish, you see? I would like to go to an address in Beken, and come back. I wish the taxi to wait. You understand?'

111

'I understand. You give me the address?'

Jessica sat at the table and wrote it out, handed it to him, waited. But he gave no sign of recognising it; he folded it and put it in his pocket.

Jessica looked at her watch again; it would not take her more than an hour to have lunch. 'I would like to leave at two o'clock, and I will be returning probably at four.'

He shook his head. 'No good. Two o'clock is no good.'

'Why not?'

'Sleep time.'

She hadn't realised that custom obtained in Turkey.

'I arrange taxi for four o'clock,' he said. 'Then you come back six o'clock, in time for dinner and the show, eh?'

'Show?'

'Belly dancing. Very good. Very . . .' He waggled his hips.

'I'm not sure that's my scene,' Jessica said. 'Okay, taxi at four.'

'I fix it. And remember, when you need man, I am the one. My name is Sami. You remember this.'

'When,' she agreed.

He grinned. 'You not think so? I have one big one.'

'I am sure you do,' Jessica said. 'Just arrange the taxi, will you?'

He closed the door and she went into the bathroom to wash her face. Presumably Merryman had no plans for coping with amorous bellhops.

Actually, the idea of a siesta was most attractive. As she lay on her bed after a surprisingly good lunch, Jessica realised just how tired she was. The two days with Tom on the farm had been delightful, but they had both been too tense really to relax, and since then she had been stretched, body and mind, to the limit.

And she had killed a man. Sometime soon that was

really going to sink in. But now, remarkably, she felt totally relaxed. Because she was under way. It was rather like flying. While she would be going through the motions of eating and drinking and sleeping and living, her life was entirely in the hands of someone else. In this case, the pilot was Merryman. Oddly, that was reassuring. He might be a bastard but he was certainly efficient.

She awoke with a start just after three, bathed in sweat. She had a shower, and contemplated her pillbox. She was extremely reluctant to take the damned thing, at least until she was fairly sure they were going to reach their target within two days. And surely it was unnecessary for this preliminary gambit. As Merryman himself had said, Korman's mob could have no concept that she would actually come to them in Istanbul. And she had no certain knowledge that Rashid ben Khalim was a member of that mob, anyway.

On the other hand, as she had been given the damned thing, and as she was about to go out into the field . . . She activated the battery, poured a glass of water from the carafe on her bedside table, and swallowed the capsule with some difficulty.

Then she considered her body armour. But the quilted underwear was simply too hot to contemplate, especially as, for concealment, it had to be worn under fairly heavy clothing. And the same argument applied; she was certain no one was going to take a shot at her this afternoon.

She put on a light summer dress instead, and, as she had half an hour to kill, opened the newspaper she had bought at Heathrow but had not actually got around to reading. The shooting in Somerset had not quite made the front page, but was fairly well covered inside. No one had apparently yet linked it to the shooting in London a few days before, although again it was being implied that it was drug related. That apart, there was little of interest. Thus the usual financial crisis, the usual Cabinet crisis, the usual crisis in the Opposition – it occurred to her that if the word 'crisis' were to be removed from the language the media would have a hard time of it – the usual inter-governmental meeting, this time in Kuala Lumpur, being attended by the Minister for Trade and Industry hoping to tie up a big export order for the UK, the usual . . . Jessica's eye flickered back to the last item.

The Minister for Trade and Industry was in Kuala Lumpur for a high-level meeting with South-East Asia businessmen. Merryman, who had originated the Cabinet-destructing theory, had not mentioned it. Well, she supposed it was none of her business, and presumably the Minister would be over-protected. But if Korman knew of it . . . she found herself smiling. If Korman was in Kuala Lumpur, all the protection Merryman had promised her here in Istanbul was a waste of time.

But as she *was* here, she had a job of work to do. She wished she hadn't taken the pill.

She went downstairs at four o'clock. Sami was waiting in the lounge. He looked at her legs with great appreciation.

'The taxi is waiting. I have told him to take you to Beken, and wait, and bring you back. He will do this.'

'Thank you. Does he speak English?'

'No, he has no English. But he is a good man. He will take you, and bring you back. You do not pay him until you are back at the hotel.'

'He knows this?'

'I have told him this, yes. He is agreeable.'

'Well . . . thanks again. See you later.'

She wondered how she was going to fend him off that

night. He was being so helpful she didn't have the heart to report him to the management, even if she knew he was only being helpful because he hoped to get between the sheets with her.

Another bridge to be crossed when she got to it, she thought as they drove over the Golden Horn.

The taxi driver wore a beard and had brilliant white teeth; he smiled a lot. Jessica sat in the back and enjoyed the view of the Bosporus on her right as they went north. The wide waterway was surprisingly busy, as the front was surprisingly built up on her left – across the strait the country looked much less developed. Asia!

She had to resist the temptation to look out of the rear window to see if they were being trailed. But if her guard had a decoder, as she had to assume he did, he would not need to follow her very closely.

There was much blowing of horns and gesticulating, for the traffic was quite heavy, but in not more than half an hour they were in Beken, and the taxi was pulling to a stop outside an ornate pair of gates. The road had now turned inland, and had also risen; Jessica guessed that the house overlooked the water. That figured.

The driver turned round to look at her, clearly inquiring whether he should attempt to drive through the gates. She pointed along the street, and he got the message, allowed her out, then drove about fifty yards and parked. Jessica hesitated for several seconds; three cars drove by while she did so, and she had to assume her watchdog was in one of them.

Predictably, the gate was locked. She rang the bell.

A disembodied voice said something in Turkish.

'Do you speak English?' Jessica asked.

'What is it you wish?' the voice inquired.

'I wish to see Mrs Rashid.'

'On what business?'

'I am a journalist. I would like to speak with her about an article I am writing.'

'You have an appointment?'

'No, I do not have an appointment. I shall only take up a few minutes of her time.'

She waited, while the voice was clearly finding out if she could be admitted. Then a small side gate slowly swung in.

Jessica drew a deep breath and stepped through, then drew another breath as it clicked shut behind her. The walls to either side were several feet high, far too high for her to scale. The only way she was going to leave was through those gates.

She walked up a paved driveway between well-filled flowerbeds. In one of these a gardener straightened as she passed, then stooped back to his weeding; if she had come through the gates she was clearly entitled to be there. Now she could see the house: white, gleaming in the bright sunshine, several storeys high, a mass of windows and television aerials, including several satellite dishes. The wide, curved front steps made her think of an hotel, and as she went up, the door at the top opened for her.

The butler wore a white jacket with brass buttons. 'Your name?' he asked in English.

Jessica controlled her breathing. 'Jessica Jones.'

He gave no sign of recognition, merely a brief bow. 'Come with me, please.'

He led the way down a mosaic-tiled hallway; the walls to either side were marked with potted plants, but no pictures, to her surprise. They passed several archways leading into over-furnished and carpeted reception rooms, then the butler opened another door at the end of the corridor, and they emerged on to a broad terrace. Here again the walls were white, and dazzling, and as Jessica had anticipated, it looked down on the blue of the sea.

A few feet along the terrace there was a table sheltering beneath a large golf umbrella, and here a woman sat. She had been writing, but she looked up as the butler approached.

'Miss Jessica Jones,' he said, in English.

Jessica was surprised. She had expected an Arab woman, or certainly Turkish.

This woman might have been Turkish, but it was more likely she was Scandinavian; she was tall – that was obvious even when she was sitting down – and extremely voluptuous, with wide hips and big breasts thrusting bralessly against the white silk of her shirt. Her tight-fitting pants were also white, as were her sandals, so that she almost merged into the generally dazzling background, especially as her long straight hair was so pale as to be almost white itself. Her face was handsome rather than pretty, the features somewhat sharp. Contrasting with the general white, the rubies and sapphires in the rings on her fingers sparkled.

Jessica put her age down as early thirties.

'I do not think we have met,' she remarked. Her voice was low, her English only slightly accented.

'No,' Jessica agreed. 'It's awfully good of you to see me.'

Mrs Rashid waved her hand. 'We shall have coffee, Osman.'

Osman bowed and withdrew.

'Sit down,' Mrs Rashid invited. 'My name is Gerberga. And you are . . . Jessica? Do you have a card?'

Jessica gave her one. Not that she would gain anything from it, as it merely said 'DC Jessica Jones' and had the address of her London flat.

Gerberga Rashid laid the card on the table. 'Osman said you were a journalist. What does DC stand for?'

Another very long breath. But she had been instructed to

117

go in with all guns blazing. The woman could only throw her out. 'It stands for detective-constable, Mrs Rashid.'

Gerberga's pale eyebrows went up. 'You are a policewoman? An English policewoman?'

'Yes.'

'And you have come here to interview me?'

'Not in the sense you are thinking, Mrs Rashid. I'm actually on holiday.'

'Explain.'

She did not appear to be either angry or afraid, or in any way put out.

'I'm in the protection business,' Jessica said. 'I stand in front of prominent people and stop them from being assassinated.'

'How interesting. Ah, coffee.'

Osman placed the predictably silver tray on the table, and poured from the silver pot. No milk was offered, but there was sugar, a tall glass water jug, and tumblers. Osman hovered beside Jessica, spoon poised.

'I don't take sugar, thanks very much.'

'I think you should,' Gerberga recommended. 'You have drunk Turkish coffee before? I mean, as made in Turkey?'

'This is my first visit to Turkey.'

'Give Miss Jones two spoonfuls, Osman,' Gerberga said.

Osman daintily placed the sugar in the cup, stirred it just as daintily, and then placed it in front of Jessica before doing the same for his mistress. Then he placed a tumbler of water beside each woman, bowed again, and withdrew.

Gerberga sipped. Jessica did the same, and nearly choked. It was both very hot and, even with the sugar, very bitter.

'You will get used to it,' Gerberga said, raising her tumbler. 'You were telling me about protecting people.'

Jessica also drank some water and told her about Alicante.

'I read about it,' Gerberga said. 'What a terrible thing. You were very lucky to escape with your life.'

'Yes,' Jessica agreed. 'The thing is, I recognised one of the bombers. His name was Robert Korman.'

Again she waited, but Gerberga's face did not change expression. 'This is important?'

'Well, yes. He is a very wanted man for a number of terrorist crimes. The point is, though, that he is supposed to be dead. Blown up by his own bomb in Buenos Aires, two years ago. But I know I saw him. The trouble is, nobody will believe me. So I took a leave of absence, and decided to see if I could find out the truth.'

'So you came here. And to me, or my husband? How can we possibly help you to find a man who may be dead?'

'I have some evidence that Korman is now based in Turkey. And, please forgive me, I also have evidence that he and your husband know each other. Or they did, once upon a time.'

Gerberga frowned, and poured some more coffee. This time Jessica helped herself to sugar.

'Have you ever heard the name, Robert Korman?' Jessica asked.

'I have never heard the name,' Gerberga said. 'But . . . you are suggesting that my husband was once acquainted with a terrorist?'

Time to think, very quickly. Was it possible that his own wife knew nothing of his background? No, it was not possible, because he had been arrested by the Turkish police as a young man. That would be common knowledge. So she had been lying from the beginning, with consummate skill. Unless . . .

'May I ask how long you have been married, Mrs Rashid?'

119

'Four years.'

Four years, Jessica thought. Four years ago Rashid had still been active in terrorism. Had he already begun his partnership with Korman? And this exquisite creature knew all about it?

'I do apologise,' she backtracked hastily. 'I just have a list of people who may once have known this man Korman, and I'm following it up. I'm sure it is just coincidental. But I'm also sure you'll understand that it is very important to me.'

'Of course I understand that. But I think it is something you should ask my husband himself.' Gerberga looked at her diamond-encrusted Cartier watch. 'He will be back in a little while.'

Jessica looked at her own Tissot. 'I'd love to, but I really must be getting along. Tell you what, though; may I call and arrange a meeting with him?'

'That may be difficult. He is a very busy man. Right now he is out of town, but I do expect him to return this afternoon. However, tomorrow I imagine he will spend all day at the office. So . . .'

'I guess I'll have to take my chances,' Jessica said, and stood up. 'Thanks a million for the coffee. And for being so co-operative.'

'But I don't think you should go,' Gerberga said, also standing. 'I know you have so much to ask him, and you may never have another opportunity.'

Jessica gazed at her, and realised that she had utterly entrapped herself. This woman knew everything, and had been considering her best course of action from the moment Korman's name was mentioned.

'Well,' she said, 'we'll have to see.'

She hurried to the doorway, and discovered it was occupied by Osman. She checked, and turned back towards Gerberga, who was walking slowly towards her.

'I hope you're not thinking of detaining me here,' she said. 'My taxi is waiting and . . .'

Gerberga spoke to Osman in Turkish, and he bowed and left.

Jessica sighed with relief. 'That was very sensible of you, Mrs Rashid.'

'I have told Osman to send the taxi away,' Gerberga said. 'After you have spoken with my husband, he will send you home in one of our cars.'

'No, no,' Jessica said. 'I wish to leave, now.'

'And I wish you to stay,' Gerberga said. 'What you have told me is very interesting. I really would like you to hear what my husband has to say about it.'

Jessica glared at her. Gerberga carried no handbag, and there was no way she could have a weapon concealed in that tight-fitting outfit. Thus presumably she was good with her hands, and she was much the larger woman. Jessica didn't doubt she could lay her out, but she had been specifically instructed to avoid getting physically involved without urgent necessity. She didn't think that had arrived yet.

'I said, I'll call him tomorrow,' she said, and went through the doorway, to find herself facing two large young men. 'Shoot,' she muttered.

'I do wish you'd come and sit down and have another cup of coffee,' Gerberga said from behind her. 'Or perhaps you would prefer something stronger?'

'You cannot do this,' Jessica said, understanding how futile her protest was. 'I am expected back at my hotel.'

'Which hotel is that?' Gerberga asked.

'The Superior.'

'Ah. My husband owns it.'

Jessica's jaw dropped.

'It was, in fact, someone from the hotel who telephoned us to say you were coming to see me,' Gerberga said. 'Which is why I received you at all.'

Jessica swallowed.

'So why do you not come back and sit down, and wait for him,' Gerberga said, and then smiled. 'Here he is now.'

The Rescue

R ashid ben Khalim looked exactly as in his photograph.

But Jessica had never seen the man accompanying him,
who was considerably shorter, and certainly not Turkish.
With his squat powerful body and lank black hair, he made
her think of a Mongol.

Both men gazed at Jessica with mild surprise. They
clearly did not recognise her.

'We have a guest,' Gerberga said. 'My darling, this is Miss
Jessica Jones. From England. She is a police detective.'

Now Rashid was clearly astonished. As was his companion. But after a moment Rashid came forward, hand
outstretched. 'Welcome to my home, Miss Jones.'

Jessica clasped the warm, strong fingers, looked into
the deep black eyes. It occurred to her that they might be
chasing the wrong man.

'Is this an official visit?' Rashid asked. 'Did I forget to
pay a parking fine, last time I was in England?'

'It is an official visit,' Gerberga said. 'She is seeking
information on a man called Robert Korman. She says you
once knew him.'

'Ah,' Rashid said. 'By the way, this is a friend of
mine.' He gestured his companion forward. 'His name
is Tugril.'

Tugril came forward to shake hands. His grip was soft,
but unlike Rashid – and very much like the immigration
officer and Sami – he allowed his eyes to roam.

'Tugril does not speak English,' Rashid explained.

Tugril made a remark, presumably in Turkish.

'He says you are a very pretty woman. He says he would like to strangle you, with his bare hands.'

Jessica took a step backwards, and found herself against Gerberga. Hastily she stepped forward again, while her brain whirred out of control. She could only think that she was in deep trouble. Her only hope was the capsule. But would Merryman's people break into the house of one of Turkey's richest men unless they definitely knew something was wrong?

'That is his way of paying you a compliment,' Rashid explained. 'You *can* speak?'

Jessica licked her lips. 'Just collecting my thoughts,' she said.

'You need to. Robert Korman is dead, Miss Jones. But you knew that.'

'Yes,' Jessica said. 'I'm sure you're right. Now, I simply must run along.'

'No, no. You simply must stay.' Rashid looked at his watch. 'I think we could all have a drink. Osman.'

The butler bowed.

'On the terrace,' Rashid said.

Jessica hesitated, then allowed herself to be returned to the terrace. The sun was drooping now, and was obscured by the house behind them.

'Have you had a good day, my dear?' Rashid asked.

'Quiet,' Gerberga said.

'And the children?'

'Noisy. They will be expecting you.'

'I shall go to them in a minute. Do sit down, Miss Jones.' He sat himself, as did Gerberga and Tugril.

'Miss Jones has an idea that Korman may still be alive,' Gerberga said.

'Of course. So you were sent here to investigate.'

'I was not sent,' Jessica said. 'I was given leave after Alicante, and decided to do some checking on my own. No one believed me when I said I had seen Korman just before the explosion.'

'How annoying for you. But . . . you say you saw him? You recognised him? Korman?'

'No, Mr Rashid, I did not recognise him. How could I? He's had a facelift, or something, hasn't he? But I recognised his voice.'

'His *voice*? You mean he spoke to you? While planting the bomb?'

He was beginning to remind Jessica of Harrison. He was certainly equally bewildered. But also, he had more or less admitted that Korman *was* alive.

'He shouted at me,' Jessica said. 'He shouted, "You fucking bitch." He had used the same words before, two years ago. I remembered both the words and the voice. And in any event, *he* recognised *me*, or he wouldn't have shouted at me.'

'I see. Ah, Osman.' Rashid waited while the drinks were placed before them, some kind of cocktail with a rum base and served in long glasses. Rashid raised his glass. 'Your health. And of course you reported all of this to your superiors when you returned home . . . and you say they didn't believe you. Most irritating. So here you are. Would you say you are the only person in England who believes that Korman is still alive?'

'Yes,' Jessica said.

'And how many people know that you are carrying out this private investigation, here in Istanbul?'

'My boyfriend,' Jessica lied. 'He is also a policeman.'

'Hm,' Rashid said, and looked up as a woman wearing a nurse's uniform appeared in the doorway. 'Ah, the children are ready to say goodnight. You'll excuse us for a moment, Miss Jones.' He spoke to Tugril, and then smiled at Jessica. 'I have asked him not to touch you, unless it becomes necessary. We shan't be long.'

He and Gerberga went inside. Jessica looked at Tugril, and Tugril looked at her, and made a remark. Presumably he was suggesting some other part of her anatomy he would like to get hold of.

He gave her the creeps. But then her whole situation was giving her the creeps.

There were so many imponderables, so many aspects of her position that needed explaining. Had Merryman known the Hotel Superior was part of Rashid's chain when he had booked her in? Just to make sure the confrontation came sooner rather than later? How long would she have to stay in this house before his people reacted? That really was an imponderable.

She looked at the doorway. But Osman was waiting there, and besides, the thought of Tugril touching her made her skin crawl.

Rashid returned; Gerberga had apparently remained with the children for the moment. Rashid sat down, finished his drink. It was starting to grow dark. 'So here you are, in Istanbul, seeking Korman. While he, or at least his people, are in England searching for you. I find that amusing. But you are far more deadly than you look, are you not? You have killed four of his people.'

'I only killed one,' Jessica said. 'You realise you are admitting not only that you know Korman, but that you have been in touch with him very recently.'

'Yesterday,' Rashid said. 'Before he left for Kuala Lumpur.'

Jessica drew a sharp breath. 'You mean . . .'

'Oh, indeed, he is a dedicated man, when he is reminded of it. What is really amusing is that I promised him I would take care of you. I did not imagine it was going to be so easy. It simply never crossed my mind that you would walk into my house.'

Jessica refused to lose her nerve. 'But as everyone knows I came here—'

Rashid held up his finger. 'No one knows you came here, Miss Jones, save for your taxi driver, who has been paid off and dismissed as you are staying for dinner. That is what he has been told.'

'And the hotel staff are all in your pay.' When I get hold of Sami . . . she thought.

'Precisely. They will not raise the alarm if you do not return tonight. However, were you not to return at all, they would eventually have to report it.' He stroked his chin, then spoke to Tugril. They engaged in quite a conversation, while Jessica waited, trying to evaluate her situation, her chances.

'You understand, Miss Jones,' Rashid said, 'that we have to kill you.'

Jessica gulped at the calm way he was spelling it out.

'Your nuisance value, your ability to identify Korman, and now, the way you connected me to him . . . How did you do that, by the way?'

'I have dossiers on several people living in Turkey who are both wealthy and linked to terrorism. Your name happened to be at the top of the list, so I started here.' Was it really her speaking in that calm, measured voice? '*You* understand that those files are from the British Special Branch, to which I belong, as does my boyfriend.'

'Ah, the famous Special Branch. Of course, your boyfriend will hunt through those files when you disappear. But there is nothing to link you to me. It is a question of how you disappear. There are three options. One is that you are found floating in the Bosporus with your throat cut. But that would lead to an investigation, and your boyfriend might well arrive in Istanbul, perhaps with support, asking questions. In that case we might have to dispose of your taxi driver as well. All very messy. The second way would be to have you just disappear. We could take you out to Korman's place in Cappadocia. It is quite something. An underground village, virtually, built hundreds of years ago for shelter from the Seljuks.' He smiled. 'Tugril is descended from the Seljuks. There you could wait for Korman's return. He should be back in a couple of days. He would really appreciate finding you there. But that would mean transporting you alive. I suppose we could drug you. Hm. But I think Tugril's suggestion is the best. Certainly the safest, even if it robs Korman of his bit of fun.'

'What is Tugril's suggestion?' Jessica asked.

'That we keep everything absolutely above board. So, you came to Istanbul, ostensibly on holiday, but in reality to see if you could prove that Korman is still alive. As you say, in your hotel room there are several dossiers on wealthy men living in Turkey who might possibly be linked to terrorism. Mine was top of the list, and besides, it indicated that I once knew Korman. So you came to see me first. You met me, and my wife and I invited you to dinner. Obviously you found nothing to arouse your suspicions or you would not have stayed. After dinner, and greatly against our advice, you decided to take a walk down into the town to find a taxi to return you to your hotel. This was a very foolhardy thing to have done, and it turned out badly. You were attacked by a gang of street louts, raped, and murdered. I'm afraid this happens all the time to unattached tourists, and not only in Turkey. I seem to remember a very similar case in your own London a few years ago. I do not think the victim was actually murdered, but she was thrown naked into a canal and could well have drowned.'

Jessica got her breathing under control. 'And you think the police will believe that story?'

'Why should they not? I will not attempt to hide anything. You certainly came here, as your taxi driver will
confirm. You certainly stayed for dinner. And then you
left. Oh, you asked me questions about Korman, but as I
know nothing about Korman, and there is no one who can
prove otherwise, you appeared satisfied. Then you left, by
yourself, and against my advice. But you are a woman who
is always doing things on her own, and no doubt against
advice. Is that not so?'

Jessica swallowed.

Rashid snapped his fingers. 'Osman, another drink before
dinner.'

Osman bowed.

'I really do not wish anything else,' Jessica protested.

'I think you do. I think you need it. You are looking a
little pale.'

Think, think, think, Jessica told herself. Merryman's
people know I'm here. As far as they know I am all right,
perhaps enjoying myself, and besides Rashid is too well
known and too wealthy for them to risk an attack which
might well set off a diplomatic incident. Therefore they are
going to do nothing, while I am being raped and murdered.
When *would* they act? Presumably they would follow the
car leaving the house, and they would certainly move in
if she was thrown from it.

But by then she might already be dead.

On the other hand, if the capsule was emitting a signal, and they were monitoring it, her whereabouts would
be revealed on their screen. How? It would have to be
directional and distance bearing, which would track her
into this house and would show that she was still here.
How sensitive would it be? It should be able to trace her
every movement, even over a few yards. So, they would
have seen it move to and fro as she had gone to the door
and then been returned to her seat. They would not be able

129

to tell what she was doing, or what part of the house she was in, but the fact that her movements had been slow and apparently controlled would leave them confident that she was not in any immediate danger.

But if there was sudden violent movement . . . It would have to cover a fair area, indicate that she was running about – even Merryman would have to realise that she would not be running around inside Rashid's house unless she was trying to escape something.

'May I ask who is going to do the raping and murdering? Will it be you, Mr Rashid?'

'No, no. I don't think my wife would care for that. You are far too attractive. No, I will leave that in the care of Tugril and his people. This is something he really wants to do. And then he can strangle you when he is finished.'

'Something else he really wants to do,' Jessica said, and accepted a second drink from Osman.

Rashid was studying her. 'You are a most remarkably calm and courageous young woman,' he said. 'Is this part of your training as a policeman, or do you have a hidden resource on which you are counting?'

'Chance would be a fine thing,' Jessica said. 'As you say, we are trained not to overreact.'

'Nevertheless, I think we should make sure. Tugril.' He spoke in Turkish, and Tugril took Jessica's shoulder bag, opened it, and poured the contents on to the table.

'Ah, Gerberga,' Rashid said as his wife reappeared. 'Would you like to tell me if there is anything unusual in the contents of that bag?'

Gerberga sifted through Jessica's belongings, while Jessica worked on her best plan. Merely to run for the door now was not good enough; she would be caught before there could be sufficient movement to alert Merryman. She needed to be able to cover some distance at great speed, and when caught – because undoubtedly she would be – some distance back again.

Gerberga was even opening lipstick tubes and the compact, peering inside. 'I can see nothing,' she said.

'I find that odd,' Rashid said. 'I think you will have to search her.'

Tugril made a remark.

'He is a randy fellow,' Rashid said. 'I think it would be best if you did it, my dear. Take her upstairs. Oh, you may need this.' He reached into his pocket and produced a small Walther PPK automatic pistol. 'But you had better take Miranda as well.'

Jessica could not believe her luck; they were actually playing into her hands.

'I hope you won't make any trouble,' Gerberga said as she escorted Jessica into the house, where they were joined by a large young woman. 'Miranda is very strong, and very capable.'

'I'm sure she is,' Jessica agreed. 'Are you just going to stand by while I am raped and murdered? That makes you as much of a terrorist as your husband. Or Korman.'

Gerberga snorted. 'I was a terrorist long before I met my husband, my dear. Recently, what with childbearing, I have found life a trifle boring. Up there.'

She indicated a flight of stairs at the back of the reception room. Once again Jessica considered her options, but still decided to wait; the two women were immediately behind her, and Gerberga had the gun. Of course, if she were to use it, that would upset her husband's plans for total non-involvement . . . but it was hardly a risk worth taking at this close range.

She climbed the stairs, and reached a first-floor corridor.

'To the right,' Gerberga said.

131

Jessica turned right; the two women followed.

'That door,' Gerberga said.

Jessica opened the door and stepped through into a darkened room; Gerberga immediately switched the light on. It was obviously a guest bedroom, with twin beds and very comfortably furnished.

She turned. Miranda closed the door, and was leaning against it. She was indeed a big woman, with a remarkably bland face.

But now they had separated, Miranda by the door, Gerberga moving across the room to a chair, where she sat down, knees crossed, the pistol lying on her lap.

'Strip,' she invited.

Slowly, reluctantly, Jessica sat on the bed, and even more slowly took off one sandal. She would in any event be better off without them if she intended to run. Then, still holding the first sandal, she leaned over and removed the second. As she straightened, she flicked the first sandal, as hard as she could, at Gerberga. Taken entirely by surprise, Gerberga was struck in the face. She gave a gasp, and tried to rise, and dropped the gun.

By then Jessica had turned and was throwing the other shoe at Miranda, much as she had done at Gabrielle in the flat. Miranda had left the door to come forward. She saw the shoe coming and ducked, but that both slowed her and left her off balance, and Jessica was in front of her before she could recover.

Jessica swung her right hand, held rigid, into Miranda's neck, and Miranda grunted and fell to her knees; Jessica's well-aimed blow had struck the aorta and for a moment the big woman was hardly conscious. Jessica continued on her way and had reached the door when Gerberga shouted, 'Stop!'

She had regained possession of the gun, and Jessica had to take the risk that she would use it. She wrenched the door open and was through and running along the corridor.

Gerberga ran into the corridor after her, and did fire, but Jessica had no idea if she had aimed or not; the bullet went wide, slamming into some expensive panelling.

'Help!' Gerberga shouted. 'She's getting away!'

Jessica had reached the stairs, and was going down as fast as she could, hanging on to the bannisters to prevent herself from falling. Gerberga stood at the top and fired again, but again the shot was wide; either she was a very poor shot or she was only intending to frighten, not hit.

Jessica reached the foot of the stairs, and skidded on the parquet. She understood that she had reached the end of the line, as not only Osman, but two other men had appeared from the back, while Rashid and Tugril were hurrying in from the terrace.

But the rest of her plan remained. She turned and ran back up the stairs, panting now. Now she was totally exposed to Gerberga, who saw her coming, and still held the gun. But she didn't shoot, merely swung the weapon as Jessica reached her. It struck Jessica on the shoulder and knocked her against the wall, but she was still able to grasp Gerberga's wrist and throw her with such force that she tumbled down the stairs herself.

Jessica regained her balance and looked for the gun, but it had gone down the stairs with Gerberga. Anyway, she reminded herself, she hadn't intended to engage in a shoot-out, which could well end up with her dead or badly wounded. The men at the foot of the stairs were shouting and coming up, while Gerberga lay in front of them, hanging on to the bannisters and swearing. Jessica looked along the corridor at Miranda, moving towards her, still holding her neck.

This really was the end of the line, Jessica decided. She

was too out of breath to run any more, or fight any more. 'Okay,' she said. 'I surrender.'

Miranda did not appear to believe her. She continued to advance, her face contorted with rage. Jessica was quite relieved to hear Rashid's voice, behind her. 'All right, Miranda. We will take care of it now.'

Jessica turned to face him, and behind him, her face as contorted with anger as Miranda's, Gerberga.

'Let me have her,' Gerberga said. 'Give her to me, tied up and stripped. I will—'

'Mark her all up in a female fashion, which will not gel with our story,' Rashid said. He smiled at Jessica, who was slowly getting her breathing back under control. 'You really are a little tiger-cat, aren't you, Miss Jones?'

'Let me at least hit her,' Gerberga begged. 'She hit *me*.'

'All right,' Rashid agreed. 'But on the body. And without nails.'

Gerberga stepped up to Jessica, who drew a breath and tensed her muscles. For the moment she was all past resisting. She could only pray that Merryman had realised what was going on.

Gerberga swung her fist into Jessica's stomach with mind-numbing force. Jessica gasped and her knees gave way. Dimly she saw Gerberga drawing back her fist again, and being checked by her husband.

'Enough.'

'You admire the bitch,' Gerberga said.

'She has a lot of guts,' Rashid admitted. 'Stand up, Miss Jones.'

Jessica struggled to her feet, panting. She felt sick.

'I do not suppose you would enjoy dinner now,' Rashid said. 'And it is quite dark. I think we had better finish it, and eat later.' He spoke to Tugril, and Tugril grinned and nodded. 'You will go with him, now,' Rashid said.

Where the hell was Merryman? Now she was helpless. Tugril grasped her arms and marched her down the stairs. His men were waiting at the foot.

Rashid spoke again, and Tugril nodded. Jessica's arms were pulled behind her back and her wrists were secured. Then a strip of wide plaster was placed across her mouth, leaving her quite unable to do more than gurgle.

Rashid also came down the stairs. 'I would like you to know, Miss Jones, that meeting you has been most interesting, and I will always have the highest regard for your courage. But there it is. We are on opposite sides, and there can only ever be one winner.'

Tugril waited for his employer to finish speaking, then grasped Jessica's shoulder and pushed her towards the other doorway. Jessica was terribly aware of eyes, watching her, all knowing that she was going to her execution. She did not wish to look at any of them, and stared straight ahead as she was taken out to the paved driveway; they hadn't replaced her shoes, and the concrete hurt her feet. Two cars were now parked at the foot of the steps, and into the back of one of these – a large black Mercedes – she was pushed. Tugril sat on one side of her, one of his men on the other. The third man got into the front beside the driver. Tugril gave an order, and the car moved down the drive. Behind them the house blazed with light. No doubt Rashid and Gerberga would now be sitting down to their dinner.

The gates opened, and the Mercedes drove through. The street outside appeared deserted. Not even a parked car. But Merryman's people had to be close, surely. Suppose they weren't there at all? The sickness grew.

They drove for about ten minutes, until they were well away from the residential area of the town. Then Tugril began pawing at the bodice of her dress, squeezing rather than caressing. His man on the other side pulled up her skirt to fumble at her legs. God, God, God! she thought.

The car swung round a corner into a darkened lane, and there stopped. The men in front got out and opened the rear doors, and Jessica was dragged out and thrown to the ground. One held her shoulders to stop her moving, while Tugril knelt above her, threw up her dress and pulled at her briefs, then began unfastening his pants . . . Suddenly they were bathed in the headlights of a car that had just come round the corner behind them.

Tugril jerked away from Jessica, turning on his knees, and she kicked him, sending him right over. The other man was facing the oncoming car, shouting and waving his arms. But the car came right up to them, and from it leapt three men. They wore black assault suits and balaclavas. They reminded Jessica of the men who had broken into her flat . . . but these were on her side.

By now Tugril's men had realised this was no mere case of an inconvenient interruption. One of them drew a pistol and was cut down by a shot from the first of the SAS men; he was using a silenced gun and there was hardly any sound save for the grunt of the man who was hit. The driver took in the situation, realised he could not get to his own car, and ran into the darkness. The third man raised his hands. Tugril was just getting up, and Jessica kicked him again, in the back, sending him down again.

Then she was being dragged to her feet by two of the SAS men, and was hurried to their car. Behind her the one remaining SAS man calmly levelled his gun and shot Tugril and then his companion, before returning to the car and getting in. A fourth SAS man had remained behind the wheel, and he now reversed the car and drove away, at no great speed.

'Mmmmm,' Jessica said.

Merryman took off his balaclava, as did McAdoo on her other side. She did not recognise the two men in front.

'Take a deep breath,' Merryman recommended, and pulled the plaster from her mouth.

'Ow!'

McAdoo was untying her wrists.

'What in the name of God kept you?' Jessica asked, pulling down her dress.

'What in the name of God possessed you to walk into Rashid ben Khalim's house and start causing trouble?'

'Because he's the man we really want. He's the brains – and the money – behind Korman.'

'You can prove this?'

'He virtually told me so.'

'No good. We'd need a lot of proof. Korman is the man we're after. Did you find out anything about him?'

'Do you have anything to drink? My throat is absolutely dry.'

He sniffed her breath. 'I'd say you've already had a skinful.'

'That was forced on me. What I want now is water.'

A canteen was produced, and she took a deep drink. 'What happens now?' They were driving along the coast road back to Istanbul.

'You tell me what happened back there.'

Jessica related the events of the evening.

'Smart thinking,' Merryman commented on her ploy to alert them. 'So, another complete foul-up.'

'My brief was to bring them out into the open. Haven't I done that?'

'Your brief was to bring Korman into the open. And you say he's on his way to Kuala Lumpur? Shit! We didn't expect him to get out again so quickly; Alicante isn't a fortnight old yet. Go to the *basha*,' he told the driver.

'Listen,' Jessica said. 'Aren't you going to take out Rashid?'

'Not without orders. This man is big news here in

137

Turkey. I'm sure the police still have a file on him, and they probably know a hell of a lot more about his activities than he realises, but the fact is that he is officially clean until he can be positively linked to Korman. And even then, until either of them commits a crime here in Turkey, there's not much to be done. Rashid is a big contributor to government party funds, knows all the right people . . .'

'You wouldn't call his attempt on my life a crime here in Turkey?'

'We can't do anything about that, either, as long as we need to keep a low profile. We're not supposed to be here at all, remember? Don't be downhearted, JJ. We have that clue: Cappadocia.'

'That is one hell of a big area,' Jessica pointed out. 'It's an entire province, or something.'

'I have some ideas,' Merryman said. 'Here we are.'

The car turned through an archway and stopped in a small courtyard. 'Change those plates, Dickson,' Merryman said as he got out; he escorted Jessica into the house, where they were greeted by an elderly Turkish man, who looked at Jessica somewhat sceptically.

'Trouble?'

'Some.'

Merryman led Jessica further into the house, which was comfortably furnished although the carpets were well worn. A woman peered at them from behind a bead curtain.

'Ibrahim's wife, Anoka,' Merryman explained.

Jessica managed a smile, and then followed Merryman up the stairs and into what was an elaborate control centre with several radios and computers.

'Quite an establishment,' Jessica commented. 'Had it long?'

'A few years.'

'And this fellow Ibrahim, is he trustworthy?'

Merryman grinned. 'Ask him.'

'Oh!' Jessica hadn't realised their host had followed them, with McAdoo.

'Coffee, Sergeant?' Merryman asked.

'Is there any chance of having something to eat?' Jessica asked. 'The Rashids invited me to dinner, but then things got out of hand. And I had an early lunch.'

'My wife is preparing a meal now,' Ibrahim said. 'What happened?'

'Nothing good,' Merryman said. He peered at Jessica. 'You all right? How close did they get to you?'

'Closer than I liked. I'm all right, really. Just a bruise or two. And some ruffled feathers. I feel dirty. What I would really like is a bath, and a change of clothing.'

'We'll eat first, then see what we can do.'

'My things . . .'

'Are at the hotel, and I'm afraid they are going to have to stay there for the time being.'

'But if I don't go back . . .'

'They'll get in touch with Rashid. By then we must be far away. Ibrahim, I need some legwork. Underground cities, or villages, or even dwellings, in Cappadocia.'

Ibrahim nodded. 'There are a lot of them. Many are of historical interest.'

'Are any privately owned?'

'Well, some are on land that is privately owned.'

'Then as soon as the relevant offices are open tomorrow morning, I want you to check out all the land deeds in that area. The property I am looking for will be owned or leased by Rashid ben Khalim.'

Ibrahim frowned. 'You think Rashid ben Khalim has land in that area? There is no reason for it. It is mostly desert.'

'I am *hoping* he has land there, Ibrahim.'

Ibrahim shrugged. 'I will find out. Supper is ready.'

The four SAS men, Jessica and Ibrahim sat around the

table downstairs. Anoka served them very tasty kebabs, rice parcelled in fig leaves, and apple tea, and then sat down with them.

'Miss Jones would like to have a bath, and can you find her something to wear?'

Anoka looked Jessica up and down. 'We are not very different in size. And a kaftan covers a wide area.'

'Just what are we going to do?' Jessica asked. 'Rashid—'

'Is going to do nothing for the rest of the night, at the very least. He sent you off to be eliminated. He certainly wouldn't want any of your friend Tugril's thugs, or Tugril himself, or the car they were using, reappearing at his house until he can be quite sure they weren't seen duffing you up. Nor, I imagine, will he expect Tugril to report in.'

'What about the driver? He got away.'

'And I should think he'll stay away, at least until he sees how things are going. So, Rashid and his wife will simply go to bed. Now, tomorrow the hotel will discover you never returned and will telephone him. But that is all part of his plan. He will say, the silly woman insisted on walking into town. You had better call the police. I would say the police will already have found the dead bodies by then, but no rape victim. So, what will your friend do then? Panic?'

'He's not the panicking kind.'

Merryman nodded. 'I bet he can be angry, though. He'll want you as badly as Korman does. But he doesn't know where you are. He may even have a problem, supposing the police manage to trace either Tugril or the car he was using back to him. But I doubt they'll be able to do that, and even if they do, with his financial and political clout he'll slide out from under them easily enough. The police will have to assume that Tugril and his people were set upon by a rival gang, who made off with you. I don't suppose that's all that far from

140

the truth. But you are loose, with an unknown number of supporters.'

'Will he try to stop Korman?'

'I don't think he can, at this late stage. But we may be able to. I'll get on the radio immediately after dinner. The conference doesn't convene until tomorrow, so we have a little time. Meanwhile, I'll see what I can do about additional support here.'

'And what do I do?' Jessica asked.

'Have your bath and go to bed. Relax. Rashid can't find you here.'

'I never expected to hear you tell me to relax and do nothing.'

He grinned. 'There's a first time for everything.'

Jessica slept heavily. She hadn't expected to. The room was tiny, the bed was narrow, and it was hard. But the warm bath had been soporific, she was exhausted, and above all, she was *secure*.

She awoke when Merryman entered the room. She sat up and hastily pulled the sheet to her throat; she had no nightclothes.

'I won't bite you,' he promised.

'I suppose I'm just feeling vulnerable.'

'That figures.' He sat on the end of the bed and she moved her feet under the covers. 'Progress. I have alerted London that Korman is back in action, and they are making the necessary adjustments to the Minister's schedule and protection. Now they know he is there, or going to be there, they are hopeful of catching Korman themselves. However, we are going to continue on the basis that they don't, and that he will be coming home sometime in the next few days.'

'Sometime, Rashid will be able to contact him and tell him about me,' Jessica said.

'Agreed, but what exactly is he going to tell him? That he was so overconfident that he could dispose of you, he agreed that Korman is alive and operating? Korman already knows you know that. That his plan misfired and you are again at large? So what's new, from Korman's point of view? Where you are now? He doesn't know. With his contacts he may be able to establish that you haven't left Turkey, but he still has to find you, here in Istanbul.'

'He will find us eventually.'

'Eventually will be too late. We are moving on today. Like I said, we are going to continue on the basis that Korman is coming home. I've been given clearance to take out his headquarters.' He grinned. 'Once I find out where it is.'

'But . . . you think he'll return there?'

'Why shouldn't he?'

'Once Rashid tells him about me . . .'

'I told you last night, there is not a lot Rashid can tell him. He doesn't know you have any links to the SAS . . .' He paused, frowning. 'He doesn't, does he?'

'No. He knows I am Special Branch, that's all.'

'And the Special Branch doesn't mess about in other people's countries, as a rule. Also, I'll bet he doesn't remember, or doesn't care, that he let slip Cappadocia. As you said, it's a huge area, and he wouldn't expect a common policewoman, even if she has friends, to be able to do anything about it. It's Korman's base, and my estimate is that he will return there, if he gets home from Malaysia. I intend to be there waiting for him. Hello, Ibrahim's back.'

He left the room, and Jessica got out of bed and dropped the kaftan supplied by Anoka over her head, then went downstairs herself.

'Guess what,' Merryman said. 'Rashid does own land in Cappadocia. Or at least he has a lease on it.'

'It is an area several miles square,' Ibrahim said. 'He leased it three years ago, for mineral exploration. There are minerals in that desert, but the capital has always been lacking to find them and bring them out. Not that Rashid has done any mining yet.'

'Three years ago,' Merryman said. 'Fits perfectly. And of course he hasn't done any mining yet. He doesn't intend to.' He prodded the map Ibrahim had spread on the table. 'Somewhere in that area is Korman's base. All we have to do is find it. Did you arrange those plane tickets for us, Ibrahim?'

Ibrahim nodded. 'Four tickets to Konya, on the noonday plane. And one ticket to London.'

'Who's that for?' Jessica asked.

'You.'

'Me? Forget it. Make that five tickets to Konya.'

'You can't be serious,' Merryman said. 'This is man's business.'

'It's my business, Captain Merryman. It's my life that's the bottom line. Besides, if I'm not there, how are you going to identify Korman? Or even his body?'

The SAS

'**S**he has a point, boss,' McAdoo said.

'For God's sake,' Merryman said. 'Do you know what you'd be taking on?'

'Tell me,' Jessica suggested.

'In the first place, this will be a surveillance operation. We will take up our positions, and we will not move, or communicate with each other, until our quarry shows. This will be out in what is virtually desert, with temperatures getting past a hundred during the day and down to just above zero at night. My men are trained to it; you are not.'

'I'll manage.'

'Should you be unable to manage I'd have to shoot you, or you could endanger the whole operation and the lives of my men.'

'I understand that. You won't have to shoot me. Have you any other objection?'

'I can think of a million. The most important being, that when we do go in, this is an SAS operation. In involves total teamwork and determination. Again, my men are trained to it; they know exactly what to do and when to do it. You are not. So once again you could endanger the whole operation.'

'I will remain a total observer,' Jessica promised. 'I'm only there to identify Korman.'

Merryman gazed at her for several seconds, then looked at McAdoo. 'Have we sufficient spare gear?'

144

The Sergeant nodded. 'We can fit her out.'

'Then do so. What time do we leave?' he asked Ibrahim.

'Three hours.'

'That even gives me time to do some shopping,' Jessica said.

'Shopping for what?'

'All my underwear is at the hotel. And you're not suggesting I go hunting for Korman wearing only a kaftan?'

'You are not leaving this house,' Merryman said, 'until you leave with all of us – and then you'll keep your face hidden. Anoka, Miss Jones needs some things. Get them for her.'

'If you will give me a list,' Anoka said.

'There's not a lot. Bra, briefs, a pair of socks, shirt, jumper, pants. Here are my sizes.' She looked at Merryman. 'Am I ever going to get my gear back?'

'I'm afraid it's unlikely. You have to stay disappeared until we can get you back to England.'

'I see. Then I think you should double up on those, Anoka.' Her bag had been left at Rashid's house, and she supposed she would have to do without things like lipstick and compacts until she got home. 'Incidentally, how are you going to get me back to England? I imagine my name and description are going to be circulated, if only as a missing person. So my passport will be a giveaway – that's if you can manage to get it back from the hotel.'

'I had that in mind and have contacted the Embassy. Let Ibrahim photograph you. He'll take the picture along and they'll give you a false passport to get you home. Then it'll just be a matter of renewing your real one.'

'How do I get the false passport?'

'It will be waiting for you at Yeşilköy, when we return there to fly out. I'm afraid that's the only international airport in the country, so we have to use it.'

'Sounds dicey.'

145

'It's a dicey business. You can still catch a plane out tomorrow; your new passport will be ready by then.'

'I'm coming with you.'

He shrugged. 'All right, Sergeant. See what you can do with her.'

Jessica followed McAdoo down a flight of steps into the basement of the house, with Dickson accompanying them. Again she was surprised – the large room, well lit and warm, turned out to be a vast storeroom.

'First,' the Sergeant said, rummaging in a large trunk, 'here is your assault suit.'

He held up the black garment.

'This is manufactured from Arvex SNZ 574 flame-resistant, anti-static and liquid-repellent fabric. You'll note that the forearms, knees and shins are reinforced with additional flame-resistant material and that the two zips are protected by flaps. You have four pockets, patches to the chest and pouches to the thighs, and you'll see that identification patches are fitted to both upper arms.'

Jessica examined the suit. It was certainly going to be hot in the desert. 'What's this? Looks some kind of a hoist.'

'It's a drag handle, to enable us to pull you to safety if you get hit or become unconscious.'

'That's nice to know. I wear this over my ordinary clothing – when I get some – is that it?'

'That's right, but you won't be wearing it at all until we get where we're going. Now your gloves.'

They were made of black leather, even on the palms.

'That's to prevent handburn should you have to do any abseiling,' McAdoo explained. 'That is Kevlar/Cordura flame-resistant and waterproof fabric, and you'll see you have completely free finger movement.'

Jessica tried the gloves and was impressed; they were the most comfortable she had ever used.

146

'Now try the boots.'

Unlike the rest of the gear these were heavy. But they were also very protective.

'You'll also need this.' McAdoo held out what looked like a neatly folded large bin liner.

'That's your bivi-bag. It's made from Aquatex. Once you're in position, you simply insert yourself, your gear and your sleeping bag into this and sit tight until ordered to move. It'll protect you from anything the weather can throw at you. In the Falklands War, some of our chaps remained hidden in observation for weeks on end, in their bivi-bags.'

'Do we get anything to eat, or drink, while we're doing this?'

'We use compos. These are packs of food and water, usually for four men for one day. You'll have one all to yourself on this do. Lastly, there's your bergen.' He showed her the large knapsack. 'This carries all your gear.'

'I don't have any gear.'

'Oh, yes, you do. First, here is your sleeping bag. You'll see it folds up into a space of five inches by three. It's made of Kevalite foil, which maximises body heat. In there, and your bivi-bag, you'll be as snug as a bug in a rug even if it snows. Now here is your escape kit, just in case something goes wrong and you're isolated.' He opened the tobacco tin. 'One button compass; you can swallow that. One wire saw. That will cut through any metal known to man. A box of matches; these are wind and waterproof. Flint and steel just in case the matches fail you. A packet of safety pins; you never know. One candle. One signal mirror. Fishing kit. I know this isn't going to be much use in the Cappadocian desert, but it's standard issue. One box of puritabs; that means you can drink almost any water you can collect. A razor blade. A packet of condoms.'

147

'Where am I supposed to put those?' Jessica asked, interested.

'They're for collecting water in, Miss Jones. One roll of snare wire. And a packet of Tampax.'

'I beg your pardon.'

'They're for lighting fires, Miss Jones. Best fire-lighters in the world.'

'Well, one learns something every day,' Jessica commented, reminding herself to be more careful in the future.

'All of that goes into the bergen, together with your spare clothing. You'll see it has waterproof inner bags, which will keep your stuff dry even when you're wading a neck-high river or caught out in a rainstorm. Now lastly, a weapon. As you will not be taking part in the assault, all you need is something for your personal protection. I recommend this Glock. It's the Model Seventeen. You'll see its body is made of plastic, so it weighs only six hundred and fifty grams. But it carries a seventeen-round box of nine-millimetre ammo, and will stop a man close to. Just remember that it has no safety catch. And of course your golok.'

Gingerly, Jessica took the knife. The thick blade was some fourteen inches long with a riveted wooden handle and was held in a canvas sheath. She drew it, tested the edge. 'It's not very sharp.'

McAdoo nodded. 'That's a constant problem with those knives. But you won't have to use it; it's intended for hacking your way through jungle, and there isn't any where we're going. But again, standard issue. Now, one last thing. Here are twenty gold half-sovereigns. This also is standard issue. And here is a pack of what we call blood chits. Again, if you get stuck on your own, you can use the money or the chits – which are basically promissory notes – to enlist help from any of the locals. You'll find the money is very useful, if need be, especially in a

perennially inflated country like Turkey. So there we are,
Miss Jones.'

Jessica gazed at the money. These people certainly left
nothing to chance. 'May I ask a question?'

'Anything you like.'

'Each of you is going to be similarly equipped?'

'We'll have slightly more firepower.'

'But each with a bergen and escape kit and money and
everything?'

'That's right.'

'You brought all this gear into the country with you?
How?'

McAdoo grinned. 'Most of it has been here for some
time. When we set up an operation like Ibrahim, we
smuggle the stuff in bit by bit, so it's here for our use
whenever we need it. Like now.'

'So Ibrahim is basically opposed to his government.'

'I wouldn't know.'

'And you don't think he might one day be tempted to
use this stuff himself?'

'It wouldn't be very wise. He's well paid. And we know
where he is.'

Anoka returned an hour later with the clothes she had
purchased for Jessica, and the two women had a giggly
fashion show. She also had news, of the great excitement
up in Beken, where the bodies of three men had been found.
The police were saying it was a gangland feud, and as yet
there was no mention of any woman being involved.

'As I thought,' Merryman said. 'The driver is lying low
for the time being. He will probably try to contact Rashid
sometime today, but by then we will be gone.'

'And what do you think Rashid is doing?' Jessica
asked.

'Tearing his hair out by the roots and beating his wife,

I would say. But then he will have to do some serious thinking, about just who got you out of trouble, and was quite happy to kill in doing so. Thinking about that is going to make him even more unhappy.'

They caught a taxi to the airport, hefting their knapsacks. They were five crazy English backpackers, out for a hike in the Cappadocian desert. They all wore dark glasses, and that the one woman in their party also kept her scarf half across her face all the time was taken to indicate that she was worried about her complexion. No questions were asked as they boarded the aircraft for the internal flight to Konya. This was a matter of roughly three hundred miles, and they were there for lunch. A car was waiting for them, to drive them into the ancient city for a meal.

'Don't tell me he's one of ours too,' Jessica whispered to Merryman as they squeezed together in the back seat.

'Not one of ours. He's one of Ibrahim's,' Merryman told her. 'Name of Mustafa.'

After lunch they drove north along a good road.

'This eventually leads to Ankara,' Merryman explained. 'That's the capital.'

Jessica knew that. She was more interested in the increasingly desolate country through which they were passing. She knew from the map that they were already some three thousand feet above sea level, but with the sun blazing down from a cloudless sky it was very hot. Around them were mountains rising much higher. And within half an hour of leaving Konya there was not a habitation to be seen.

Then their driver swung down a track leading away from the road, and now they proceeded in front of a plume of dust, bouncing and thumping over the uneven surface.

'What happens if we break down?' Jessica asked.

'We walk.'

She gulped, but the car kept going for perhaps an hour, and then stopped. Merryman got out, and the others followed.

'This is Rashid ben Khalim's lease,' the driver said, in surprisingly good English.

'And the underground city?'

'It is only a village, I believe. It is about three miles away, bearing three seven two.'

'Right,' Merryman said. 'You have my call sign.'

Mustafa nodded.

'It will be just that, nothing more. Then I will expect you to meet us here, within three hours.'

'I shall be here,' Mustafa said. He got back into the car, made a four-point turn on the track, and drove back behind his plume of dust.

'How will he know the exact spot?' Jessica asked.

'He has one of these.' He showed her the small, virtually hand-sized decoder.

'It's called a GPS, which stands for Global Positioning System. It picks up signals from a variety of satellites, and gives you your position to within a few yards.'

Jessica was beginning to realise how little she knew about this kind of secret warfare.

'Now,' Merryman said, 'I don't know how many people Korman has in his hideaway when he is not there, but we can be pretty sure there are some, and that they will be keeping a lookout.' He looked at his watch. 'Half past four. We'll move away from the track, half a mile, and camp, as if we were settling for the night. Once it's dark we move on and take up our positions.'

He was totally in command, and totally confident. With all the high-tech gear at his disposal, Jessica could understand that; her own confidence was growing. But she also felt a rising sense of excitement, and of comradeship, too. She knew she was only a passenger, and regarded, probably even by McAdoo, as a handicap, but it was still thrilling to belong to such a team. What was even more impressive was that, while they ate and drank instant coffee heated in a battery-controlled thermos, there was no discussion of what lay ahead, or might lie ahead. Every man knew exactly what he had to do, in whatever circumstance.

The meal over, they relaxed for an hour, each man communing with himself; there was almost no conversation. Darkness came suddenly, and there was as yet no moon. Without a word they all put on their assault suits, rendering themselves all but invisible in the darkness. McAdoo packed up the gear; Dickson and Lister covered all evidence of their having been there with dust and stones. Merryman and Jessica waited until the work had been done, then Merryman set off. They walked in single file, Jessica immediately behind the leader, the three men following.

Merryman had his meter, and after just an hour he held up his hand. 'Jones first,' he said. 'Up there.'

Jessica blinked into the darkness and saw the rising ground to her left. 'How high?'

'Not too far. Say fifty feet. Find a good spot and get into it. And remember, you don't move again until I come to get you. Whatever you have to do must be done on the spot. Right?'

Jessica swallowed. 'Right. Where exactly is the village?'

'I have no idea. We know it's somewhere very close, in this valley, so we are going to cover every angle and wait. They should reveal themselves soon enough, but in any event it's not the people who are there now, but the people who will be coming, that we want.'

'Am I allowed to wish you good luck?'

'Why not? Not that we believe in luck. Now for Christ's sake don't make a noise getting up there, and don't fall and break your neck.'

152

The Search

Jessica began the ascent, grateful for the gloves protecting her hands from the rough stones and earth. The climb was by no means steep or difficult, but was rendered so by the darkness and Merryman's insistence that he did not want her kicking down any noisy stones. That meant every foot and handhold had to be carefully tested before given any weight.

She went up, slowly but surely, for some fifty feet, then began looking for a vantage point. Finding this took her an hour, but at last she located a small gully just big enough for her body, and with a high rim which rendered it invisible from below. She unpacked her bergen, spread her sleeping bag and got into it, then inserted the whole lot into her bivi-bag. By wriggling around she was able to make a little hollow for herself and discovered she was quite comfortable.

Then she placed her weapons, pistol and knife where she could reach them at a moment's notice, took out her carton of food and drink, and settled down to watch and listen. But there was nothing to see in the darkness, and no sound either, above the whine of the wind. To all intents and purposes she was entirely alone, in the middle of a desert.

Now the temperature began to drop, sharply, but inside her bag she was completely warm, and when she drew her head down as well she was even comfortable. Well, she reflected, Merryman hadn't said anything about not sleeping.

When she awoke it was broad daylight, and already warming up. She looked out at an empty landscape, with ground rising to either side but at some distance, leaving a valley perhaps half a mile across, a desolation of tumbled rock and stone with an occasional stunted tree, and decreasing shadows cast by the rising sun. There was nothing to indicate there was a living soul for a million miles.

She wriggled out of her bags and attended to what needed to be done, hoping that Korman wasn't going to be too long in returning, as the gully wasn't all that large. Then she breakfasted, and settled down in her bags again. The day grew steadily hotter, and by noon she was out of her bags and wishing she could discard the assault suit as well.

Then she saw movement in the valley below her. A man walked slowly through the stones. He was casually dressed and had a broad-brimmed hat. He did not appear to be armed.

Where had he come from? She hadn't been issued with binoculars, and she would not have dared use them anyway, just in case there was a reflection. But there was no indication of where the underground headquarters might be. On the other hand . . . She remained absolutely still while the man walked almost to the foot of her hill. Clearly he was merely taking a constitutional, because having reached the hill he simply turned and walked back again.

Jessica stared at him, eyes watering in the glare. He was there, he was there . . . he was gone. Damnation, she thought. But at least she had narrowed down his disappearance to a small area. And presumably Merryman had been able to do so too.

The day drifted by. Jessica played word games in her mind, remembered things which could be strung together in a series of incidents, wondered how Judith and Megan were getting on, wondered too if what she was doing was a total waste of time, and if the security forces in Malaysia had managed to get Korman. But that still left Rashid, and she was now certain he was the more dangerous man. Korman could be replaced, but if Rashid were to go the whole Will of God would collapse.

Something else she would have to convince her superiors about.

She now began to suffer cramping in her calves. She made sure there was no one in the valley, then lay on her back and kicked vigorously for several minutes; she did not dare stand up.

Then darkness again, dropping on to the valley. Jessica had a meal – she was really not very hungry – and settled down for another night. Merryman had said something about his people having remained in position for *weeks* in the Falklands. Well, they each only had rations for four days, so he would have to pull out after that.

She slept fitfully, awoke, and went through the same routine as before. Now she was beginning to dream of hot baths. Or even cold ones.

Remaining in one place and virtually in one position for hour after hour caused a considerable drop in her metabolic rate. She wondered if anyone had worked out how to combat that. She found that she was constantly nodding off as the temperature again rose.

Then she heard the sound of an engine.

Instantly, tension and increased heartbeat flooded her body and had her fully awake. The noise was quite close, but she couldn't see what it was until the helicopter dropped straight past her position to come to rest on the floor of the valley.

Three people got out. She was too far away to make out any of their faces, but one was a woman with long black hair. That had to be Gabrielle. Of the two men . . . She couldn't identify them. One had fair hair, certainly, but she thought he was too big for Korman.

They appeared to be in a high good humour, laughing as they shouted their farewells to the helicopter pilot, who almost immediately lifted off again.

Each of the three arrivals carried overnight bags, and these they hefted as they walked together, away from

Jessica's hill, taking the same route as the man yesterday had. And suddenly the man was there again, standing amidst the rocks and bushes, waiting for them.

The helicopter noise had faded. It was already several miles away, and it had to be Merryman's decision as to when it would be out of sight.

But he had already made that decision. The blast of a whistle cut across the morning, and the four people greeting each other turned in astonished alarm, to run into a hail of fire as the four black-clad soldiers scrambled from their hiding places, shooting as they did so. They were each armed with a sub-machine gun; the terrorists never stood a chance. Gabrielle managed to draw a pistol but was cut down in the very act, spinning round and crashing to the ground. Three members of the assault force were already past the scattered bodies; the fourth remained behind to fire the final shots into the twisting half-corpses.

Jessica stood up. Regardless of her orders she clambered down her hillside, panting and slipping on the uneven ground, now dislodging stones in great numbers. From beyond the first exchange there came explosions, as the assault force tossed CS grenades down the opening leading to the underground village.

As she approached she saw that the remaining SAS man was wearing a gas mask and breathing apparatus. He saw her coming, and waved his arm, signalling her to keep clear, but she continued to move forward until she reached him. She stood above the scattered bodies. All were dead, ripped to pieces by the fearsome assault. None had been wearing masks, and their faces were indicative of total surprise and the understanding that they had been destroyed.

But the only thing about any of them that she recognised was the long black hair of the woman Gabrielle.

*   *   *

'Well?' Merryman barked as he led his assault force back out of the underground village.

'He's not here.'

'How can you be sure?'

'I don't recognise any of the faces. And none of them can speak, can they? So I can't recognise their voices.'

He glared at her. She was feeling slightly hysterical. She wondered if he was too, or if this was just another job of work.

'You are saying none of these are Korman?'

'I am saying I recognise none of these as Korman. What about inside?'

'Three. But obviously none of them would be Korman.'

'I need to be sure.'

Another glare. She could tell what he was thinking: just who the hell is running this show, anyway? But he knew they had to be sure.

'Dickson,' he snapped. 'Give her your mask.'

Dickson obliged. Jessica strapped the oxygen mask on, made sure it was breathing properly, and followed Merryman to the concealed entrance. Lister stood at the top. She followed Merryman down the steps, where the unmistakeable figure of McAdoo waited.

At his feet there was sprawled a dead body.

Merryman waved his arm, and they crossed the reception room to the communications centre. Here there lay another body, before an impressive display of both sending and receiving equipment, as well as television screens: one still beamed an internet item, not apparently relevant.

Merryman still carried his sub-machine gun. Now he fired several bursts into the equipment, scattering it into a cloud of microchips; he had apparently already removed all the relevant software.

Jessica stepped back outside, and he joined her a moment later, indicating the living quarters. Here there were several comfortably furnished bedrooms, all empty. Merryman led her to the master suite, a place of television sets and more computers and CD players, together with a huge double bed. And another body, a woman wearing maid's clothing, sprawled on her back, cut to pieces by the storm of bullets.

Jessica turned and went outside; she felt sick. She climbed the steps to the upper level, took off her mask and inhaled fresh air.

Merryman stood behind her. 'Did you recognise *any* of them?'

Jessica shook her head.

'And these?'

'The woman with the long black hair was part of the gang who raided my flat. I'm only going on the hair. I never saw her face.'

'What a shitting mess,' he commented.

'Was it necessary to kill the maid? She wasn't armed.'

'What were we supposed to do, leave her behind to tell the police exactly what happened? Anyway, she worked for Korman. That makes her a terrorist in my book. And where the hell is he?'

'Maybe they did get him, in Kuala Lumpur, after all.'

'If they did, his people would hardly have returned here, in such a good humour.'

'Then he must have stayed in Istanbul. Probably to help Rashid look for me.'

Merryman nodded. 'That's most likely. Go get your gear. I've called for Mustafa, and he'll be at the rendezvous in a couple of hours. So we'll need to be there too.'

'What about these people?'

'What about them?'

'Well . . . aren't we going to bury them?'

'Why?'

'You can't just leave them here to rot, and be eaten by crows.'

'They'd rot just as fast underground, and the crows would go hungry. We don't bury them, Jones. My guess is that the next person to come here will be Korman, maybe with your friend Rashid in tow. What they see here will shake them up a bit. Time's passing. Get your gear.'

Jessica obeyed, climbing the hillside while her mind tumbled in rhythm to her stomach. By the time she was packed up and had climbed down, the others were waiting.

The sun seemed to be hovering exactly overhead. Was she imagining it, or was there already a stench of death filling the valley; there was no breeze. Merryman signalled, and the little group moved out.

Jessica walked beside him. 'What do we do now?'

'We get out of here just as fast as we can.'

'And Korman?'

'We've missed him. This time. But we've destroyed his base, and his people. He'll have problems.'

'You said we were here to get him, no matter how long it takes.'

'The position will have to be reassessed, and new orders given, in London.'

'Couldn't we just wait here for him to come?'

'We don't know when that will be, and we've only rations for two more days.'

'Well, then, what about Istanbul? We're fairly sure he's there . . .'

'We don't know where, unless he's staying with Rashid. If he's staying with Rashid, he's taboo as far as we're concerned. What is more, at some time the various police forces are going to do some correlating and get their act together. We certainly can't use you any more, right now. No, we get out fast, reassess, and receive fresh orders.' He

159

grinned at her. 'Maybe they *will* let us go after Rashid. But somehow, I doubt it.'

'And meanwhile Korman goes free.'

'I told you, he'll have to start from scratch. Even with Rashid's backing, that's going to take time.'

Mustafa was waiting at the rendezvous. 'All has gone well?'

'Not entirely,' Merryman said. 'We missed our target.'

'Ah,' Mustafa said. 'You will have to try again.'

'Yes,' Merryman agreed. 'Tell me, is there any news?'

'News?'

'Overseas news. We've been cut off the past couple of days, remember.'

'Overseas news,' Mustafa said thoughtfully. 'Ah, yes, there has been a bomb.'

'Oh, shit,' Merryman commented.

'Where?' Jessica asked.

'A place called Kuala Lumpur. It is in Malaysia. You know this place?'

'You mean he got through,' Jessica said. 'You did send that warning?

'Of course I did,' Merryman snapped angrily.

'Was anyone hurt?' Jessica asked Mustafa.

'Oh, yes, there are many dead. Including some British. One was a very important man. A minister.'

'Shit!' Merryman said again.

'So you'll see that this woman is becoming a serious threat,' Rashid said.

He and Korman were seated on the terrace of his house in Beken, looking down at the water.

'I always said she was,' Korman pointed out. 'And you didn't believe me.'

'We all make mistakes,' Rashid said equably. 'Actually,

160

it is not the woman in herself who is so dangerous; it is the back-up with which she seems to travel. When your people raided her flat in London there was another policeman, heavily armed. When my people raided the house of that child, again she had another gunman to assist her. Now on this last occasion, according to Idris the chauffeur, there were four men, wearing assault gear and heavily armed. This is not a private organisation we are dealing with, or a police group. This sounds like an army.'

'You think she is linked to the SAS?'

'It starts to look that way.'

'So what are you planning to do about it? I mean, about what happened here?'

'There is nothing I can do about it,' Rashid said. 'At present there is no link between me and what happened in the town. Nor can there be. So, we must just let it go.'

'With respect,' Korman said, 'you were over-elaborate. You had her, and you let her go. You should have killed her on the spot.'

'My own feelings exactly,' Gerberga said, joining them, as elegantly dressed as ever.

Korman stood up at her entry; her husband did not.

'Again, that is not as easy as it seems,' Rashid said. 'If one intends to eliminate all risk of a trace. I think I did the best thing. What I did not know, because I lacked the information, was that this woman travels in the company of a heavily armed hit squad.'

'And by now she is back in England, safe and sound. And now she not only knows what I look like, but she knows that you and I are linked, and she knows that I have a base here in Turkey. This is very bad.'

Rashid nodded. 'I agree. But it is not all bad. You have had another triumph.'

'It was a damn near run thing,' Korman said. 'The security was tighter than I have ever known it. There was no way we could use a car; they simply weren't letting any but official vehicles through.'

'So you found a volunteer. Your people must be very faithful to you.'

'They are fanatics.' He grinned. 'They are the Will of God.'

'Absolutely. Well, I suggest you disappear into your hole and stay there for a while until we see how things lie.'

'The Jones woman will put the finger on you.'

'I do not think that will have any important consequences. The entire British action is based upon a single fact: that Jones identified you as the bomber in Alicante, and that she knows what you look like. There is no other proof against you, and there is none at all against me. In fact you could say she blew it, whether she did come under her own steam or was ordered here – even if her back-up were from the SAS. Now, as you say, she has definitely linked me to you, but she cannot prove it, any more than she has any substantive proof that you were in Alicante. And of course there is no proof at all to link you with Kuala Lumpur.'

'So you think she can just be ignored.'

'No, no, I think we must do something about her. But obviously it cannot be a simple hit job; she is too good for that. So when we go after her again, it must be very carefully planned. However, there is one concrete piece of information she has obtained from her visit here: that you are based in Turkey. So as I say, you go out to your desert hideaway and stay there for a few weeks while we see what, if any, action the British Government is going to take. Always remember that while we may have lost some people, we are ahead of the game. Two British ministers are dead, and we are still in business. The ball is in our court. That is the bottom line. We will have dinner.'

*　　*　　*

Robert Korman lay in bed and listened to the hooting of sirens in the Bosporus.

He knew Rashid was right in his calm estimation of the situation. They *were* ahead in real terms. The British Government must be ready to fall apart, with two of their most senior and respected politicians dead. Whereas against them, the only threat to their existence – and their continued success – was a single little policewoman. That she received massive support when she needed it made no difference to that assessment. Without her, the back-up would have nothing to go on.

Then why couldn't he sleep? He supposed the reason was that she was a woman.

Throughout his life he had used women as and when he needed to, either for sex or as part of his organisation. He had never loved, because he had loved Arsinoe, and since her death he had never found a replacement. Yet they had been useful as both toys and tools . . . until Buenos Aires.

That should have been one of his greatest coups. He and his team had infiltrated the International Culture Centre the night before the reception. They had merely to set the device and the timer and make their way back out of the building. When he had seen Todo about to connect the wires the wrong way, he remembered thinking, as he hurled himself behind one of the packing cases in the cellar, this cannot be happening to me. Then oblivion.

Claus had dragged him clear. They had been the only survivors of the team. Claus had saved his life, had nurtured his shattered body, had helped him escape.

The woman Jones had been responsible for Claus's death!

Their great stroke of fortune had been that the Argentine police had assumed there had been no survivors at all. His great stroke of misfortune was the discovery that one of the flying pieces of metal had slashed into his genitals and left him only half a man.

The surgeons had been able to put his face back together – rebuilding it bone by bone – and even given him a new look, which he had assumed would protect him forever. They had done the same with his broken body. But they had not been able to restore his manhood.

Then the amused contempt he felt for the female sex had turned into vicious hatred. And now he was being dogged by one of them. Jessica Jones knew nothing about him, save that he was there. She knew nothing of the tormented hell in which he lived, the frustrated existence that could only be relieved by violence. She was merely doing a job of work, no doubt. Her duty.

Which would destroy him, unless he destroyed her first.

His head turned as the door opened, and his hand closed over the pistol that was always by his head. Then, to his surprise, the light came on.

Korman sat up, the pistol levelled. Gerberga Rashid wore a dressing gown, and he did not think there was anything underneath.

Quietly, she closed the door and came forward. 'Put that thing away.'

Korman obeyed; he was still too surprised to do anything else.

'This is the first night you have slept in my house,' Gerberga said, and sat on the bed beside him. 'Are you not pleased to see me?'

Korman licked his lips. 'Where is Rashid?'

'Rashid is out. He goes out most nights after dinner. He goes to one of his mistresses. For at least an hour, more often two. He will not be back before midnight.'

'Rashid is married to you, and he goes to a mistress?'

Gerberga shrugged. 'He finds me cold, unresponsive. Also he likes variety.'

'My God!'

'That is the way of men. Of men like Rashid, anyway,' Gerberga said. She frowned, as Korman had still not moved. 'Are you afraid of him?'

Korman knew he probably was, but he was not going to admit it. Yet his silence was eloquent.

'Rashid has told me you are the most dangerous man in the world,' Gerberga said.

After Rashid himself, Korman thought. 'He is my friend.'

Gerberga snorted. 'Rashid does not have friends. You mean, he is your employer. That means I also am your employer. I would like to employ you, now.'

She began to move the sheet, and Korman caught her hand. 'Has Rashid not told you about me?'

She smiled. 'Oh, yes. He says you are only half a man. He regards you with contempt.' She leaned forward to kiss him. 'But you have hands. And perhaps, a desire to hate him as well.'

The helicopter dropped out of the sky into the valley. It had circled once, as usual, while the pilot had endeavoured to establish radio contact. There had been none, and now Korman was inspecting the valley through binoculars, his heart slowly coagulating.

But then his heart had perhaps coagulated the previous night, when the woman had left him to realise just what he had done. He presumed he had satisfied her; she had seemed satisfied. Or would she have been satisfied by anything, so long as it had enabled her to avenge herself on her husband. Last night he had realised how little he, who hated everybody, actually knew about hating.

And for him, another long frustration, dissipated only

165

by his momentary domination of the woman. But he had not been able to hurt her. He had not risked that.

And now he was in her power, as well as Rashid's. As well as . . .

The pilot was pointing.

Korman peered at the dead bodies. They were definitely human. But there was no sign of any other movement. He pointed down, feeling his blood start to boil. It was not possible.

But it had happened. The helicopter touched the ground, and Korman leapt down, drawing his pistol as he did so. The pilot remained at the controls, ready to take off again at the first sign of trouble.

Korman ran forward, checked some distance away from the bodies, while the vultures, disturbed at their feast, circled sullenly overhead.

Korman stared at the hideous remains, already half-reduced to skeletons.

He ran past them to the still open entrance to the underground village. Out of the entrance there drifted the unpleasant tang of the CS gas. Still he went down, overwhelmed by the sense of catastrophe. The smell of gas was stronger inside the village, but it was overhung by the stench of death. These bodies were already being attacked by the ants.

We are on top, Rashid had said. We are in control. Why worry about a few deaths? The ball is in our court.

Robert Korman uttered a scream and ran back up the steps.

The Visitor

The returning party was met at Heathrow.

There were two cars. McAdoo, Dickson and Lister were placed in one and driven off, Merryman and Jessica went in the other, accompanied by three Special Branch Officers.

'May I ask where we are going?' Jessica asked; it obviously wasn't the training ground, where the rest of her clothes were. She had had a quick bath at Ibrahim's before catching the flight, but she was not looking her best and she dearly wanted to get under a shower with a good shampoo.

'Downing Street,' one of the officers said.

'Downing . . .' She looked at Merryman, who pointed to a newspaper stand they were just passing: CABINET MINISTER KILLED. SECOND OUTRAGE IN A FORT-NIGHT.

'Looks like we have a crisis,' Merryman said.

The drive took an hour, and there was little conversation.

'How many were killed in Kuala Lumpur?' Merryman asked.

'Forty-one,' one of the officers said.

'It was a suicide job,' said another. 'There's no defence against those.'

Merryman and Jessica exchanged a quick glance. But it couldn't possibly have been Korman himself.

167

The headlines were even bigger in Westminster. Then they were at the gates to Downing Street, and the car was stopping. As both Merryman and Jessica were wearing civilian clothes, they attracted no attention except from the odd passer-by, perhaps wondering what two such scruffy individuals were doing entering the hallowed precinct.

One of the officers accompanied them, showed his pass, and they were ushered up to the famous door, where a knock had them immediately admitted. Jessica had never been inside Number Ten before, and gazed in some awe at the panelling and the portraits while experiencing the utter quiet of the place.

'In here, if you please,' said the secretary. 'The Prime Minister will be with you in a moment.'

Jessica entered first, blinked at the two men already there. One she didn't know. The other was Commander Adams.

'Good morning, JJ,' the Commander said. 'I gather you've been working.'

'Yes, sir,' Jessica said. 'In a fashion.'

'This is General Owen, of the SAS,' Adams introduced.

Jessica stood to attention. Merryman had already done so.

'At ease,' Owen said. 'Did you get your man?'

'No, sir,' Merryman said.

'And your telephoned warning didn't have the desired effect, either. It never occurred to us that he'd use a suicide bomber. Well . . .' He turned as the door opened, and stood to attention as the Prime Minister came in, followed by the Home Secretary and two assistant secretaries. 'Please sit down.' The Prime Minister, as always, gave the impression of being in a great hurry.

They all sat down.

'I assume we are agreed that the Kuala Lumpur bomb was the work of this man Korman?'

168

The senior officers looked at Merryman.

'Yes, sir. It was undoubtedly his work.'

'And have you succeeded in eliminating him?'

'No, sir. We traced him to his base, and attacked and destroyed it. Unfortunately, he was not there. However, sir, it is my estimation that we have severely inhibited his ability to carry out another attack on the scale of either Alicante or Kuala Lumpur for some considerable time.'

'But the man remains free, and will undoubtedly strike again, given time.'

'I would say that is certain, sir. Miss Jones has some additional information.'

All heads turned towards Jessica.

'I have discovered that Korman is, and I believe has been for some time, funded by a wealthy Turkish businessman named Rashid ben Khalim. Now that his base of operations has been destroyed, Korman will go to Rashid for the means, both financial and physical, of re-establishing himself. If Rashid can be neutralised, Korman might never be able to recover.'

The Prime Minister looked at his assistant secretary.

'Rashid ben Khalim is on file, Prime Minister.' The secretary went on to outline Rashid's background, as it was contained in the file Jessica had been given. 'There is nothing presently known to connect this man with Korman, or directly with terrorism.'

The Prime Minister looked at Jessica, but Merryman spoke for her.

'Miss Jones managed to penetrate Rashid's house in Istanbul, Prime Minister, and there obtained the information.'

'And you have this proof with you?'

'No, Prime Minister, I'm afraid not. I was taken prisoner by Rashid, and just escaped with my life.'

The Prime Minister looked pained, as if he did not

169

really wish to know the gory details of how his security services worked. 'But there is documentary evidence of his involvement?'

'No, sir. He told me he was.'

The Prime Minister frowned. 'Did this man know you are a British policewoman?'

'Yes, sir.'

'And he just came out and admitted he was involved in terrorism, with a man like Korman? I find that incredible.'

'Not so incredible, sir. He told me because he was about to execute me.'

The Prime Minister gazed at her for several seconds, then looked at Adams, who gave a nervous smile. 'I'm sure what happened is as Detective-Constable Jones has described it, Prime Minister.'

'Extraordinary,' the Prime Minister commented. 'What it boils down to is that we have nothing against this man Rashid that could possibly stand up in a court of law.'

'With respect, Prime Minister,' General Owen said, 'we have nothing against the man Korman that would stand up in a court of law. Only Detective-Constable Jones's observation.'

'Yes,' the Prime Minister said, regarding Jessica with a not altogether pleased expression. 'What about the Turkish authorities? Do they know anything about this?'

'If you mean the raid on Korman's headquarters, no,' Owen said. 'I authorised it, based on your instructions that Korman was to be taken out at any cost.'

'But he wasn't,' the Prime Minister pointed out. 'You're sure this place you raided *was* Korman's headquarters, Captain Merryman?'

'Ah . . .' Merryman looked at Jessica.

'I see,' the Prime Minister said. 'Some more information given you by Mr Rashid, Miss Jones?'

'Something he let slip, sir.'

'I see. What I was really asking was, do the Turkish authorities know anything about Mr Rashid?'

The secretary turned a page. 'He is undoubtedly on their files. He was arrested for possessing seditious material, once, but that was fifteen years ago. Since then he has become an extremely successful businessman, and one of the principal contributors to the ruling party's campaign funds. I think we would need to have very definite proof of his involvement with Korman before they would take action against him.'

The Prime Minister looked at Jessica.

'The man is a cold-blooded killer, sir,' Jessica said. 'In my opinion he is far more dangerous than Korman.'

'Yes,' the Prime Minister said thoughtfully. 'Well, gentlemen, and Miss Jones, let me attempt to summarise the situation. Three members of my Cabinet have been murdered. I am not going to remind you that they were talented people, and also dear friends of mine of very long standing, because with them were killed some two hundred other people, taking both Kuala Lumpur and Alicante together, and in fact if you include Buenos Aires, the death toll climbs higher still. At the present time, we have confined ourselves, publicly, to making the usual condemnatory noises, and the media seem content to treat it as a ghastly coincidence that each bomb should have killed an important member of my government. Now, reluctantly, I gave the security services *carte blanche* to find this man Korman, and, ah . . . execute him, as I accept that bringing him to trial and hopefully conviction in this country would be a very long drawn-out and difficult proposition, if it could be achieved at all. Such a trial would also necessitate revealing many of the secrets of how our security services operate, and that would be unpleasant.'

He paused, again to look around at the faces. 'Unfortunately, this has not happened.'

171

'I don't think you can blame my people, Prime Minister,' Owen protested. 'They did all they could.'

'I am not blaming anyone, General. I am merely assessing the facts. Captain Merryman may well be right when he says Korman's offensive capacity has been destroyed, for some time. I hope he is right. However, the facts are that Korman is still alive, and has apparently once again disappeared. So we may take it for granted that he will surface again, as soon as is possible for him. We have also slipped a couple of notches in our actual, shall I say, relationship with him. Down to a week ago, while he knew that he had been identified in Alicante by Miss Jones, he felt the ball was in his court, not only to do something about her whenever he could, but also to continue his activities. Our secret weapon was Miss Jones, our ability to use her in an offensive rather than a continuing defensive role. That is now blown. Korman, and his friend Rashid – if it is true they are working together – now know Miss Jones is being used in an offensive capacity. And Rashid, I am told, also now knows just what Miss Jones looks like. It seems to me that we have got ourselves into an impasse here. Miss Jones is the only person we have who can identify Korman; but Korman and his associate will react immediately they catch a sight of her, and go to ground. Meanwhile, the lives of all my colleagues are at risk. Thus far we have kept this secret. Now matters are getting out of control. I need to make two urgent decisions. The first is, do I put the facts before my Cabinet, which, with the best will in the world, may involve some resignations – most of them are married men with children, who may well feel the risk is not worth it. That would mean that Korman is effectively holding my Government to ransom, which is apparently what he wishes to do. It would also of course mean going public on the whole thing, with the damage it would do to the credibility of this Government.

It's a miracle there hasn't already been a leak. The second decision is, do we use this respite of a few weeks that Captain Merryman says he has earned us again to attempt to seek and destroy this terrible man, allowing for the fact that we now have no idea where he may be, and only one of us has the least idea what he looks like. And also understanding that the longer we keep this thing secret, should we fail to deal with Korman and the facts of the matter then became known, the bigger will be the explosion of public resentment and anger.'

Not to mention that of his Cabinet colleagues, Jessica thought, at being kept in the dark about being on an assassin's hit list. 'With respect, Prime Minister,' she said.

All heads turned towards her.

'May I repeat my argument, sir, that Korman stands or falls by Rashid ben Khalim. Take him out of the equation, and Korman is yesterday's man.'

'But you'll agree you have no proof of the relationship between Korman and this man. Save what Rashid himself told you.'

'He told me the truth, sir.'

'So you believe. But as we have agreed that his telling you something will not stand up in a court of law, when you say take him out of the equation, you mean . . .' He paused, waiting to hear the fateful words from her deceptively sweet mouth.

'I believe it is necessary for him to be killed, yes, sir.'

The Prime Minister sighed, and produced a handkerchief with which to wipe his forehead.

'I'm afraid Miss Jones may well be right, sir,' Owen said.

The secretary had continued to look at the file. 'He has a wife and two children.'

'His wife is every bit as vicious as he is, sir,' Jessica said. Once again the Prime Minister regarded her, contemplatively. No doubt, Jessica thought, he is wondering just how vicious *I* am.

'You say these people, ah, roughed you up and threatened to kill you,' the Home Secretary said. 'You're sure there isn't an element of a desire for revenge in your recommendation?'

Of course there is, Jessica thought. But she said, 'I regard them as the two most dangerous people on earth, sir.' And that was no lie.

'It goes against the grain,' the Prime Minister said. 'But . . . how would it be done?'

'It would have to be a straightforward hit, sir,' Merryman said.

Owen was nodding. 'A specialist team . . .'

'Not a team, sir. One man. The very best we have.'

'Hm. I suppose you're right. But if Detective-Constable Jones is right, the hit would have to include Mrs Rashid as well.'

'And leave two children orphans,' the secretary muttered.

For God's sake, Jessica wanted to shout. Didn't those thugs leave Megan Lynch an orphan, just for starters?

'Very sad,' the Prime Minister said. 'But apparently a matter of necessity.'

'Very good,' Owen said. 'Make your recommendation, Captain Merryman.'

'Myself, sir.'

'You? But you have just had to get out of Turkey in a hurry.'

'That was necessary, sir, both to safeguard our identity, our man on the ground, and of course, Miss Jones.'

Thank you for those kind words, Jessica thought. But she did not suppose he was intending them kindly. He was back to his old ways of regarding her as a nuisance.

'But we left without hindrance. The police had not yet linked Miss Jones to the killings in Beken.'

'They have now,' Adams said. 'Well, in a manner of speaking. It has been reported to us that a British tourist, identified as Miss Jessica Jones, went missing from her hotel on the night of the killings. She attended a small supper party at Mr Rashid's, and after that insisted on walking down into the town by herself. That is Rashid's story, you understand. Then she disappeared.'

'Then there is no direct link between Miss Jones and the killings,' the Home Secretary said.

'Not direct. The Turkish police find it coincidental that the last time Miss Jones was seen on that night was close, both in time and space, to where the three bodies were found. What they find disturbing is that they have now discovered that three nights later Miss Jones left the country without ever having returned to her hotel to collect her belongings, which are now in the hands of the police.'

Once again the heads turned towards Jessica.

'Was there anything incriminating in those belongings, Miss Jones?' asked the Prime Minister.

'Only six files relating to wealthy Turkish residents who could have links to terrorism.'

'Amongst them, of course, Rashid ben Khalim.'

'I'm afraid so, Prime Minister.'

'In other words, Miss Jones, in real terms, you are *persona non grata* with the Turkish police. At the very least they will want to know where you were and what you were doing during those three days. I'm surprised they have not applied for your extradition.'

'They have not sufficient proof of any wrongdoing on Miss Jones's part for that, sir,' Adams said.

'Have they identified Tugril and his people?' Jessica asked. 'That could provide another link to Rashid. Maybe something positive.'

'If they have,' Adams said, 'they're keeping it quiet.'

'But basically,' the Prime Minister said, 'they have a lot on us.'

'No, sir, they do not,' Merryman said. He had been keeping quiet with difficulty. 'The point is, sir, that no one in Turkey knows who I am or what I am, save for Ibrahim and his wife. I can simply walk in, do what has to be done, and walk back out again. I know where Rashid lives, and Miss Jones has provided me with a ground plan of the house. I can be in and out in a day. And should anything go wrong' – he gave a deprecating smile to indicate that was not even a remote consideration – 'there will be no possibility of anyone linking me to this Government, to the SAS, or even this country, except by virtue of having been born here.'

'A dirty business,' the Prime Minister commented. 'But . . . needs must where the devil drives.'

'Then, sir,' Owen asked, 'will you authorise the return visit to Istanbul of Captain Merryman, in order to take out Rashid ben Khalim? It being understood that there can be no written confirmation of this order, and that should Captain Merryman be arrested by the Turkish police he reveals nothing of who or what he actually is.'

The Prime Minister nodded, and looked around at the faces. 'I authorise the order and require that it be carried out as soon as possible.'

'Immediately, sir,' Merryman said.

'Then the matter is closed . . . until the order has been carried out. I need hardly remind you gentlemen that everything that was said here today is top secret. Thank you.'

He rose and left the room, followed by his secretary.

'You'll keep me informed, General Owen,' the Home Secretary said. 'And good luck, Merryman.'

He also left the room.

'You'll come with me, JJ,' Adams said.

'Yes, sir. May I have a word with Captain Merryman first?'

Adams glanced at Owen, then nodded. 'Of course.'

The two senior officers waited outside.

'I wish I was coming with you,' Jessica said.

'So do I. But it's not practical.'

'I realise that. So, like the man said, good luck.'

To her consternation, he put an arm round her and kissed her. 'You have been growing on me, over the past week.'

'Slowly,' she suggested, holding back a nervous laugh.

'When I return, I'd like us to get together.'

Jessica gulped. How do you tell a man, who is at once your superior and about to depart on what is virtually a suicide mission, that he doesn't turn you on?

'Call me,' she said, 'when you get back.' It was the least she could do.

Jessica sat in the back of the police car with Adams.

'Quite an adventure,' the Commander remarked. 'You must be very glad it's all over.'

'Is it over, sir?'

'For you, JJ.'

'Korman . . .'

'If Merryman's claim is right, and his base has been destroyed . . . Do you know how many of his people were involved?'

'I was there, sir. The base was utterly destroyed. And seven of his people were killed.'

'Together with four who were shot coming after you over here. Well, then, I think we may agree with the Captain's assessment that Korman is effectively out of action for the foreseeable future. And if *you* are right, that he has been financed all along by Rashid's money, then if Merryman succeeds in his mission there won't be a foreseeable future – for Robert Korman. No, JJ, I think you have done wonderfully well. A total credit to the force. There will be a commendation, and promotion as well, I can promise you. But for the time being, after what you have gone through, I think you need a fortnight's leave.'

'To go where, sir? I've had all the travelling I can stand, for the moment.'

'The department has a flat in Mayfair. We use it for visiting VIPs and the like.' He smiled. 'Right now you can be classed as a VIP. Move in there. You'll find it very comfortable.'

'Thank you, sir. I have a partner.'

'Oh, yes, Sergeant Bainbridge, isn't it? I'm not sure where he is at the moment, but he'll be given the address and told to join you as soon as he's free.'

'Thank you, sir. I also have quite a lot of gear, scattered around the country.'

'Collect it.'

'Does that include from my old flat, sir? The one that was raided?'

'Of course, JJ. You need to get it through your head that, as I said, it's over for you. You're free. Free as air.'

Free as air, she thought. Was she? Could she ever be free of her memories? When she thought of Tugril tearing at her clothes and her body like a hungry animal, of crouching in her gully above Korman's hideaway, of watching all of those people shot to pieces . . . No, she would never be free of those. Just as she would never be free of having condemned Rashid, and no doubt Gerberga as well, to death. And Merryman? No, she thought Merryman would survive, even if he was captured and tried for murder by the Turkish authorities. The British Government would get him out, somehow.

But Korman . . . she could never be free of him, either,

until he was dead. Because she knew that however long it took, he would return; he was that kind of man.

On the other hand, she was certainly free for the next few weeks. There were so many things she wanted to do, so many things she needed . . . principally to lie in Tom's arms. But that would have to wait until he turned up.

She took a taxi to the address she had been given, and was impressed. The furnishings were comfortable, the décor impeccable. If it had a somewhat cold and unlived-in aspect, she reckoned she could soon change that.

Megan!

She telephoned Judith's home number, which took a lot of doing as one went through various security checks before it actually rang, and then she was told by the female voice on the end of the phone that Assistant Commissioner Proud was out.

'I knew that,' Jessica said; Judith would be at her office. 'I actually would like to speak with Megan Lynch.'

There was a brief silence on the other end of the phone.

'Are you there?' Jessica asked. 'You do have someone named Megan Lynch staying with you, don't you? She's a little girl, seven years old.'

'Who are you?' the voice asked.

'Detective-Constable Jessica Jones. I'm a friend of Megan's. I introduced her to Miss Proud.'

'I think you had better talk to Miss Proud about it,' the voice said, and the phone went dead.

Damn, blast and shoot, Jessica thought. Was that Judith practising ultra-security? She hoped so. Because if not, something had gone wrong.

She tried New Scotland Yard.

'Who is calling, please?' asked the switchboard when she asked for Judith.

'Detective-Constable Jessica Jones.'

Another one of those silences. This time because Assistant Commissioners did not normally accept calls from constables, even detective-constables.

'She really will wish to speak with me,' Jessica said.

Still there was no reply, but there was a series of clicks and thumps, and then Judith's voice. 'JJ? My God. Where are you calling from?'

'The VIP flat.'

'Good lord! How did it go?'

Jessica had never heard Judith sound so humanly concerned and excited.

'It's a good and bad situation.'

'No Korman?'

'No Korman. I'll explain it when I see you, ma'am. What I'm really calling about is Megan. Is she all right?'

'Megan is fine. She'll be so happy to see you again.'

'When can that be?'

'I'll pick you up at six.'

Sheer relief. It was all working out. It was already five. Jessica had a hot bath and changed into the second set of clothes Anoka had bought for her. They were really no better fit than the first, and she continued to feel like a scarecrow. But she could start collecting her own gear tomorrow. Her principal aim was to reclaim Megan.

'Say that again?' Rashid asked his helicopter pilot.

'There were bodies everywhere, sir. And the underground facility was utterly wrecked, all the equipment shot to pieces.'

Rashid look at Gerberga.

'There can be no doubt about it,' she said. 'That sort of total destruction is the work of the SAS.' She turned to the pilot. 'And Mr Korman?'

'Well, like I said, ma'am, for a few minutes I thought he'd gone mad. He ran about the place, screaming, then he rolled in the dust. It took me some time to calm him down and get him into the aircraft.'

'And then you flew him back to Istanbul. Where is he now?'

'I do not know, ma'am.'

'What do you mean, you do not know?'

'Well, ma'am, when we left the aircraft, we went to the car, to come here, and Mr Korman suddenly said that he had something to do, and walked off.'

'As he was, with his clothes disordered and dirty?'

'Yes, ma'am.'

Gerberga looked at her husband, but like him, she did not suppose a disordered-looking man was going to attract too much attention on the streets of Istanbul.

'He is probably looking for a woman to beat up,' Rashid said. 'That is his hobby when he is angry.'

How little you know, Gerberga thought. 'I hope you are right,' she said. 'The question is, what are we to do now? If Korman's base has been destroyed . . . You spent so much money on creating that set-up . . .'

'It needs discussing,' Rashid said, and nodded to the pilot. 'Thank you, Hanif.'

Hanif hesitated. 'The site . . .'

'Was there anyone around?'

'No, sir. Only vultures.'

'Then we will leave the site, for a while at least. No one ever goes there.'

'Yes, sir.' Hanif looked uneasy, but he left the terrace, and Osman closed the door behind him.

'What we really need to find out is who told the SAS where to find the site,' Rashid said.

'Who could have done it? It is known only to you, me, Korman, and Korman's people. And if they are now all dead . . .'

'It is also known to Hanif.'

Gerberga frowned. 'Hanif has been your pilot for years.'

'The most faithful of men is capable of being suborned.'

'Will you kill him?'

'I shall have to consider the matter.'

'This thing has cost so many lives,' Gerberga said. 'All because of that bitch of a policewoman.'

'All because of Korman's obsession with her, you mean.'

'I don't agree. But the question still remains: what are we going to do?'

'That is something else I shall have to consider.'

'You will have to rebuild his organisation.'

'You think so?'

'Well . . . he is the best bomber, and incidentally, the best hit man, in the business. His record proves that. Buenos Aires wasn't his fault.'

'He is also forty-nine years old.'

'That is not old,' Gerberga snapped. And flushed.

'It is getting old,' Rashid said. And frowned at his wife. 'Why this sudden anxiety about Korman?'

Her flush had faded. 'I can only say again, he is the best there is. You will not find a better, and you will never find a man so dedicated to the job in hand. Just to discard him would be sheer stupidity. All he needs is a new organisation, a new base. And I suggest this time that you select both yourself; I think where he has been let down over this Jones woman is in the failings of his people.'

'It is something to be considered,' Rashid agreed.

'First time I've been in here,' Judith Proud said, looking around her. 'Comfortable?'

'Very,' Jessica said. 'Or I will be when I can get some of my gear in.'

In strong contrast to Judith, spruce in a dark blue business trouser suit, Jessica was still wearing the scarecrow kit Anoka had bought for her in Istanbul.

'I can imagine,' Judith said. 'Was it rough?'

'It had its moments.'

'But you didn't get your man?'

'He simply didn't turn up. But we got his base. And a lot more besides. You were right about Rashid ben Khalim being his financier. That's being cleaned up now, I believe.'

'Great stuff. That must be a relief to you.' Judith led the way down the stairs.

'It'll be a relief when Korman is finally done. But I suppose it's out of my hands now. And anyway, once his source of supply is cut off, he should be rendered useless.'

'And about time. The Commander tells me you're on leave.'

Jessica sat beside her in the BMW. 'A fortnight. He was going to see if he could organise Tom.'

Judith nodded. 'He's given that one to me. I'm afraid Tom is away right now, but he should be back in a day or two.' As might have been expected, Judith drove as expertly as a London taxi driver.

'And Megan?'

'She's a treat.'

'You really mean that?'

'I do. Makes you think . . . realise, perhaps, that's there more to life than money and pats on the shoulder. I don't know when I've been so happy.'

'Oh. I'm so glad.'

'But you'd like to have her back.'

'It's not that. I, well, I feel responsible for her. And I did foist her on you.'

'You did not,' Judith argued. 'I foisted her on myself.

Don't get me wrong, JJ. She's your baby. I mean, literally. But as you say, until Korman is finally sorted out, she's probably safer as my responsibility. And do you really want her under your feet when you have a get-together with Tom?'

Jessica couldn't think of an immediate reply to that. But Judith could see she was unhappy.

'Which is not to say she can't come and visit with you,' she said, pulling into the underground car park beneath her apartment building.

'JJ!' Megan threw both arms round Jessica's neck for a hug and a kiss. Lurking in the background was a hard-faced woman whom Jessica assumed was the dragon who had fended her off on the phone.

'Having fun?' she asked the little girl.

'Oh, yes. Judith is super. Great fun.'

Jessica could not repress a hasty glance at her superior. She had never heard anyone describe Judith Proud as fun before. Judith merely smiled.

'She gave me this.' The child produced a vast single-volume encyclopaedia. 'It has everything about everything in it. Look, I'll show you . . .'

'Miss Jones will be staying to supper, Louise,' Judith told the housekeeper.

Later, when Megan had gone to bed, Judith wanted a detailed breakdown on everything that had happened.

'What an experience,' she remarked, clearly taken aback at the idea of one of her officers being subjected to rape, even if it hadn't come off. 'I think you need danger money as well as everything else you've been promised. But you think it will all be wrapped up tomorrow morning; I suppose if anyone can do it, Merryman is the man. You may not like the sonofabitch, but you have to admit he's good.'

Tomorrow morning, Jessica thought. How she wished she could be there.

Next morning, Korman had still not appeared. Rashid and Gerberga were having a pre-lunch cocktail on the terrace, Gerberga keeping her agitation under control with some effort, when Osman appeared in the doorway.

'Mr Klemperer is on the phone, Mr Rashid. He says it is urgent.'

Rashid nodded, and Osman put the cordless phone on the table beside him.

'Yes?'

'I think you should know, Mr Rashid, that I have been visited by Mr Korman.'

'Have you, now.' Rashid was frowning again. Klemperer was his armourer in Istanbul. 'How did he look?'

'I would say he was upset, Mr Rashid.'

'That seems about right. What did he want?'

'A great deal, sir. Let me see . . . two handguns with spare magazines and one Minimi, with both belt and box cartridges.'

'You gave him these?'

'I had no instructions not to, Mr Rashid.'

'I understand. Well, well. Any explosives?'

'No Semtex, sir. But a dozen grenades.'

'I see. Did he give you any indication as to what he required this weaponry for? He can hardly be meaning to leave the country with that lot. Certainly by air.'

'He had a car, sir. One of ours, with several false bottoms and hidden compartments.'

'I see. How long ago was this?'

'He left half an hour ago, sir.'

'And you have only just called me?'

'Well, sir, I did not know whether it was necessary to call you at all. It was only after Mr Korman left, and I began to think about his appearance and, well, his general demeanour, that I felt I should check it out.'

'I see. Have you any idea which passport he was using?'

'I'm afraid not, sir.'

'Thank you, Klemperer.' Rashid replaced the phone. 'He's gone off on his own, armed to the teeth.'

'My God!' Gerberga clasped both hands to her neck. 'You think he is coming here?'

'There is no reason for him to arm himself so thoroughly to come here. He is using one of our special cars, which means he intends to leave the country. And he is carrying a Minimi rifle. That is deadly at six hundred yards. And incidentally, he has taken a belt of ammunition as well as a box. That belt holds two hundred cartridges. That sounds as if he intends to fight a battle.'

'Where?'

Rashid shrugged. 'I would say, England. He has gone quite off his head. What Hanif said suggested this.'

'He must be stopped. He cannot have reached the border yet. You can telephone and have him stopped.'

'And let the whole world know he is my partner?'

'It can be an anonymous call.'

'Which will result in a huge shoot-out, if Korman is in the mood I think he is in. With the same end result, if he is not killed outright. Korman is a nihilist. He will know that only I could have ordered him stopped, and he will happily take me, and you, down with him.'

Gerberga bit her lip. 'So you will just let him go . . . to do what?'

'I would say he is going after Jessica Jones. He blames her for every disaster that has happened.'

'Without any back-up, any organisation? He'd be mad.'

'Precisely. At the moment he is quite suicidal. Well, we will have to let him get on with it.'

'But' – again Gerberga bit her lip – 'he will be killed.'

'If that is what he wants, so be it. Perhaps he will come to his senses before he commits himself. After all, it is not possible to drive across Europe in less than three days. He will have plenty of time to reflect. He may even get picked up before he can do anything. The essential thing is that if he is captured alive, he must be quite sure that we have done nothing to betray him.'

'You are letting a madman loose on the world,' Gerberga said. 'Supposing he does take out this Jones woman? Who is to say he will stop there?'

Rashid shrugged. 'I don't care if he does or not. As you say, he is a madman on the loose. Perhaps he means to go after another Cabinet Minister, with a gun. Well, good luck to him. But as you say, my dear, without a back-up or any organised plan, he must come to a dead end eventually.'

Gerberga glared at him. Everything he was saying made sense, and even more sense for her. Korman was the first time she had ever cheated on her husband. Although she had known about Rashid's peccadilloes for a long time, she had been too afraid to react, and in any event, the opportunity had been lacking; the house and the servants and the cars and the gardeners were all Rashid's people. There was no way *she* could go out at night without first telling Rashid exactly where she was going and why.

That night had been the first she and Korman had ever slept under the same roof. She had found the idea irresistible. Not merely from a desire for revenge. There was also the excitement of sleeping with the most deadly man in the world. And then, the knowledge that he was impotent had made him more attractive still.

The anticipation of what might, or might not, happen, had been all but overwhelming. And the result had exceeded all her expectations. It had been the best sex she had ever known – even if he had been unable to complete –

simply because he had wanted to please her. Rashid knew how to please a woman, but when he did so it was because he was pleasing himself. He enjoyed the sight and feel of a woman in orgasm, but it was for the feeling of power it gave him, not any desire to make her content.

Power! That was all Rashid had ever wanted. And with his money and his companies and his own tame team of international assassins she sometimes felt he thought he was God.

The odd thing was that she yearned to have power too. She had had it as a young woman; with her beauty and her sexuality she had dominated the small group of anarchists to which she belonged. When she had given that up to marry Rashid, she had supposed she was moving up to a higher form of power.

And he had given her none.

But Korman represented power. Rashid supposed Korman was all his. She had known differently, after that night. Korman had admitted he hated all women since the death of his sister, and the hatred had turned to a continuing anger since Buenos Aires. But Gerberga had discovered it was all compounded of frustration and grief, an inability to relate to any human being, man or woman. His team had respected him and feared him; none of them had had any affection for him. His own fault? Undoubtedly. But that did not change the truth. Outside his team he had no one. Even Rashid had always been his employer, never his friend. His being, his identity, had rested in moving from one terrorist attack to the next.

But when he had lain in her arms, and she had talked to him, and told him how much she admired him and wanted to be with him, he had wept.

There was power. Until today. She could understand that the sight of his home destroyed, his people lying scattered about the desert, eaten by vultures, might have driven an essentially unstable character mad. She had hoped that he would come to her in his despair. But she could understand his wishing to go charging off, resolved to end it all in action.

She could understand it, but she didn't want him to die. And it was slowly dawning on her that her husband *did* want that. Because of his obsession with that bitch of a policewoman, Korman was becoming a liability. Rashid would be very happy to be rid of him, for all his talents, so long as when it happened he was not in any way involved.

It occurred to Gerberga, as she gazed across the table at the handsome face smiling at her, that she also could hate . . . her husband.

'And in the meantime,' Rashid said, 'I will start rebuilding the team, and finding it a base.'

'Who will lead it?' Gerberga asked. 'Supposing Korman doesn't come back?'

'I will find someone,' Rashid said, and looked up as Osman appeared before him.

'There is someone to see you, sir. A Mr John Smith, from England.'

The Hit

G erberga and Rashid gazed at each other for several
   seconds.

'John Smith,' Rashid said. 'These people must think we
are fools. Did he say what he wished to see me about,
Osman?'

'Just that it was an urgent matter, sir.'

'I do not think you should see this man,' Gerberga
said.

'If I do not, how will I find out who sent him, and with
what in mind? He could be from Korman . . .'

'That is hardly likely.'

'Agreed. Or he could be another policeman, investigating
the strange behaviour of Miss Jones. He could even be an
agent of the British Government, asking what I require to
cease this campaign. In effect, surrendering.'

'Or he could be a hit man.'

'That is possible. You had better search him, Osman,
before you show him in. Arm yourself. And call in the
boys to back you up.'

Osman bowed, and withdrew.

Gerberga opened her handbag and took out her little
Walther, laid it on her lap below the level of the table.

'You are too nervous for your own good,' Rashid
remarked. 'Osman will not let Mr Smith bring a weapon
in here. I must confess that I am quite intrigued. If this
man is an emissary from the British Government, they have

acted very promptly. Jones and her accomplices can hardly have got back to England before yesterday afternoon . . .'
He looked up as the door opened again. 'That was quick. That—' He gasped, and began to rise, then fell back again as Merryman shot him in the chest with his silenced pistol.

Rashid hit his chair with another gasp, then slid from it to the floor. Merryman had already turned towards Gerberga, but was too late; he had not seen the concealed gun. Gerberga shot him through the head.

Merryman spun round and crashed to the floor, scattering blood. Gerberga stood up, waited for a moment. Her gun had not been silenced, but it made very little noise. She laid it on the table. Then she stooped over her husband.

He was panting, and there was blood on his lips. 'I am a fool,' he muttered. 'Get a doctor, Gerberga. A doctor. I am not killed.'

'I can see that,' Gerberga said.

Merryman had dropped his gun when he fell. Gerberga carefully wrapped the gun in a napkin from the table, arranging the cloth so that she could grip the butt and also the trigger. Then she straightened and stood above her husband.

'Gerberga,' he gasped. 'I am losing blood. Gerberga . . .' His face contorted as he took her in, the gun in her hand, the look on her face. 'Gerberga . . .'

'I think you would be certain to die from such a wound, anyway,' Gerberga said, and shot him through the heart.

Gerberga then replaced the gun where it had fallen from Merryman's hand, removed the napkin, folded it and placed it in her handbag. She stood above Merryman for several seconds, then stooped for a closer look. His face was shattered, but she did not think she had ever seen him before in her life. She had no intention of disturbing either the way he was lying, or his clothes; that was a police matter, and in any event she did not suppose he would be carrying any identifying documents.

John Smith!

She stood up and staggered into the house, just in case. But there was no one there, save Osman, lying on his back, dead. He had been shot twice. Gerberga immediately knew what had happened. Merryman had followed Osman into the house, and when the butler had returned – before summoning assistance – had shot him. How innocent even men like Osman, or Rashid for that matter, were when confronted by a professional assassin.

Whose professional assassin?

She threw back her head and screamed. 'Aaaagh! Help me! For God's sake, help me.'

The two under-butlers – who were also Rashid's bodyguards – ran in from the pantry; the upstairs maid appeared at the top of the stairs; Miranda from the office.

'Madam?!' Miranda cried, running forward to catch Gerberga as she seemed about to fall. 'My God! Osman!'

'My husband,' Gerberga moaned, nestling into her servant's arms. 'Oh, my husband!'

Miranda sat her on a settee, then ran on to the terrace.

'Mr Rashid!' she screamed.

The two bodyguards continued to stare at Osman's dead body. The upstairs maid had collapsed on the top step.

Miranda ran back into the house. 'Madam . . . that man . . .'

'He just walked in here and shot my husband. After he had shot Osman.'

Gerberga pulled herself together with a very obvious effort. 'Call the police. Hurry.'

Miranda put her mistress to bed. This suited Gerberga; she always looked her best in bed.

The Search

In a matter of minutes the house was swarming with policemen.

'What a terrible tragedy,' commented Inspector Kurio. He was embarrassed, to be sitting in a chair next to the bed of a beautiful woman in such a state of dishabille. 'I mean, why? Had your husband any enemies, Madam Rashid?'

'Not that I knew of,' Gerberga said. 'But I never interfered in my husband's business affairs.'

'And this man . . .'

'Just appeared. He said he had an urgent message for my husband. From England. He gave his name as John Smith.'

'And Mr Rashid agreed to see him?'

'I imagine my husband had no reason to fear this man. Yes, he agreed to see him. But then this man shot Osman, walked on to the terrace, and as you saw, shot my husband twice. Just like that. One, two.'

'And then . . .?' He held up the Walther by a pencil thrust through the trigger guard.

'Oh, I shot him, Inspector. With that gun. I think I would have done so anyway, but after he shot my husband he turned his gun on me.'

'And you killed him with a single shot to the head. You are a very good shot, madam. Do you always carry a gun?'

'That gun, yes. Rashid gave it to me years ago. It is to protect me against kidnapping. My husband is a wealthy man.' She gulped. 'Was a wealthy man. Yes, I have practised with it, often enough, but I have never used it in earnest, before today. Will I be charged?'

'No, no. You acted, as you say, in self-defence. But this man, this killer, you have never seen him before?'

'Never.'

Kurio nodded. 'Well, I must go and see if my men are finished. I'm afraid they will be around for some time. Will this upset you? Your children? Where are your children?'

'They are at school. They do not come back until after three.'

'You mean, they do not know their father is dead?'

'Not yet.'

'Are you going to send for them?'

'When I feel better, yes.'

He nodded again. 'Well, if there is anything I can do for you . . .'

'You can answer me a question.'

'Of course.'

'Am I restricted in any way? I mean in my movements.'

'Certainly not.'

'You mean I can leave the country?'

He frowned. 'Now?'

'Well, perhaps tomorrow.'

'To go where?'

'It is a business matter.'

'I hope you are not thinking of going after this hit man's employers, madam.'

'Nothing is further from my mind.'

'I am glad of that. These things should be left to the police. Of course you may leave the country, if you wish to do so, madam. You will be required to give evidence at the inquest, but that will not be for a week or two. You will be back by then?'

'I will be back inside a week, Inspector.'

Things to be done. But in the right order. She called Miranda, sent her out to get the children. At times like these, children were a nuisance. Gerberga had always found her children a nuisance. They had been Rashid's idea; he had had in mind total respectability. But he didn't have to look after them, or see them more than once a day.

Then she telephoned Marco, Rashid's lawyer. 'Have you heard the news?'

'I am hearing unbelievable rumours. My God! Is it true?'

'Yes. Will you come here, immediately?'

'Of course.'

Gerberga got out of bed, put on a negligee, and went into Rashid's private office. She knew the combination of the safe, and within seconds was sitting at his desk, turning the pages of his files.

Power! She was the one with the power now, if Marco told her what she wanted to hear. But power meant Korman as well as money. Somehow he had to be stopped from committing suicide. So . . . Korman's file was detailed. Every move he had made over the past four years, every move he had had made by others.

Korman was going after Jessica Jones, a woman for whom he had conceived a quite unnatural hatred. Well, Gerberga thought, she hated the bitch herself. But where in all Britain's sixty millions was he going to find her?

He had found her the first time because, unsuspecting the future, she had been living in a flat owned in her own name.

He had found her the second time by tracing the address of a little girl she had befriended in Alicante. That had been a very long shot, but it had worked. Like a total innocent, and in the midst of all the turmoil with which she must have been surrounded, Jessica Jones had gone to visit Megan Lynch, and walked right into a hit stake-out. And, being Jessica Jones, had shot her way out.

Korman had not had to find her the third time, because she had come looking for him, backed up by Britain's most feared fighting force.

So, now . . . Jessica would surely have gone to ground in a secret location. There was no hope of finding such a location. She would have to be drawn from her lair, and the only way that could be done was by using someone who was very important to her. That was certainly how Korman would be thinking, and how he would intend to act, when he got to England.

But driving across Europe, he could not possibly get there until the day after tomorrow. By flying, she could be there tomorrow morning.

She copied out Megan Lynch's address in Southley, Somerset, put the slip of paper in her handbag, returned the files to the safe, and locked it again.

'It is such a shock.' George Marco took out his handkerchief and wiped his brow.

'And for me,' Gerberga assured him. She was fully dressed, but looked impressively distraught. This was not entirely acting; the children had come home half an hour before and had been fairly hysterical, although they were both too young properly to understand what had happened. 'Now I need to know exactly where I stand.'

Marco raised his eyebrows. 'Don't you know?'

'Confirm it.'

'The bulk of the estate is in trust for the children. But you, Rashid's principal banker and myself are the trustees, with you having sole discretion as regards to income. This means that while you cannot sell any of the assets or break up any of the companies without our agreement, you are not going to be short of funds. However, I'm afraid there are a good many things to be gone through, shares in various companies, etc, etc. There are also some unexplained items, large withdrawals in cash from various accounts, but' – he shrugged – 'you know what Rashid was like. He never let his left hand, much less his lawyer, know what his right hand was doing.'

'Or his wife,' Gerberga said. 'I will look into it, when

I have time. What I want to know is, how much am I worth?'

'It's very difficult to put a figure on it. Shares fluctuate, and so do markets.'

'Put a figure on it,' Gerberga said.

'Well, very approximately, a minimum of fifty million.'

'Are we talking in lire, dollars, or pounds sterling?'

'That is in pounds sterling. Rashid did most of his trading in that currency. There is very little in Turkey, you understand. He kept foreign balances.'

'I see.' Power, she thought. 'That is the capital. What is the income?'

'Several millions a year.'

'Very good. You and I will have to have a long get-together when I return, and make one or two decisions.'

'When you return? You are going away?'

'Yes. Tomorrow morning. It is a business matter.'

'But . . . the police? The children? The funeral? The inquest?'

Gerberga raised her hand and ticked off her fingers. 'The police have given me the okay. The children will be in the care of Miranda while I am away. I am only going for about forty-eight hours; the funeral can wait until I get back. And the inquest will not be for another two weeks. Does that answer your queries?'

Marco looked as if he might have liked to ask more, but decided against it. 'Of course. By the time you return I will have prepared detailed lists of all your husband's holdings and investments, and his various bank accounts. As I say, there is quite a lot of money that has disappeared, and which I imagine is in various accounts unknown to me. Perhaps you may be able to find it by going through Rashid's private papers.'

'I will see what I can do, when I come back,' Gerberga said.

She wondered what Marco would say if he knew that a couple of millions of the missing money had gone into creating Korman's desert hideaway!

'Megan Lynch?' asked the staff nurse on the reception desk. 'No, I know nothing about her. Perhaps you should ask Miss Lovelace.'

'Ah,' Gerberga said. 'Yes. I was given her address in Southley, but when I went there, the house was shut up, and the neighbours told me there had been some crime committed, and that Miss Lovelace had been brought to this hospital. So I naturally supposed . . .'

'Oh, quite, Miss . . . ah . . .' She looked again at Gerberga's card, and then at Gerberga herself, obviously wondering how the DSS had got hold of this glamorous creature. 'Elliott. And you are from the DSS . . .'

'Well, you see,' Gerberga said, 'the child is really our responsibility. Not in a physical sense, of course, but in view of the deaths of her parents and the severe injury to her grandmother, there is quite a large compensatory payment due, and it is a little disturbing to have her just disappear.'

'Oh, absolutely,' the staff nurse agreed. 'I'll have you taken out to Miss Lovelace. She'll be able to tell you where Megan is. But . . . please be careful. Miss Lovelace is still suffering from shock.'

'I understand. Do you know what actually happened down in Southley?'

'I'm afraid I don't know the details. There was a shooting, and a man was killed. Two, I think.'

'Good heavens,' Gerberga said. 'And this Miss Lovelace was involved?'

'Only in so far as she was looking after the girl Megan at the time.'

'Are you saying the girl was involved?'

'I really do not know, Miss Elliott. It's all been rather

hushed up. I strongly recommend that you do not raise the matter with Miss Lovelace.'

Gerberga nodded. 'Of course.'

Another nurse had arrived, and Gerberga was escorted out the back of the nursing home into the grounds, which were bathed in the bright afternoon sunlight. Here there were quite a few people of both sexes, mostly elderly, some fully dressed and others in dressing gowns, sitting or walking, watched by several more nurses.

'Over here,' said Gerberga's escort, leading her to where one woman sat alone, staring at the ornamental pond. 'Miss Lovelace? You have a visitor.'

'Me?' Miss Lovelace half-turned her head.

'Gwen Elliott, for the Department of Social Security,' Gerberga said. 'I actually need to speak with Miss Megan Lynch. Are you her guardian?'

'Megan? They took her away, you know. Well, really, I wasn't all that sorry. Those people, shooting at her, shooting at me . . .'

'It must have been terrible,' Gerberga said sympathetically. 'You mean they were shooting at Megan?'

'I think they were shooting at that Jones person. But we were there.'

'I know,' Gerberga said, more sympathetically still. 'There is going to be compensation.'

'Money?' For the first time Miss Lovelace looked animated.

'Yes, indeed. Quite a lot. But I really do need to see Megan before I can complete the paperwork.'

'She telephoned to see if I was all right,' Miss Lovelace said. 'Didn't come to see me, mind. Just telephoned.'

'From where did she telephone?' Gerberga asked, with great patience. 'From Miss Jones's address?'

'No, no. She's not staying with Miss Jones. She spends so little time at home. She's staying with Miss Proud.'

'Miss Proud,' Gerberga said. 'Would you have her address?'

'I don't have her address. She's a policewoman too. Very high and mighty, from what Megan said.'

'I see. Well, thank you very much. I shall probably come down and see you again, after I've spoken with Megan.'

'You said there'd be money.'

'Oh, indeed. A great deal. As soon as I've spoken with Megan and completed the paperwork. Bye.'

She went back into the hospital.

'Any luck?' asked the staff nurse.

'She was very helpful. Now it's just a matter of completing the paperwork. By the way, a colleague of mine may come down here, probably tomorrow. He will likely wish to see Miss Lovelace as well. If he does, will you ask him to contact me?' She wrote out the phone number of her hotel and added a brief message. 'He may seem surprised, as he assumes he is handling this case; he doesn't realise he's been replaced. If he seems doubtful, perhaps you could describe me to him. And show him that message.'

The staff nurse studied the paper. Gerberga had written: *R has resigned and I am in complete control of this matter. Please call me and prepare to co-operate fully. G.*

'I'll give him this, yes.'

'I'd be most grateful. Now I simply must rush.'

She hurried from the hospital before the nurse could ask her the name of her colleague.

Gerberga drove back up to London, returned her hire car, and took a taxi to her hotel. She was well pleased with what she had accomplished, and so quickly. Now it was just a matter of waiting.

And reflecting, on how much she now had, on how much she could now do.

The Search

Things had happened so fast over the past twenty-four hours that she had not had the time to think. Save about reaching Korman before he got himself killed.

She lay in bed and gazed into the darkness. Power! To do anything she wished in life, always with her faithful hit man at her side. He would need to be relocated, of course. Somewhere out of Turkey. No one could blame her for wishing to leave the house, and indeed the country, in which her husband had been murdered. Especially if the assassin's employers were not discovered.

She did not doubt it had been the British Government. They were not to be taken lightly. But if they had been tipped that Rashid had been financing Korman, it could only have been by the Jones woman. That meant Mr John Smith *had* been instructed to kill her also. She hadn't been certain of that at the time; she would have shot him anyway.

Another reason for disappearing, just as far and as fast as possible. They would be able to trace her eventually, she did not doubt. But since she was not as arrogantly self-confident as Rashid, if she handled things properly they would have a difficult time reaching her.

And she would have Korman.

And Jones? Oh, she would get to Jones. When she was ready.

Gerberga spent the morning in her room, waiting. She would have liked to get out and walk about London, a city she had only visited once before, but that was not practical until Korman arrived. She had a lot to do, hunting through phone books, until she found what she wanted: Assistant Commissioner Judith Proud. That had to be the high-up policewoman mentioned by Miss Lovelace.

Lunch came and went. She ate little. She was becoming quite anxious. She had ordered several newspapers, but predictably there was no report of recent events in Istanbul in any of them. The murder of a wealthy Turkish business-man would not be regarded as worthwhile news by any English editor. And she doubted it would be so regarded by any French or German editor either.

Korman would have reached those countries last night. Now all he had to do was cross the Channel . . . She kept looking at her watch as the minutes ticked away. Had he been picked up, the amount of hardware in his car detected? At six o'clock she watched the news. Surely the arrest of a man smuggling weapons into England would be reported. But there was nothing.

She gazed at the telephone. What to do? It had all seemed so simple. She had been certain he would follow the same track as herself, simply because it was the only track he *could* follow, if he was to trace Megan Lynch and thence Jessica Jones. Just as she had been certain that on receipt of her message he would come to her, at least out of curiosity as to what had actually happened.

But what if he was in one of his paranoically suspicious moods, and thought the message might be a trap? Suppose he was not going to let anything deflect him from his purpose? Then there was only one place he could be going, to begin with.

Gerberga got up and dressed, hurriedly.

'What do you think?' Jessica asked.

'I think it's super,' Megan said, looking around the room. 'Not as nice as Aunt Judith's, of course.'

'She says the sweetest things,' Judith remarked, glowing.

She had certainly made a conquest, Jessica thought. And why not? She felt a great sense of responsibility towards Megan; but she knew her lifestyle, if she was going to return to Protection, was no way to bring up a child who was already somewhat traumatised.

There was also the matter of Tom's point of view.

While Judith, with more money than she knew what to do with, and a nine-to-five job, would make an ideal foster or adoptive mother.

'This will be your room.' She showed Megan into the spare bedroom. 'Make yourself at home.'

She returned to the lounge, and Judith.

'I'm only letting you have her for one night, mind,' Judith said.

'I understand that, ma'am.'

Jessica had spent the previous day collecting her gear and having her hair trimmed. Going back to the Docklands flat had been frightening, but the neighbours had merely stared. And at least, the lock having been replaced, nothing had been stolen. Now she was ready to resume normal living, as far as she could.

'You won't want her around tomorrow, anyway,' Judith said. 'I've an idea Tom Bainbridge will be back.'

'Will he?' Jessica's heart leapt.

'So you can drop Megan off at my place, and be here to welcome him. And by the way, JJ, as we have become rather thrown together, I think you can stop calling me ma'am, in private. The name's Judith. In public, of course . . .'

'I understand, ma'am . . . Judith. Thank you. May I ask if you have any news of Captain Merryman?'

Judith raised her eyebrows. 'I had gained the impression that you and he didn't get on.'

'I don't think we could ever be bosom buddies, if that's what you mean. But I did discover just how good he is at his job. He should have returned from Istanbul by now, surely.'

'As far as I know, he hasn't,' Judith said. 'But we know he completed his mission.'

'Oh!' What a relief.

'That's all we know. Our Consulate in Istanbul has reported that prominent businessman Rashid ben Khalim was shot and killed yesterday morning. There are no further details, as yet; the police are keeping it very much under wraps, and there is some suggestion that the assassination may have been political.'

'And the assassin?'

'Nothing has as yet been released about the assassin. So it is quite possible that he is under arrest. If he wasn't, one would suppose they'd have released a description.'

'Yes,' Jessica said thoughtfully. 'If he has been arrested, you'll get him out, won't you?'

'Of course, although it may take some time. But I'm sure Peter Merryman can stand up to a Turkish prison for a few months.'

'Peter? Is that his name?'

'Didn't you know?'

'Oddly, we never got around to first names.'

'I must rush,' Judith said. 'Have a good evening. And I'll expect Megan back for tea tomorrow. As it's Saturday, I'll be home all day.'

She was really quite possessive.

Judith hummed a little tune as she parked the BMW in her allotted space in the underground car park and got out. She was glad Jessica had accepted the obvious and not made a fuss. Not that she was in any position to make a fuss; she had no rights to the child. Neither did she, of course, but Judith intended to obtain those rights just as soon as possible. This woman Lovelace was clearly a write-off. The first thing to do was fly down to Alicante and see Mrs Lynch, explain the situation to her. The woman would have to be guaranteed unlimited access to the child, as and when she was able, but Judith did not really see her objecting to Megan's being adopted.

Then there would be the application and then . . . Judith was well aware that there were some local bodies who were against singles adopting children. She did not imagine any of them was going to resist Assistant Commissioner Judith Proud for very long.

And then . . . she would have a child of her very own. That was something she had always wanted, even if she would have admitted it to no one but herself. What she had *not* wanted was the discomfort of pregnancy or the horrors of delivery. Nor had she ever wanted to change a nappy or suffer the time-wasting of caring for a babe in arms. But a seven-year-old, bright and quick-witted, and obviously intelligent, who had an unbearable past from which she would be rescued by her adoptive mother . . . that could be the beginning of a very fruitful relationship that might well stretch into her old age, the possible loneliness of which was beginning to prey on Judith's mind – she had no family.

So, then . . . She strolled to the lift, and checked. She had not noticed the woman standing in the shadows beside the door.

'Miss Proud?' Gerberga asked.

The Attempt

Judith blinked at the stranger, aware mainly of a forceful voluptuousness. 'I am Miss Proud,' she said. 'Do I know you?'

'Not at all,' Gerberga said. 'But we are going to get to know each other very well.'

Judith frowned, and was distracted by the arrival of the lift, the doors of which opened.

'Shall we go in?' Gerberga asked.

'No,' Judith said. 'I will go in, and you—'

'Will come with you,' Gerberga said, moving with sudden and unexpected speed as she seized Judith by the collar of her jacket and the seat of her pants and hurled her into the lift car.

Judith could not stop her head hitting the opposite wall with a thud that knocked her senseless for a moment. She gasped, and slid down the wall to land on her knees. Only vaguely was she aware that the door had closed and the car was moving upwards, and that her assailant was kneeling beside her, fingers thrust into her hair, pulling her head back.

Think, she told herself. I must be able to deal with this. I was trained to it. But as she had never actually had to face physical violence she was only aware of pain.

'Which floor?' Gerberga asked.

Judith inhaled, slowly and noisily. 'Get stuffed,' she muttered.

In response, Gerberga swung her heavy shoulder bag into Judith's face. Judith cannoned into the opposite wall with a force sufficient to send her head spinning again. She had never experienced such primeval violence, and from a woman who was at once well-dressed and appeared to be cultured. She gasped, and tasted blood; her lips had been cut.

Gerberga left her lying there, and opened Judith's handbag, which she had dropped at her initial assault.

'Number Four,' she said. 'Now tell me, Miss Proud, is there anyone in the flat? I saw a woman leave, about an hour ago. I presume she was your servant. Is there anyone else? Where is the little girl?'

Judith looked up at her through a blood-red haze, half of pain, half of anger. This could not be happening to her. She was Assistant Commissioner Proud. She was trained in unarmed combat. She should be able . . . But she hadn't practised any of her skills for years, whereas this woman . . .

Gerberga was kneeling in front of her, and slapping her face, very hard, sending her head to and fro, bringing her hair down from its bun to drop past her shoulders.

'You must learn to co-operate,' Gerberga said.

To her horror, Judith realised she was afraid, not so much of what her assailant might do next, but simply of being in this position, of anyone finding out.

The lift had gone past four. Gerberga stood up and pressed the requisite button, and it came back down. Judith gathered her thoughts and her strength, and launched herself at Gerberga's legs. But Gerberga had not taken her eyes off her, and saw her coming. A well-aimed kick had Judith lying on the floor of the car, rolling to and fro, holding her face and wondering if her jaw had been broken.

One of her shoes came off.

'Silly bitch,' Gerberga commented.

The door opened, and she looked into an empty lobby.

'Up.' She seized Judith by the collar and dragged her to her feet, picking up the shoe with her other hand. Judith's knees started to give way and Gerberga had to hold her up, but Judith was past fighting her for the moment. Tears streamed down her face as she was pushed against the wall. Gerberga used her key to unlock the door; then she was pushed into the flat, where she fell to her hands and knees, panting.

Gerberga placed her foot on Judith's buttocks, and pushed. Judith fell to her face on the floor. Gerberga tossed the shoe to the floor beside her, then deliberately stepped on her back as she moved to the inner doors, opening them each in turn.

Judith gave a little moan of pain, but didn't move.

'Nice,' Gerberga remarked. 'Get up.'

Slowly Judith got to her knees, and then stood up, holding on to the doorjamb. Her face was a mask of blood, and her white shirt was stained; her jacket had swung open.

'In here,' Gerberga said.

Judith half-fell into the lounge. Gerberga had already checked that there was no one else in the flat.

'Go and wash your face,' she said. 'You look terrible.'

Judith stumbled across the lounge and into her bedroom, then went on to the bathroom, conscious of Gerberga just behind her. She was trying desperately to think of a weapon . . . but she did not keep weapons in her flat. There were only the knives in the kitchen, and she knew very little about knives.

Golf clubs! Hers were in her wardrobe. But would this woman just let her take out a club?

She stared at herself in the mirror above the basin, did

not recognise herself. Then stared at the woman standing beside her, hardly ruffled by the violence she had been expending.

Gerberga smiled at her. 'You'll feel better.'

Judith ran water, scooped it over her face and even her hair, trying to dim the aching of her head. When she dried her face the towel was bloody. She looked at herself again. She was beginning to swell.

'I think you need a drink,' Gerberga said.

She waited, and Judith went past her again, into the lounge. Now she was trembling, almost uncontrollably. Partly it was outrage, that this should be happening to her. Equally it was an immediate fear, that the woman might start hitting her again. But underlying both of those was the sudden realisation that she had inadvertently stumbled into the orbit of people like Korman, that her very life was in danger.

She did feel like a drink, and poured herself a small brandy; she glanced at the woman hopefully.

'I will not, at this time,' Gerberga said.

Judith sipped.

'Drink it all,' Gerberga said.

Judith gulped the brandy. Perhaps it would help her to think. The woman did not appear to be armed, save for her extraordinary strength, and her willingness to use that strength. But was she any less strong? She had been taken entirely by surprise. The woman had stolen the initiative. Now it was a matter of summoning the mental will to use her own strength. But once she started that, she knew she would have to go all the way. Half measures would not do with this woman.

Gerberga was able to read what was going through her mind.

'Does that feel better?' she asked. 'Now, lie on the floor, on your face.'

Judith hesitated, the brandy coursing through her stomach.

'If you do not,' Gerberga said, 'I will break your arm.'

Judith found she was kneeling without even intending to.

'Right down,' Gerberga said.

Judith lay down, cheek against the carpet.

'Spread your arms and legs,' Gerberga said. 'Wide.'

Judith obeyed.

'Now stay like that,' Gerberga said. 'I can get back to you long before you can get up, and if you try to get up, I will kick you hard enough to break your ribs. Remember this.'

She got up and went into the kitchen. The door was wide open, and Judith could see her watching her while she opened drawers and cupboards. From the cutlery drawer she selected a large knife. Judith's heart sagged. She had just had that knife sharpened.

Gerberga continued hunting through the various cupboards, but could not find what she wanted; Judith's flat was too well equipped with modernity to have such things as clothes lines.

Gerberga returned to the lounge, surveyed her prisoner. 'Roll on your back.'

Judith obeyed. Now, she told herself. Now! Sit up and grapple with her. But the thought of being hit again . . .

'Be a good girl,' Gerberga recommended, and unbuckled Judith's belt. It was a cloth belt, but made of strong material. 'On your face,' Gerberga commanded.

Judith sighed, and rolled over again. She needed to catch her off guard. Surely there would be an opportunity . . .

Gerberga brought Judith's legs together and bound the ankles with the belt. 'Don't move,' she reminded her, and went into the bedroom. Judith watched her pull open drawers and throw the contents on to the floor. She selected a pair of tights, and returned to the lounge. 'Hands behind back,' she said.

Judith realised she had lost her chance; the woman was anticipating every eventuality. She put her hands behind her back and had her wrists tied together, expertly.

'Now we should be able to have a civilised conversation,' Gerberga said, holding Judith's shoulders to pull her to a sitting position and prop her back against the settee, on which Gerberga now sat.

'I am hoping we will be joined by a colleague of mine,' she remarked. 'However, as he will be seeking the same information as myself, I may as well anticipate him. I will introduce myself. My name is Gerberga Rashid. My husband was murdered yesterday morning, I think by a member of the British Security Services.'

Judith found she was panting; Jessica had told her how frank Rashid had been with her . . . because he intended to kill her. There was no way this woman could leave her alive and hope to get back out of England, after having revealed her name and identity. And anyway, Jessica had described her as a cold-blooded killer.

'I hope he was not a friend of yours,' Gerberga continued, 'because I shot him. I suppose it was a knee-jerk reaction. Had I been thinking clearly I would have taken him prisoner and held him for questioning. But there it is. And it is not important. I just want you to be sure that you are dealing with something big. As opposed to which, you are nothing. You are my servant, until I choose otherwise. Do you understand me? Say it. You are my servant.'

'I am your servant,' Judith muttered. The only thing that mattered now was survival, for as long as possible, until . . . But Louise would not return until nine o'clock on Monday morning, and in any event she didn't think Louise would be able to cope with Gerberga Rashid.

Well, then, Jessica. She thought Jessica might be able to handle the situation. But Jessica was not coming until late tomorrow afternoon.

'Good,' Gerberga said. 'Now we understand each other. Now that you know who I am, you will realise that I know everything that has been going on. There is just one missing link. I know that the child Megan Lynch was given into your custody . . .'

'It was not custody,' Judith muttered. 'It was protective care.'

'As you wish. So, where is she?'

Judith licked her lips, and winced. 'Megan is no longer here. She has been handed over to the local authority to be placed in an orphanage.'

Gerberga looked down at her for several seconds, then she thrust her fingers into Judith's hair and pulled her head back. Judith gasped with pain.

'I know you are lying,' she said. 'If the child is not here, it is because she has returned to the care of Miss Jones. Is that not the truth?'

Judith stared up at her, mouth sagging open because of the pressure being exerted on her scalp.

'So all you have to do,' Gerberga said, 'is give me Miss Jones's new address, and you will save yourself a lot of pain.'

'Please let go of my hair,' Judith begged.

Gerberga gave it a last tug, then released it. Judith's head sagged forward.

'The address,' Gerberga said.

'I don't know Jones's address,' Judith said. 'She is in a safe house, a hideaway.'

'And you, a senior police officer, do not know where it is?'

'Why should I?' Judith asked. 'We have several such houses in London alone.'

'But you could find out.'

'Yes,' Judith said. 'I could find out. A telephone call . . .'
She bit her lip, realising she had been a shade too eager.

Gerberga got up and picked up the knife, then she sat
astride Judith's thighs, drawing her dress up to her knees.
Judith panted.

'You are lying,' Gerberga said. 'You and Jones have
been working closely together, have you not? Did you not
send her to Istanbul to track down Robert Korman? I know
all about that. And while she was gone, you looked after
Megan Lynch. Now Jones is back, and you are no longer
looking after Megan Lynch. Because you have returned her
to Jones. Is that not the truth?'

Judith licked her lips. 'I have told you, Megan has
gone to—'

'And I say you are lying.' Gerberga's voice was like
the crack of a whip, and she swung her hand to and fro,
slapping Judith's face as she did so. Blood from her cut
lips dribbled down her chin.

'No,' Judith moaned. 'No.'

'Now,' Gerberga said, 'working so closely together, you
will certainly know where Jones is living. With Megan, eh?
Give me the address.'

'No,' Judith muttered. 'No.'

'You still do not understand,' Gerberga said. 'You are
my prisoner and my servant. I can do anything I like to
you.' She picked up the knife and prodded Judith in the
stomach, not hard enough to penetrate the material of her
pants, but enough to bring another sharp intake of breath.
'I can cut little bits off you,' Gerberga said. 'I can burn
you. Or I can just go on beating you. Do you really want
that to happen?'

Judith stared at her from pain-filled eyes. 'No,' she
whispered.

Gerberga got up, went to the sideboard, and poured

another glass of brandy. Then she knelt beside Judith. 'Drink this.'

'No,' Judith said.

'I have said you will.' She grasped Judith's hair with one hand, pulling her head back and forcing her mouth open, so that with the other hand she could pour the brandy between the bleeding lips. Judith gasped and choked; at least half the alcohol went down her shirt front, but the other half went down her throat, adding to the confusion in her brain.

Gerberga got up, and went to the window to look out. What had happened to Korman? Could he possibly have got Jones's address from some other source? But there was no other source.

While this woman . . . she had a lot more guts than Gerberga had first supposed. Could the address be tortured out of her? It probably could. But did she want it? She would very much like to have Jessica Jones tied up in front of her as she had this woman, but it was not a prize she intended to risk her life for. Her business was to stop Korman risking *his* life in a search for insensate revenge.

Where *was* he? She had been so sure he would come here, because there was nowhere else he could go. Equally she had been sure he would arrive this evening, as it was three days since he had left Istanbul. Something must have happened . . . Of course he could have been delayed.

Her brain was going round in circles.

And now this woman . . . She had to be highly intelligent, and probably very experienced as well, Gerberga thought, to have got to her position. So she was thinking, trying to work things out, trying to decide what to do . . .

The sensible thing for *her* to do would be to cut Judith Proud's throat, return to her hotel, pick up her bag, and catch the first available flight out of England – she had an open ticket and did not in the first instance care where she wound up. Once she was out of the country she could easily find her way back to Turkey, and there would be nothing to connect her to a policewoman found dead in her flat.

But that would mean abandoning Korman. If she could give him another twenty-four hours . . .

She went into the spare bedroom, looked at a child's clothes, one or two soft toys . . . Wherever she had gone, Megan Lynch was certainly coming back.

She returned to the lounge, knelt beside Judith's feet, picked up the knife and cut away her tights to expose her toes. Then she ran the reverse of the blade over the little toe on the right foot.

Judith gasped, and drew up her legs. Gerberga pulled them straight again.

'Listen to me,' she said. 'Very carefully. I am going to ask you some questions, and I wish the truth. Or I will cut off this toe. And then this one, and so on until you have none left. Then I will start cutting off other things. Do you understand this?'

Judith licked her lips.

'Right. First, do you go into your office on a Saturday?'

Judith hesitated, then said, 'No.'

Gerberga studied her for several seconds, then got up and went to the desk in the corner of the room, opened the desk diary lying there, flicked the pages. The dates of Saturday were usually things like golf or coffee with a friend. Tomorrow's was blank.

'Then what are you doing tomorrow?' she asked.

'I am doing nothing tomorrow.'

Gerberga nodded. 'Does your servant come in on Saturdays?'

'No.'

'I believe you. Now, you are doing nothing tomorrow because you are expecting Megan Lynch to return here, is that not correct?'

Judith inhaled, sharply.

'Very good,' Gerberga said. 'What time is she coming back?'

Judith licked her lips again.

Gerberga knelt beside her and held her little toe. 'I will count to five.'

'She will be back for tea,' Judith said.

'Excellent. And will she be brought by Miss Jones?'

Judith stared at her.

'That is better yet. You see, I do not even have to press you for the address. Now, I tell you what I will do. I will prepare supper for us both, and we will have a quiet evening at home together. Won't that be nice?'

Judith made a hissing sound, like a snake.

And if we are lucky, Gerberga thought, Korman will arrive in the middle of it.

'Did you sleep well?' Jessica asked over breakfast.

'Oh, yes,' Megan said. 'It's a very comfortable bed.'

'It's a nice flat,' Jessica said.

'Is it yours?'

'No, worse luck. I'm just borrowing it for a few days.'

'Can't I stay here with you?'

Jessica frowned at her. 'Don't you like staying with Miss Proud? I thought you did.'

'She's very nice,' Megan said. 'But' – she screwed up her eyes – 'she isn't you, is she?'

'Ah . . . no, she isn't. Now, what would you like to do this morning?'

She was anxious to get off the subject of what happened next in this unfortunate child's life. She had already accepted the fact that there was nothing she could do about it – unless she resigned from the force, and she wasn't about to do that. Whereas Judith . . . That might seem the best possible solution – supposing Megan would go for it.

More heartbreak for the little girl.

216

'I'd like to go for a ride on the river,' Megan said. 'I've never been for a ride on the river.'

'Oh, right,' Jessica said. 'We'll go down to Greenwich and look at the *Cutty Sark* and the museum and the observatory. We can lunch down there.'

'Oh, super,' Megan said.

'So, you run along and have a bath and then get dressed,' Jessica said, and switched on the television to look at the morning news. There wasn't a lot, save that the Prime Minister was also making a trip on the river that morning, to inspect some new aspect of the Dome development. Damn and blast, Jessica thought. That meant the river would be swarming with media and security people, not to mention spectators.

But Megan had seemed so keen . . . And anyway, they were going to the other side.

The street bell rang. Jessica cocked an eye at it, then slowly got up. Only the people at New Scotland Yard knew where she was. So . . . she drew a deep breath and picked up the phone. 'Yes?'

'Guess who.'

'Tom!' she shouted. 'Oh, Tom!' She released the street door, then opened the flat door and went on to the landing to watch him come up, carrying his travel bag.

'It seems forever since I last did this,' he said, taking her into his arms for a long hug and a longer kiss. 'Does this mean you're still in hiding?'

'Only in a manner of speaking.'

She led him into the flat and he looked around. 'Impressive. How long have you got it for?'

'A couple of weeks, at least. How long have I got *you* for?'

'A couple of days, at least. Hello.'

Megan had come out of the bathroom, wrapped in a dressing gown. 'I heard the shouting,' she explained.

'That was me,' Jessica said. 'Tom, this is Megan Lynch. I told you about her, remember?'

'Yes.' Tom shook hands.

'Megan, this is Tom.'

'Is Tom your husband?'

'Ah . . . no. Tom is my partner.'

'I know what that is,' Megan said. 'You're lovers.'

'Spot on,' Tom said. Do you think—'

'Yes,' Jessica said. 'You go have your bath, Megan, then get dressed and sit down and watch telly. Tom and I have a lot to talk about.' She led Tom into the bedroom and closed the door.

'She's not permanent, is she?' He was anxious.

'No, she's not. Although sometimes I wish she could be. But right now she belongs to Judith Proud.'

'Say again?'

'I know. It's a long story.'

'Which I hope you're going to tell me,' he said. 'But first things first.'

'Have you breakfasted?'

'Yes. Join me in the shower.'

'Oh, yes.'

They stood together and kissed while the water bounced off their bodies and ran down the hills and valleys.

'We supposed to be going down to Greenwich,' Jessica said. 'Will you come?'

'There's time.' He switched off the water, handed her a towel. 'First, we have things to do.'

'If you'll shave,' she said.

Lying naked in his arms, mutually exhausted, she told him about the last few days.

'So, you see, I've turned into a callous, cold-blooded killer,' Jessica explained.

'That makes you more exciting,' Tom said, beginning

218

to nuzzle her again. 'How many of them did you kill yourself?'

'Just the one, at Southley. Patrick did for the other. Then the SAS took over. My God, I've never seen anything like it.'

'But you're happy they were around.'

'If they hadn't been, I wouldn't be here. But you see, then I pressed for Rashid and his wife to be executed. Just like that. As if I were God or something. I was so fired up. It's only since I've had the time to think about it . . .'

'After what they did to you, they had it coming,' Tom said.

'Um.' She moved his hands. 'We have to make a move. Megan's waiting.'

'Back to the shower. When did you say she's going back to Judith?'

'This afternoon.'

The river was as crowded as Jessica had presumed it would be. It was a lovely morning with hardly a cloud in the sky, and apart from the steamers carrying sightseers up and down, and the barges moving to and fro, there were also a considerable number of pleasure craft. Megan was fascinated, and although their boat was fairly crowded she kept rushing from side to side to gain different vantage points.

'She's certainly lively,' Tom commented. 'How does Judith cope?'

'Imagination boggles, doesn't it?' Jessica agreed.

The boat jam was even thicker as they reached the deep bend, with the Dome rising on the north bank, the more prosaic buildings of the Royal Naval College on the south, and beyond that, the gentle slope of the hill up to the Observatory. Here there were a good number of police launches to be seen, but as Jessica, Tom and Megan were travelling by public transport they were less harried than most. Even so, it was eleven thirty by the time they got ashore, and if they were going to get Megan to Judith's in time for tea they would have to catch the two o'clock boat back upriver.

'Just the *Cutty Sark*, I think,' Jessica said. 'Then a quick lunch, then off we go.'

'For a long evening's nooky,' Tom said.

Jessica stuck her tongue out at him.

'What's nooky?' Megan asked.

'It's what people do when they've been separated for a long time,' Tom explained. 'Providing they like each other enough.'

The child looked about to make one of her penetrating ripostes when there was an explosion of sound from the north bank. They all turned, as did thousands of others, at the sudden pop-pop, followed by the thud-thud of grenades. People screamed, and swayed back and forth. Boats cannoned into each other; some of their crews fell overboard. The noise swelled into the morning air.

Now they could see smoke rising on the north bank, and the sound of more explosions hurried into the morning.

'Here!' Tom pushed them to one side, where he had seen a uniformed policeman chattering into his radio.

'Watch it!' The policeman wasn't armed, but he was signalling a colleague.

'Relax,' Tom said, and showed his badge.

The policeman peered at it, then looked at Jessica.

'Her too,' Tom said. 'But not the girl.'

The policeman ignored the wisecrack. By this time he had been joined by his sergeant. 'You on duty?' the sergeant asked.

'No we're not,' Tom said. 'Just trying to find out what the hell is going on.'

'There's been an attempt on the life of the PM, that's what's going on.'

'You don't mean . . .'

'He's been hit, that's all we know.'

'And the assassin?'

'He got away, hurling grenades. There's a mess over there. Maybe you'd better report.'

Tom looked at Jessica. 'You don't suppose . . .'

'Throwing grenades? My God, Tom, it has to be.'

'Right. You get the kid out of here. Take her to Judith's, where she'll be safe. You stay with her until I come for you.'

'But you—'

'I need to get across the river, see if I can help.'

'But if it is Korman, and he's got away, only I know what he looks like. Shouldn't I—'

'We'll line up everyone we arrest and let you have a look at them,' Tom promised. 'Now get out of here. Can you get me a boat across the river?' he asked the sergeant.

'Let's go.' Jessica held Megan's hand.

'What's happening?' Megan asked. 'Aren't we going to look at the *Cutty Sark*?'

'Some other time. There's a very bad man on the loose. Right now, we have to get you somewhere safe.'

She hurried the child through the throng, and out into the street. They were lucky. A taxi was halted on the corner, the driver looking utterly bemused by the pandemonium with which he was surrounded.

'Will you take us into Westminster, please?' Jessica asked.

'You heard what's happening, miss?'

'I know there's trouble on the north bank,' Judith said. 'I want to get my niece out of it.'

'Yeah,' he said. 'I want to get out of it too.'

They got into the back seat, and he drove away as fast as he could through the packed streets.

'Is this the terrorist who killed my Mummy and Daddy?' Megan asked.

'If it is,' Jessica promised her, 'this time we're going to nail him.'

If only she could believe that.

Gerberga spent most of the day sitting at the dining table playing patience, with the television on, muted, so that she could watch the various news items. None of them were very interesting.

Judith lay on the settee, still bound hand and foot. The two women had shared her bed last night; neither had undressed. Gerberga had actually appeared to sleep from time to time, whereas Judith had endured increasing discomfort, both from the bonds and her various cuts and bruises. And mostly from the torment in her mind. Her captor was waiting . . . for what? It could only be for the return of Megan . . . and Jessica.

Pray to God they'd have Tom Bainbridge with them.

To her great relief, Gerberga had untied her first thing in the morning, so that she could wash herself and have some breakfast. Once again, temptation mingled with fear; Gerberga sat opposite her, and the knife was next to her hand.

'You are being very sensible about this,' Gerberga said. 'And this time tomorrow, it will all be a bad dream.'

Judith's nerve cracked. 'How can you say that,' she shouted, 'when you mean to kill me? You *have* to kill me.'

'You almost sound as if you wish me to,' Gerberga said. 'If you become hysterical, I will have to gag you as well. What happens to you depends on my friend. When he gets here.' *If* he gets here, she thought; she was feeling fairly hysterical herself.

'Your friend being Robert Korman,' Judith said.

222

'Why, yes,' Gerberga agreed. 'He wishes to kill Miss Jones, you see. It will be a pleasant surprise for him, when she arrives here.'

'And you expect me just to sit back and watch that happen?'

'There is nothing you can do about it, if you want to live,' Gerberga said. 'Now come and be tied up again.'

'Please,' Judith said. 'If I gave you my word . . .'

'Sorry,' Gerberga said. 'No words. Anyway, I want to take a shower.'

She tied Judith up again and disappeared into the bathroom. Judith made a few efforts to tug against the bonds, but Gerberga was an expert. Judith's whole body slumped in despair. She looked at the clock on the mantelpiece as she couldn't see her watch. It was half past nine. Jessica was unlikely to appear before half past three, at the very earliest.

But even when she did, she was unlikely to be armed. Perhaps Tom would be with her. But what if Korman arrived first? Judith didn't doubt *he* would be armed.

'That feels better.' Gerberga had even washed her hair, and then wrapped it up in a towel. Then she resumed her interminable games of patience.

The minutes ticked by; suddenly Gerberga's head jerked, and she reached for the remote. '. . . condition not known at this time,' said the newsreader. 'But it seems apparent that he was badly hurt. The casualty list has now grown to seven dead and thirty-two injured. This is due to the grenades that were thrown at the police and spectators. No one was prepared for it, and as a result of this extreme terrorist attack the gunman has for the moment escaped. However, we are told that several cordons are being set up, one round Millwall itself, another further back through West Ham and Tower Hamlets, and a third around Westminster. Unfortunately, due to the ferocious nature of the attack, a good description of the gunman has not been obtained, but he is believed to be of average height, nondescript features, wearing a dark coat and carrying a small bag. However, police suspect that he may have changed or discarded the coat, and also the bag, as it would have been used to carry the grenades.'

'What's happened?' Judith asked.

'I think he's assassinated the Prime Minister,' Gerberga said. 'Oh, the crazy fool.' But there was admiration in her voice. She had supposed he was only after Jessica Jones.

'In broad daylight, just like that?' Judith asked. 'How can he hope to get away with it?'

'I don't think he means to get away with it,' Gerberga said. 'It is just part of something he wants to do.' Just part, she thought.

'But—' Judith said, and Gerberga held up her hand.

'To recapitulate the situation as we know it,' the newsreader said, 'at eleven forty-two this morning, as the Prime Minister walked up the street from the river towards the Millennium Dome site, three shots were fired, by a man standing in the front row of the crowd. It is believed the shots were from a handgun, and were fired through the pocket in which the gun was concealed. The range was about thirty feet, and the Prime Minister was hit at least once. He has been taken to hospital.

'In the few seconds after the shooting, while everyone was too shocked to move, the gunman threw several hand grenades. One of these landed amidst the security guards, who had already identified the gunman but were now blown apart. The other grenades were thrown closer at hand, into the crowd, killing several people, including women and children, and injuring many more. People close to the gunman attempted to grapple him, but he fired again several times. When his would-be captors fell back, he threw another two grenades. As a result of all

224

this he was able to make his escape. A massive manhunt has been mounted.

'I have with me Chief Superintendent Maurice Bingley. Superintendent Bingley, what can you tell us?'

The Superintendent looked shell-shocked. 'I can tell you that we have in our midst a madman who is totally careless of human life, who has already killed a dozen people, and who is undoubtedly still armed and dangerous.'

'May I ask, Superintendent, if any of your policemen at the scene were armed?'

'Yes. Several of them. Unfortunately they were all situated close to the Prime Minister, in a normal protection pattern, and were thus affected by the grenades. One of them is dead, three more are in hospital. You must understand that this kind of suicidal attack is not something we have ever had to face in this country.'

'Is it not customary to have armed men on rooftops, overlooking the scene of a possible terrorist attack?'

'It is, when such an attack is regarded as possible. This one is right out of the blue. There has been no terrorist activity in this country for the past three years. There is no known group active in England or in any part of western Europe. It is the act of a madman.'

'He is incoherent with shock,' Gerberga commented, and muted the sound.

'You think Korman did this?' Judith asked.

'Who else?' Gerberga said. 'The question is, what will he do next?'

As she spoke, the street bell rang.

The End of the Search

B oth women's heads jerked. But both were thinking the same thing: Korman could not possibly have got from Millwall to Westminster so quickly, unless he had a car. And even supposing he had a car, and had not been stopped, it would have to be a miracle, as he would first have had to escape the crowds and regain his vehicle.

The bell rang again.

'Who are you expecting?' Gerberga asked.

'No one, at this hour,' Judith said. 'I swear it.'

'I believe you.' Gerberga released her bonds, pulled her off the settee, and half-carried half-pushed her across the room to the phone by the door. Then she stood behind her, the knife in her hand, the point resting on Judith's back. 'Please don't attempt to be either foolish or heroic,' she warned.

The phone rang a third time.

Judith had been rubbing her wrists together to restore her circulation. Now she picked up the phone. 'Yes?'

'Oh, thank heavens,' Jessica said. 'I was beginning to think you were out.'

'I was watching the news. But . . . Jessica, why have you come now?'

'Well, the news. We were actually in Greenwich when it all happened, so Tom pushed us into a taxi and said to come to you.'

'Is Tom with you?' Judith's voice went up an octave.

'No, he stayed to see what he could do. May we come up, Judith?'

'Say yes,' Gerberga whispered.

Judith drew a deep breath. She could scream, now. She *should* scream, now. But to do that would be to die; Gerberga had the knife at her throat. And it would do nothing to find Korman. The breath was exhaled in a sigh. 'Of course you can,' she said. 'I'll just release the door.'

She pressed the catch, and Gerberga took the phone from her hand and hung it up.

'How convenient,' she said. 'Quickly, now.'

She pushed Judith back to the settee, made her lie down, and tied her wrists and ankles together again. She had just finished when there was a ring on the door of the flat itself. She drew a deep breath, put her finger to her lips, and went to the door, releasing the catch and pulling it open in the same movement as she stepped behind it.

'Judith?' Jessica asked, and stared at the woman on the settee. 'Judith!' she shouted, and ran forward.

Gerberga stepped up to her and hit her a chopping blow on the back of the neck. Jessica went down on to her hands and knees. Megan, who had followed her into the room, screamed, but Gerberga grasped her by the shoulder and jerked her forward, at the same moment kicking the door shut. Then she put her arm round the girl's waist and held the knife to her throat. 'Stop wriggling or I'll cut you,' she said.

Jessica was slowly recovering, rising to her knees and turning to look back.

'The woman with nine lives,' Gerberga remarked. 'Hello, Miss Jones. Please don't try anything silly. If you do, this little girl's blood will make an awful mess. And besides, you don't have your heavy mob to back you up, do you?'

Jessica inhaled, slowly. She didn't want to believe this

was happening. It had been all over, for her. Adams had said that and she had believed him.

'You don't look at all pleased to see me,' Gerberga remarked. 'However, I am very pleased to see you. Get up.'

Jessica rose to her feet, sizing up the odds. Gerberga was bigger and stronger than she was. On the terrace in Istanbul she had felt she could perhaps take her, but not while she was armed with a knife, and especially while she was holding the knife to Megan's throat.

Equally depressing was the sight of Judith's badly bruised face, the expression in her superior's eyes. Judith was very frightened. Now that was something she had never expected to see.

'What do you want?' she asked. 'Me?'

'In time. What I want is Korman.'

'He'll never make it,' Jessica said. 'Even if he knows where to come.'

'He knows where to come,' Gerberga said. 'And he will make it.'

'Then you'll both have had it,' Jessica said.

'I don't think that follows,' Gerberga said. 'Is this not the very last place anyone would look for him? And no one knows anything about me. I do not think we will have any trouble.'

'You'll never get out of the country,' Jessica said. 'They'll have closed all seaports and airports by now.'

'When you say closed, you mean they will force every-one to be scrutinised,' Gerberga said. 'But as I have said, there is no reason for anyone to suspect me of anything. And Korman is travelling on a false passport, and there is no accurate description of what he looks like, nor, in fact, does anyone outside this room even know that it is Korman involved.'

Jessica opened her mouth and then closed it again. Tom!

Tom had to convince his superiors that it was Korman. Would he also be able to figure out that Korman would go to Judith's flat? That would take a lot of deduction. But eventually, when she didn't come home after dropping Megan off, Tom would come looking for her.

Unless Korman got here first.

'So you see,' Gerberga said, 'all we have to do is wait. Why don't you sit down and relax.' She sat down herself, Megan beside her.

'Are you a very bad woman?' Megan asked.

'Oh, very bad,' Gerberga said. 'You don't want to make me cross.'

'I'm hungry,' Megan explained. 'We were going to have lunch in Greenwich, but then we had to leave in a hurry.'

'We'll have to wait awhile,' Gerberga said. 'We'll have lunch when Mr Korman gets here.'

Megan looked at Jessica. 'Is it going to be all right, JJ?'

'Yes,' Jessica said. 'It's going to be all right, Megan.'

She stared at Judith, and Judith stared back. Between them they ought to be able to do something. But then she realised that even if she could get Judith free, her nerves were too shattered for her to be of any use at all.

She could only pray.

'So, you are convinced the assassin is this man Korman,' the Home Secretary said.

'Absolutely, sir,' Tom replied.

The Home Secretary looked at the other officers seated round the table. 'What do we have on him?'

'We have absolutely nothing,' said Commander Adams. 'He was supposed to be dead. My woman Jones claims that she saw him, alive, just before the Alicante bomb went off. On the Prime Minister's orders she was seconded to the SAS as part of a team to find out if he actually was alive,

229

and deal with him. Unfortunately, this does not appear to have been successful.'

'What group does he work for?'

'Himself. Nobody else. And as you know, he seems to be targetting our Cabinet Ministers.'

'And has now gone to the very top.'

'Will the PM survive?'

'He's in intensive care. One must hope he does. As to whether he'll be able to continue in office, that's another matter. It's Korman we have to worry about. It is quite intolerable that our Prime Minister can be shot in broad daylight on a crowded street while surrounded by armed guards.'

'It was the grenades that did the trick,' Adams said.

'I can see that. But it is equally intolerable that he should have escaped. The attack took place three hours ago. The area is cordoned off and people are being stopped and searched. But he has still not been found.'

'Well, Home Secretary,' Adams said, 'there was no very good description. Just an average man in a dark coat . . .'

'He fired through the pocket of that coat,' the Home Secretary snapped. 'Surely that should have been picked up?'

'Not if he got rid of the coat, and his guns, and his grenades. You must realise, Home Secretary, that the throwing of those grenades indiscriminately into the crowd left everyone stunned for several minutes. No one knew if any more were going to be thrown. Your average Englishman, while he may have got used to indiscriminate bomb blasts during the IRA troubles – and even the IRA usually telephoned a warning – is simply not used to suddenly having a series of grenades tossed into his midst.'

'Not cricket,' Tom murmured.

The Home Secretary glared at him, then turned back to Adams. 'All right, we know he is a maniacal mass murderer, who has managed to disappear. So let's get some concrete facts. You say he can only have made his escape by discarding his coat and his weapons. I accept that. Thus he became an ordinary, inoffensive citizen, who could submit to a search without fear of arrest. But that means, from our point of view, that he *is* an ordinary inoffensive citizen, walking the streets of London unarmed.'

'Unless he has another source of supply to which he can turn, sir,' Tom said.

The Home Secretary again glared at him. 'Where would this be?'

'I have no idea, sir. But he usually has a pretty formidable back-up.'

'And what would he need this additional armament for? I would have thought he'd just be anxious to get out of the country as quickly as possible.'

'Unless he was planning another assassination,' Adams said.

'Does he suppose another Cabinet Minister is going to appear in public, today?'

'Well . . . I suppose not.' Adams looked at Tom.

'There is another possible target he may have in mind,' Tom said, 'before fleeing the country.'

'Who?' the Home Secretary inquired.

'DC Jones, sir.'

'*Who?*'

'You met her at Downing Street. DC Jones is the constable who first alerted us to the possibility that Korman might still be alive,' Adams said.

'She was also behind the destruction of his base in Turkey,' Tom said. 'We know he has already made at least two attempts on her life.'

'And you think he would risk going after her, with all the police in England after *him?*'

'Yes, sir, I do, for three reasons. The first two are linked. You say all the police in England are after him . . . but none of them knows what he looks like. Only Miss Jones knows that. So quite apart from a personal hatred he has for Miss Jones, he has a compelling reason for getting rid of her.'

'And the third reason?'

'Well, sir, as we have just seen, the man is a psychotic killer, one who has tremendous belief in his own powers. But his entire organisation has been destroyed, and also, so we understand, his financier. He may well be out of action, on the scale we have seen in the past, for a very long time. So he makes this grand gesture. If he is forced to suspend his war on the British Government, or perhaps even abandon it altogether, he will take out the head of the British Government first, even without a back-up team or by the use of his favourite weapon, the large bomb. That being so, it is entirely in keeping with his psychological profile that he should also take out the one person in England who can identify him. Then he can comfortably disappear for as long as it takes him to rebuild.'

'Hm,' the Home Secretary commented, and looked at Adams.

'I think that probably sums up the situation,' the Commander said.

'Where is Miss Jones now?' the Home Secretary said.

'That's the good news. Korman can't possibly know where she is. She is actually living in one of our safe houses.'

'And she's there now?'

'No, as a matter of fact. She's with Assistant Commissioner Proud, at her flat. I'm to pick her up in an hour.'

'I think it isn't a good idea to have her moving about,' Adams said. 'I think you should telephone AC Proud as see if JJ can spend the night there. I mean to say, there can hardly be a safer house in London than Judith Proud's. That way we can all concentrate on finding Korman without constantly having to look over our shoulders.'

'Well . . .' Tom hesitated. Bang goes my long evening of nooky, he thought. But what the Commander was saying made sense – quite apart from the fact that it was the Commander who was saying it. 'Yes, sir.'

Adams smiled. 'Don't look so despondent, Tom. As we need every man to be on duty over the next twenty-four hours, you wouldn't be able to spend the evening together anyway. And I tell you what I'll do: you can have an extra day's leave. When we have Korman in the bag.'

Gerberga changed her mind about waiting for Korman to have lunch. She had Jessica cook a meal, while she kept Megan at her side as a precaution. She kept the television on all afternoon. The news coverage was continuous.

'It's so boring,' Megan complained.

'It's not boring. It's fascinating,' Gerberga said.

She was very worried, but she wouldn't show it to her prisoners. The Prime Minister had been shot just before twelve. It was now nearly three. And Korman was still at large. So where was he?

'How far is it from the Dome site to where we are?' she asked.

'About seven miles,' Jessica said.

Seven miles, Gerberga thought. Three hours? He should have been here by now. Unless . . . But if he had been arrested it would surely be on the news.

Jessica could see that she was agitated. The temptation to make a move before Korman got here was enormous. But anything she did might involve Megan's death. The little girl was bearing up magnificently, refusing to let either Gerberga or the ever-present knife get her down, but Jessica could tell she was terrified. Besides, if she waited, Tom would eventually turn up.

The phone jingled, and all their heads turned.

'Who would that be?' Gerberga asked.

233

'It could be anyone,' Judith muttered. She was still tied up, uncomfortable, and utterly depressed.

They waited, and it continued ringing.

Gerberga chewed her lip. Presumably whoever it was was expecting Judith to be at home on a Saturday afternoon. She carried the phone to beside the settee. 'Be very careful what you say,' she said, still holding Megan's arm. 'And if it is a summons for you to go on duty to help them look for Korman, tell them you are not feeling well.'

She lifted the phone and held it to Judith's ear and mouth, bending her own head so that she could hear what was being said.

'Yes?' Judith said.

'Oh, good afternoon, ma'am.'

'Tom! How good to hear your voice.'

There was a brief silence. The Assistant Commissioner had never greeted him like that before. 'I assume Jessica and the child got to you safely, ma'am?'

'Oh, yes,' Judith said. 'Jessica is expecting you to pick her up.'

She gazed at Gerberga, and Gerberga gazed back.

'Hello, Tom!' Megan shouted.

Gerberga slapped her hand over the girl's mouth.

'Hi, Megan. The thing is, ma'am, what with this manhunt that's going on for Korman, and his connection with Jessica, the Commander feels it would be best for Jessica to spend the night with you. I can pick her up in the morning, by which time hopefully this flap will have ended.'

'Oh, no . . .' Judith stared at Gerberga, who was holding the knife to Megan's throat and nodding vigorously.

Jessica had risen and was standing behind her, but even to touch Gerberga would mean Megan's death.

'Ma'am?' Tom asked.

'I'm sure she'll be very disappointed,' Judith said.

'May I speak with her?'

Judith looked at Gerberga, who gave another nod, at the same time tightening her grip on Megan, who squirmed helplessly.

Jessica's brain raced. There had to be some way of letting Tom know the situation.

'Hi,' she said. 'What's this about abandoning me?'

'Orders from the top. But I think the old man is right. And he's going to make it up to us: I'm getting an extra day's leave.'

'Great. So what are you going to do all by yourself, tonight?'

'I'm working. So is every other policeman in the country. Save you.'

'Lucky me. But if you do get a moment, Tom, do run through that new CD and see if it is any good.'

'Eh?'

'You're not thinking, Tom,' Jessica said. 'The one I just bought you, the reissue of *The Desert Song*. It's supposed to be the best ever.'

'Ah . . . yes, I'll do that.'

'I really would like your opinion, a.s.a.p.'

'Oh . . . right. I'll get on to it right away. Take care, now.'

The phone went dead.

'Replace it,' Gerberga said.

Jessica obeyed.

'Well, that takes care of the evening,' Gerberga said. She released Megan's mouth. 'I hope I didn't hurt you, child, but you were really very naughty, interrupting adults like that.'

Megan had tears in her eyes. 'I hate you,' she said.

'I'm sure you will discover I am a very nice person, in the course of time,' Gerberga said. 'I think you could prepare some tea, Jessica.'

As with lunch, she and Megan went into the kitchen with

Jessica. Jessica's brain continued to tumble. Had Tom got the message? He would have to, surely. And then . . . how soon would he respond, and how? She knew Gerberga was approaching a decision. If Korman didn't turn up in the next hour or so, she would abandon him. To do that, and leave the flat and go to an airport, she would have to kill her three hostages. But it wasn't as simple as that. Just as the necessity of keeping hold of Megan all the time had prevented her tying Jessica up, so she would have to know that for her to start killing would leave Jessica with nothing to lose. Therefore, she would have to be the first to go. Then Megan and Judith could be dealt with at her leisure.

She made the tea, watching the knife all the time. The attack, when it came, would be without warning and very violent. It was so tempting to try to anticipate it. But that was simply not on while Megan was in the line of fire.

They continued to watch the television. The police had found the coat and the bag that had carried the grenades, discarded in an alley within a hundred yards of the shooting. But they did not appear to be any closer to catching the as yet unnamed killer.

Jessica looked at her watch. A quarter to four. Half an hour since she had spoken with Tom. Perhaps he hadn't got the message after all.

The street bell rang.

Commander Adams looked at Tom somewhat impatiently. He was beginning to wonder if the Detective-Sergeant was using his peculiar position as JJ's partner to become a monumental nuisance. Now to insist on an interview to outline a quite ridiculous theory while he, and everyone else, was supposed to be out looking for Korman . . . If it was Korman . . .

'Korman?' he asked. 'In AC Proud's flat? Really, Bainbridge. You say you spoke to Miss Proud yourself?

And then to JJ? How on earth could they speak to you if they were in the hands of Korman? And how did he get there? *Why* should he go there?'

Tom kept his patience. 'I spoke with Miss Proud, sir, and with Jessica, yes. But I believe they were . . . are . . . under restraint. Jessica gave me a quite absurd message about some new CD we'd just bought. We haven't bought any new CD, sir. And this thing is supposed to be a reissue of *The Desert Song*. That's got to be a reference to Korman. His base was in the desert. As for how he traced her there, I have an idea. The only way he could have done that was to pick up the trail in Southley. If he did that, and managed to trace the girl Megan to Miss Proud, he'd use that knowledge to find out how to get at Jessica. It's just his luck that Jessica should turn up there.'

Adams gazed at him for several seconds. Then he said, 'If Korman is in Miss Proud's flat, with AC Proud, JJ and Megan Lynch, aren't they all certainly dead by now?'

'They were alive half an hour ago, sir.'

'If this is true, how do you propose to handle it?'

'Well, sir, as you say, this man is a killer, and their lives are certainly in danger. We have got to go in, secretly, and very hard.'

'That's a high-risk strategy, Bainbridge. The three women could be killed.'

'The three women *are* going to be killed, sir, at any moment. I think the SAS can handle it. Especially if we can get hold of the same team as supported Jessica in Turkey. They'd be dead keen.'

'Very well. I'll set it up. But . . . it can't happen for at least a couple of hours – you say the women may be murdered at any moment.'

'Yes, sir. If you'll set it up, I'll see if I can keep them alive until it happens.'

*　　*　　*

Christopher Nicole

'Answer it,' Gerberga told Jessica. 'And be careful.'

'Yes?' Jessica said into the phone.

'I have an urgent message for Miss Proud,' the voice said.

A voice she would have recognised anywhere. She went quite cold, then became very hot. 'I'm sorry,' she said. 'We're not taking any messages.'

But Gerberga and Megan had been standing right behind her. Now Gerberga pushed her aside.

'Robert?'

'I thought you might be there.'

'Oh, Robert. Come up.'

She released the catch. 'You,' she told Jessica, 'open the door and wait.'

Jessica obeyed. But now they were in the deepest trouble. What to do?

She watched Korman emerge from the lift, on the other side of the lobby. He checked when he saw her, and his hand dropped to his pocket. Then he saw Gerberga behind her.

'It is all right,' Gerberga said. 'She's tame.'

He came right up to Jessica, and she backed away from him. He was carrying a suitcase. He stepped into the flat and closed the door, looked at Judith.

'She's a big wheel,' Gerberga explained. 'You crazy man.'

'Is he dead?'

'There's been no report of it on the television. Where have you *been*?'

'Taking care of things. Do you have anything to eat? I am starving.'

'Are you armed?'

'Of course I am armed.'

'Well, then, let us get civilised. Keep that bitch covered while I tie her up.'

238

Korman drew an automatic pistol. Gerberga at last released Megan. The little girl ran to Jessica, who hugged her.

'Just don't move,' Gerberga advised, and went into Judith's bedroom for some more tights. With these she bound both Jessica and Megan hand and foot, making them lie on the floor.

'I hate you,' Megan said again.

'If you say that once more I'll tan your bottom,' Gerberga told her. She went into the kitchen and prepared a meal for Korman, who sat at the dining table and ate wolfishly. 'Now tell me what happened. Where have you been all afternoon? Why didn't you contact me? And how did you get this address?'

'Make some coffee,' Korman said.

Gerberga did so.

'I need that,' Korman said. 'It has been a difficult day. I got this address the same way you did.'

'Then you also got my note. But you ignored it.'

'I did not like the sound of it. Rashid resigned? That did not make sense.'

'Rashid is dead.'

Korman's head came up.

'He was shot by a hit man. We think he must have been sent by the British Government. Because of that bitch.' She pointed at Jessica.

'And the killer?'

'Oh, I shot him.'

Now Jessica gave a sharp intake of breath, while Judith sighed.

Gerberga smiled at them. 'I think I was next on his list.'

'And Rashid was killed,' Korman said, amused. 'By a single shot.'

'No,' Gerberga said. 'It required two. If I was to take control.'

He stared at her.

'So tell me what you have done since deciding not to contact me,' Gerberga said.

'I drove up to London and booked in at a small hotel. Then this morning I went down to Greenwich. The English newspapers are very good. They spell out exactly where their important people are going to be, every day and virtually every hour.'

'You drove down to Greenwich?'

Korman grinned. 'I used a bicycle. I told the hotel staff that I was a tourist and that I had worked out that the best way to get around London was a bicycle. They agreed with me. So this morning off I went. And afterwards, while the people were still recovering from the grenades, I went back to where I had left my bicycle, dropped my coat and my gear, and cycled back into town. It is amazing how sympathetic the English are towards a man on a bicycle.'

'You killed twelve people!' Judith shouted.

'I thought there would have been more,' Korman said regretfully. 'And the Prime Minister is still alive.'

'Just,' Gerberga said. 'And it has taken you four hours to cycle from Millwall to here? Seven miles?'

'Well, of course it did not,' Korman said. 'It took some time, mind you. Although I left very promptly, the police were setting up roadblocks within minutes of the shooting. It was the bicycle that saw me through. They could not believe an innocent, unarmed man on a bicycle could have carried out such an attack. So I went back to my hotel, collected the things I had left there, checked out, and came here. I have a plane ticket on the eight o'clock flight to Paris; the hotel got that for me last night. Have you a ticket?'

Gerberga nodded. 'An open ticket. I will see if I can get on the same flight.'

She telephoned the airline, gave her name and ticket number. There was no problem with a seat on the eight o'clock to Paris.

She replaced the phone and looked at her watch. A quarter to five. 'We should check in by six, so we should leave here at half past five. That just gives us time to clean up here.' She went into the kitchen, returned with a roll of tape. 'We don't want them screaming and shouting and upsetting the neighbours.'

She slapped a length of tape across Judith's mouth; Judith made a little moan of protest.

'You're not just going to leave them?' Korman asked.

'No, no.' Gerberga put tape over Megan's mouth as well. 'That would be too dangerous. I will cut their throats.'

She stood above Jessica.

'Please,' Jessica said. 'Not the little girl.'

'She has seen us. She knows who we are. She must die, Jones. That must be obvious even to you. And then, you see, no one will ever know we were here at all.' She slapped the tape across Jessica's mouth, then turned to Korman. 'Will you do it, or would you like me to?'

'Oh, I will do it. But you say we have forty-five minutes?'

'We still have to find a taxi. And be careful. There must be no blood on your clothes.'

Korman grinned, and took off his jacket, then his shirt. Then he pulled off the tablecloth and wrapped it round his waist. He made Jessica think of a butcher. He *was* a butcher.

'I would like to play with her a little before I kill her. This woman has caused me more damage than anyone else in the world.'

'Oh, very well. Amuse yourself. Fifteen minutes.' Gerberga sat down and crossed her knees. Jessica strained against her bonds, without the least effect. Judith stared at her

241

with enormous eyes. Megan was crying, great sobs that wracked her body.

Korman stood in front of Jessica and felt her nose. 'This will come off. That is how they punish recalcitrant women in the Middle East.' He squeezed her breasts. 'And these. Then you will die less of a woman. Then—'

The street telephone rang.

Korman spun round, knife thrust forward, as if he would attack the phone itself.

'Who the fuck is that?'

Gerberga looked from one woman to the other, then picked up the phone herself.

'Yes?' She spoke in a low voice.

'Is that you, ma'am?'

Tom! Jessica thought. Oh, my God, Tom! He had understood her message after all. But, if he was alone . . .

'I am speaking for Miss Proud,' Gerberga said. 'What do you want?'

'I want to speak with Korman,' Tom said.

Gerberga stared at the phone. Korman made a strangled exclamation.

'I know he's there,' Tom explained. 'Holding the girls hostage. I also know he's up the creek without a paddle. Only I can get him out.'

Gerberga looked at Korman, who looked about to have an apoplectic fit.

'Are you alone?' she said into the phone.

'At the moment. But if you don't rush, there's going to be a lot of people here soon.'

'What is your name?'

'Tom Bainbridge.'

'And why are you doing this?'

'Let's say I'm hoping you'll be grateful.'

Again Gerberga looked at Korman, who was recovering

his nerve. 'You have to let him up. We can deal with the situation when he is here.'

Tom! Jessica wanted to scream. Don't come. But how she wanted him to come.

'Come up,' Gerberga said, and released the street door.

'Take this.' Korman gave her his pistol, then placed his suitcase on the dining table and took out the various parts of the Minimi rifle, expertly fitting them together.

'You are expecting to fight a battle?' Gerberga asked, when she saw the box cartridge.

'If I have to,' Korman said, and nodded at the door as the handle turned.

Jessica strained at her bonds, with no more success than earlier. But surely Tom had to know what he was doing.

The problem was, he didn't know about Gerberga.

The door swung in, and Tom stepped into the room. His eyes swung from left to right, taking in the situation: the two bound and gagged women and the little girl; Korman, just fitting the last piece of the gun together. The temptation was too great, and his hand moved to his jacket.

'Don't do it,' Gerberga said from behind him, at the same time presenting the pistol to his neck.

Tom checked, and Korman stepped up to him and took the gun.

'You offered to help us, not arrest us,' Gerberga said.

'It was a sudden idea,' Tom explained. 'You all right, JJ?'

Jessica nodded.

'Right,' Tom said. 'By the way, you *are* Robert Korman?'

'I am he,' Korman said.

'And you?'

'I am Gerberga, wife of the late Rashid ben Khalim.'

'Ah. Right.'

'Is it important?'

'Just like to know who I'm dealing with. Were you involved in the assassination attempt?'

'No. What is it you have to say?' Gerberga asked.

'Just that this building is entirely surrounded by the SAS. Nobody is being allowed in or out except by their permission.'

'You expect us to believe that?' Gerberga asked.

'I'd have thought you have some idea of what they can do,' Tom suggested. 'But have a look.'

Both Gerberga and Korman moved to the window, keeping their guns pointed at Tom. There were quite a few people in the street below, being marshalled by the police. There had been no sirens, no shouting – just an orderly evacuation of the other flats in the building.

Only Tom knew that the SAS had not yet arrived. Some of the police were armed, but in a strictly defensive capacity.

'Shit,' Korman muttered. 'Well, then . . .'

'Wait,' Gerberga said. 'This idiot didn't come here to commit suicide. You said you could get us out.'

'I can,' Tom said.

'How?'

'I happen to know this building very well. There is an underground walkway beneath it. I can take you out through there to surface two blocks away. Outside the cordon.'

Gerberga turned her head as Judith gave a sharp intake of breath.

'He's lying,' Korman said.

'It's his life,' Gerberga argued.

'In exchange, you won't harm any of these ladies,' Tom said.

'That is not possible,' Gerberga said. 'They know who we are, and where we are going when we leave here.'

'I will give you my word they will not repeat that information.'

'You must take us for fools,' Korman said.

'As a matter of fact, I do,' Tom said. 'For getting yourself into this situation in the first place. But my offer is the only one on the table. Once the SAS come busting in here, you are going to be killed. I'm at least giving you a chance.'

Gerberga and Korman looked at each other. Jessica tried to calculate what they might be thinking. Korman had to know he was done. But his coming to England at all had to have been a suicide mission, driven on by the destruction of his home and his organisation. But Gerberga . . . The only crime she had committed in England was to hold them hostage. If she could just get out of the country and back to Turkey, extradition proceedings might simply not be worth it. She had come here to save Korman from committing suicide. But now that he had done that – to all intents and purposes, that is – was she really going to go down with him?

Korman made his decision first.

'We are done anyway,' he said. 'So let's take on the bastards, and take some of them with us to hell. But first we'll settle with this bitch.'

He swung the Minimi rifle towards Jessica. She drew a deep breath, and tensed herself for the coming, fatal shock.

Then she heard a roar of sound from above. Korman checked, looking up. 'Helicopter! They're coming down on the roof.' His face was a mask of rage.

Tom started forward, and was checked by Gerberga's pistol.

'Bastards!' Korman shrieked, and swung his rifle back towards Jessica. Again she tensed herself, and heard the crack of the pistol as Gerberga shot her lover in the back. Blood flew and Korman went down with a crash.

'The deal is on,' Gerberga said, and pointed at Jessica. 'I saved your life, Jones. Remember that!' She gestured with her pistol. 'Take me out.'

Tom hesitated for a moment, then went to the door. Gerberga followed, the pistol pointed at him. She seized her shoulder bag and slung it as she went through the door.

'Not the lift,' Tom said. 'Down here.'

He turned along the corridor, then dived to the floor as they heard the shattering of wood and glass.

'Bastard!' Gerberga shouted, but instead of firing at him she looked up at the three black-clad men who had appeared further along the corridor. She levelled the pistol, and was struck by several bullets at the same time. She gave a shriek and fell backwards, the gun flying from her hand.

'You all right, Mr Bainbridge?' Sergeant McAdoo asked.

Tom looked down at the shattered body of Gerberga. He had never seen her before today, but he did not doubt she had been a formidable female.

Now his sole thought was for the women. 'I'm all right,' he said, and ran back along the corridor. As he did so, the door swung open and Korman stood there, swaying, bleeding . . . but holding the Minimi rifle.

'Down!' McAdoo shouted.

Again Tom hit the floor, as did McAdoo and his men.

'There are women in there!' Tom shouted as they levelled their guns.

Korman had seen that he was staring death in the face, and slammed the door shut. McAdoo signalled his men and they rose and ran forward. Tom picked up Gerberga's pistol before leading the rush.

'That bitch,' Korman snarled. Blood was mingling with his saliva. 'But you . . .' He swung back to face the helpless Jessica, and the window shattered as a black-clad SAS man swung himself through it at the end of a rope.

Korman turned and fired, and the soldier, hit in the chest,

tumbled back out of the window again. Tom hurled his shoulder against the door with such force that the latch snapped and it swung inwards. Korman swung back, rifle levelled, and Jessica threw herself forward, rolling across the floor to strike him across the back of the legs with her own.

Korman stumbled, and his shot went wide. At close range, Tom shot him through the head.

'Quite a fall-out.' Judith was as spruce as she had ever been, although her face remained puffy from the beatings Gerberga had given her. 'One prime minister retiring, one SAS captain shot dead, all those people killed.' She smiled at Jessica, who today was wearing uniform, to receive her promotion. 'At least there is one new sergeant.'

'And?' Jessica asked.

'Oh, one retiring Assistant Commissioner.'

'You don't have to.'

'Perhaps not. But I have to. Can you understand that? I learned something the other day. That I'm not as strong or as tough as I thought I was. Quite literally, that woman knocked the stuffing out of me. I was terrified. I made no effort to resist her. Well, almost none. Knowing that about myself, how can I send my people out to risk their lives? So I'm taking early retirement.'

'We'll be sorry to see you go, ma'am,' Tom said.

'You'll get over it. I'd like to take Megan on a world cruise, JJ. Is that okay with you? You know I've filed papers for adoption.'

'Then it really has nothing to do with me any more,' Jessica said. 'But . . . have you talked with Megan?'

Judith nodded. 'We had a long talk. She'd rather stay with you, of course. But as that isn't on . . .'

'It isn't on, I'm afraid,' Jessica said. 'I'm not retiring.'

'I understand.' She gave a sad smile. 'So I suppose she's

settling for the next best thing. We're flying down to Spain tomorrow to see her grandmother, but I've already spoken with her on the phone and she seems content. Relieved, actually, that the child is safe and will be well looked after. I want you to know, JJ' – she flushed – 'that I intend to devote the rest of my life to that girl. But . . . you're always welcome.'

'Is that a tragedy, or a happy ending?' Tom asked as they returned to the VIP flat.

'Her career is a tragedy, ending like that,' Jessica said. 'But if she can make Megan happy, and maybe find some happiness herself, it could be a happy ending.'

'What about us? If you really wanted to quit, and take her on . . .' He paused uncertainly.

Jessica considered what he was saying. She supposed it really was over, for her. But when she thought of all the people so senselessly killed, the property so senselessly destroyed, the brave men who had given their lives to seek and destroy one madman – no, she thought, two madmen, and a mad woman – she had a duty to all those who remained, and might need protecting, because there would be other madmen in the future.

'I'll stick around awhile.'

He squeezed her hand. '*We'll* stick around, Sergeant Jones.'